----------- ★ -----------

A DATE WITH TERROR

She stood at the appointed spot on the south side of Rivington and waited. She was stiff, poised, her whole body ready to run.

She looked at her watch again. Twelve-ten.

On the other side of the street, the shadow stirred. Hard-soled boots hit the sidewalk as the figure moved out the doorway into the light.

Louisa put her hands to her mouth to stop the scream that rose in her throat. She was frozen, hypnotized, unable to do anything but stare at that silent figure moving toward her, each slow step punctuated by the crack of boot heels on concrete. Step by step, closer and closer...

----------- ★ -----------

PAINT HER FACE DEAD

PAINT HER FACE DEAD

Jane Johnston

WORLDWIDE®

TORONTO • NEW YORK • LONDON • PARIS
AMSTERDAM • STOCKHOLM • HAMBURG
ATHENS • MILAN • TOKYO • SYDNEY

PAINT HER FACE DEAD

A Worldwide Mystery/November 1988

First published by St. Martin's Press Incorporated.

ISBN 0-373-26013-X

Printed in U.S.A.

ONE

"I'M AFRAID!"

"Of what?"

"Someone wants to kill me!"

The girl's voice was nasal and whiny. Louisa had to twist around in her chair to catch a glimpse of her. She saw glassy blue eyes, which were rimmed with black and smudged with shadow the shade of a bruise. A round face, chalk white. A slash of purple lipstick. The girl's hair was dark where it was cropped at the sides and back, and it erupted over her forehead in a tangle of spikes dyed a brilliant emerald green.

She looked like a child playing grown-up with forbidden cosmetics and clothing. She wore a long man's jacket with heavily padded shoulders and a pair of black cotton tights. Her elaborately beaded and sequinned cardigan was buttoned partway up over what appeared to be a man's thermal undershirt.

Louisa could no longer hold her contorted position. She turned around in her chair. Facing the platform was almost as uncomfortable. Deprived of her watch, she guessed that she had been sitting for nearly five hours, and all that time she had been observing, with a disturbing fascination, the man on the platform, Tony Cazzine.

Behind her the girl wailed, "Someone wants me dead!"

Louisa winced. The day had started with gut-spilling. It had progressed to paranoia.

The ambiguity of her situation was another unexpected irritation. She was not there to seek enlightenment by sitting thigh-to-thigh with one hundred and ninety-nine other people locked into the ballroom of the Park Summit Hotel. She was there to get material for a magazine article—an exposé of SUM, the new human-potential movement that had unashamedly adopted the authoritarian methods of its predecessor, est.

Her agent, Hal, had talked her into SUM. She had talked him into the assignment. Hal had the fervor of the recently converted. "I swear, Louisa, SUM took everything in my head, shook it up, and laid it down in new patterns. I've quit smoking, cut down on booze, stopped needing—"

"Spare me, Hal! I'll do it, but you've got to promise—"

"Anything!"

"I do an article on it, and I do it *my* way. If I think it's a con, I say so."

"You won't say that. When you get on-line, you'll thank me. You'll be a different person two weeks from now."

Two weeks! If she wasn't a mental and emotional basket-case after SUM's battering, she would have material for one of the best articles she'd ever written. She shut her eyes and began to think about her lead paragraph.

The Self Utilization Marathon took sixty hours, spread over two weekends of "interfacing" and "programming." What happened during that time was described in an incomprehensible babble of sports metaphor and computer jargon.

"Finishers," such as Hal, went without food, water, and toilets for hours at a stretch. The coach questioned their values and bullied them into admissions of fear and failure. Finishers who "got on-line" at the end of the marathon claimed that they experienced such total self-awareness that they were able to throw away their emotional baggage and sweep aside their barriers to personal and professional success.

It was a con. It had to be. Getting free from guilt and fear took years of work, not two weekends. Louisa's three years of therapy following a painful divorce had taught her that, and she still succumbed to bouts of self-recrimination and insecurity. What was happening made her angry. SUM played on the human weakness for a quick fix. Its devotees were deluded by the catharsis of public confession into believing they were miraculously changed.

She was honing the sharpest edge of her attack for the coach. Tony Cazzine had to be the most seductive con man she had ever seen. He confronted the marathoners without mercy. They adored him.

"No one's going to kill you, Deirdre!" he was saying patiently to the sniffling girl. "Are you ready to get rid of that bullshit?"

Bullshit. The *mot juste* for what was going on in this room. "Bullshit" was Cazzine's response to every confession of guilt, rage, or impotence that marathoners spewed out.

Louisa sighed. Cazzine's eyes flicked to hers. His look was cool, neither curious nor critical. This was not the first time their eyes had met. If he knew who she was, he might be trying to gauge the amount of damage she could do to SUM.

Her articles appeared regularly in *New York* magazine and the *Village Voice*. Her zest for exposing hypocrisy and pretension had made her, in three years of free-lancing, well-known. She heard the word "ruthless" as often as she heard "hard-hitting." Both adjectives sometimes filled her with dismay. She loved what she did. She wanted to be known for her service in the interests of her readers.

Louisa wasn't the only person in this marathon with a degree of public visibility. SUM was "in" right now. She recognized performers, a producer, several artists, and one very successful novelist. Most were in their twenties to forties, with a handful of older men and women at one end and teenagers at the other. That put her, at age thirty-two, right in the middle.

She began a mental list of adjectives to use in her article—marathoners were young, professional, urban, trendy. SUM met a generation's demand for self-importance. Marathoners would scorn the idea of whispering their confessions to an unseen priest behind a grille. Their confessions were electronically amplified, and their high priest transformed sins into wrong attitudes and absolved them of "bullshit."

Tony Cazzine leaped off the platform and strode up the center aisle toward Deirdre, who was now snuffling audibly into the hand mike. While he didn't seem to be trying to project a macho image, he moved like an athlete—or a dancer. The undistinguished beige shirt and brown pants he wore did not neutralize the power of his lean, hard body. He was in his late thirties, she guessed. There were lines in his forehead and around his mouth that did not seem to have been put there solely by his years. His hair was lightly flecked with gray, and his eyes were so dark they were almost black.

She was sure every woman in the room was as aware as she was of Tony Cazzine. A few men, too, judging from the ones who had already leaped up to declare their eagerness to come out of the closet.

Cazzine showed no sign of fatigue after more than five hours of intense interaction. He was energetic, even eager, as he bore down on Deirdre.

"Thirty seconds!" An assistant coach called the warning from the back of the ballroom. A marathoner was limited to three minutes of "input," unless the coach deemed the situation worthy of further exploration.

"You can have more time, Deirdre," Cazzine said. "I want you to bring that fear to the screen and look at it!"

Deirdre had a death grip on the mike. Tears were making her eye makeup run in grayish streaks. As her punk image dissolved, she looked more and more like a messy child.

"Time!"

Cazzine's voice had become soft, more persuasive. "If you get that fear on the screen, Deirdre, you can read it out and delete it from your life. Are you willing to do that?"

First bully, now father confessor! He'd get this miserable girl to sob out her secrets and expose her fears in front of one hundred and ninety-nine people, and he'd go back to the platform well pleased. Then he'd pick another victim. Someone else who had paid five hundred dollars for the opportunity would strip off his dignity and flash his naked soul. Louisa began a list of nouns—masochists, exhibitionists, egotists, show-offs....

For a few seconds Deirdre's snuffles were painfully amplified. Then she seemed to pull herself together. She drew a wad of tissues from the pocket of her huge jacket, swiped at her face with it, took a deep breath, and said, "This sucks!"

"Read it out, Deirdre!"

"Okay, it's like this," she said firmly, clearly enjoying the attention she was getting. "I have this relationship—ex-relationship, I shoulda said—and I don't know what the fuck he was so totally pissed about! I mean, like, he didn't have to go crazy-like and get me thrown outta the place! So, I told him, I said—"

Cazzine cut through her chatter like a knife. "Right! That's the fear you're letting run you, isn't it?"

Deirdre's mouth hung open. Her eyes, in a raccoon-mask of smudged mascara, stared at him.

"You'd like to punch the escape key for now, wouldn't you?"

Surprise and doubt clouded her face. "Yeah, I guess so.... I mean, like, okay, if you say so."

"Thank you, Deirdre." Cazzine said the words with finality and turned back to the platform. After a few seconds, as if Deirdre wasn't the only one having difficulty grasping that the exchange was over, a patter of applause followed. The applause was a recognition that an "interface" or an "input" was ended. Deirdre handed the mike back to a hovering assistant coach and sat down.

Anger almost choked Louisa. Cazzine couldn't just walk away! She had intended to keep silent for the duration of the marathon, but she could not allow him to get away with it. Deirdre was a silly bitch, who shouldn't have gotten up in the first place, but fear of murder should not be callously dismissed. He had interrupted Deirdre in mid-sentence.

She raised her hand.

"Louisa?" Cazzine wasn't looking at her. He seemed to have seen her out of his peripheral vision. He didn't need to look at her name-tag to see who she was.

She stood up and waited for the mike. Up to this moment she had been bored, restless, hungry, and aware that she needed to go to the bathroom. All those discomforts vanished in a sudden excitement. She was going to take an adversary position. He would be a powerful adversary.

The mike was placed in her hand. "I think what you just did is very damn dangerous!" She heard gasps. She had the shocked attention of everyone in the room.

Everyone but Cazzine. He had seated himself in a high director's chair on the platform, and he was looking at a notebook that lay open on a lectern in front of him. He turned a page. Then glanced at her. "I read you, Louisa," he said.

"Deirdre thinks someone wants to kill her. You act as if you think it's in her mind!"

"Thank you for that input." He turned another page.

"Is that all you have to say?"

"What else do you want me to say?"

She made her voice cold. "I've expressed my concern. I'm sure I speak for many in the room who are as appalled as I am at the way you interrupted Deirdre. I demand the courtesy of an answer. Why aren't you taking Deirdre seriously?"

He closed the notebook. He stood up with slow, casual movements that seemed almost an insult. He came to the edge of the platform. His eyes were on her. She felt as if she had stepped into the path of an electric current. In the waiting silence she knew they were sizing up each other. The room was still. She was utterly unprepared for what came next.

"I *am* taking Deirdre seriously," he said. "I'm also taking *you* seriously. What's the truth you're not willing to admit?"

Louisa gasped. A nervous laugh bubbled up and almost escaped. The question was so direct, so damning, that words formed in her head so forcefully that she had to choke them back—*I came here to get material for an article that will expose SUM for the rip-off I think it is.*

For a few seconds she wavered. What would happen if she admitted the truth? She'd get involved. She'd be committed to looking into her own psyche instead of researching an article. She'd be a participant in the marathon. She'd have to submit to its discipline and use its ridiculous language. If she locked herself into a deeper confrontation with Tony Cazzine, she'd lose her objectivity. She might lose more than that. All these realizations flashed through her head while she stood holding the mike, her eyes on Tony Cazzine.

"Louisa?" He made it sound like a polite inquiry.

Damn him! *Put up or shut up, Louisa,* she said to herself. Then she shook her head. She handed back the mike and sat down. Cazzine held her gaze through the few seconds of ritual applause. Then he said, "The marathon will go into a thirty minute shutdown."

An earnest young assistant coach, whose name tag identified him as Kevin, came to the platform to give the location of the restrooms and to state the conditions of the shutdown. "It is now one-thirty," he said. "Be back in your seats, ready to begin at exactly two o'clock!"

Louisa got to her feet. She was utterly sick of Cazzine and the marathon and was once more aware of all her discomforts. Her muscles, used to a vigorous workout every day, ached from disuse. She inched her way out of her row and into the stream moving sluggishly up the aisle toward the doors at the back of the ballroom.

She found herself face-to-face with Deirdre, who was pushing against the flow, shoving aside everyone between herself and the platform, clearly intent on Tony Cazzine. Louisa ducked out of the way and went on. Behind her she heard angry grunts from those Deirdre had bulldozed aside. A confrontation was inevitable.

There was a muffled snarl, then Deirdre said sharply, "Outta my way, Pop!" Louisa looked around. Tom, one of the oldest men in the marathon, was glaring in undisguised hatred at Deirdre's back.

"Freak!" he yelled.

Deirdre, without pausing or looking back, raised her hand above her head and gave him the finger.

Louisa found her bag on the table at the back of the room where she'd been told to leave it. She moved into the mob pushing toward the doors. A glance over her shoulder showed a long line of marathoners waiting for private interface with Cazzine. Deirdre had managed to get there first. She was waving her hands in excited gestures as she talked. She seemed to have his attention. Then Cazzine was speaking, and Deirdre seemed to hang on his every word. Louisa wondered if toughness was his nature or merely an act that the coach's role demanded.

An interview with Cazzine could be the lead-off for her article. Surely he'd agree to talk with her if she could persuade him that an interview would be his opportunity to defend SUM. She would try to get him to admit that he intimidated marathoners and manipulated them psychologically. The interview would demand all her skill. It would be challenging and exciting.

"You'll never get on-line that way, Louisa," said a voice behind her shoulder. She looked around. Ernie, a newly confessed gay who had input tediously this morning about the strain of his years pretending to be straight. For a startled moment she thought he was talking about the line for the restroom.

"You'll never experience any change in your programming until you plug into the real power source," Ernie said solemnly.

"What's that, Ernie?"

"Your own integrity. Look what telling the truth did for me. I feel fabulous! You should trust Tony, Louisa. He's fabulous!"

She resisted the impulse to laugh. SUM was, among its other failings, so damn humorless. Still, she had to admit, Ernie looked, if not quite as "fabulous" as his overworked adjective, a lot more chipper than he had this morning. And he would go out of here claiming that SUM had saved his soul by forcing him to tell the truth about himself.

Absurd! Nothing in this exercise in self-abuse would make public confession look appealing to her. She could imagine the havoc she'd create with herself if she admitted to bouts with the demons of self-doubt and self-pity. She was the only one who knew how tenuous her hold was on the self-esteem she'd pulled together after her divorce. Let the Hals and Ernies get their minds shaken up and put down in new patterns. She'd hang on to what she had.

In the press of bodies near the door, she was shoved into a man who turned on her sharply. No wonder. It was Tom, the man Deirdre had so ruthlessly pushed aside. In his sour expression, she thought she saw cynicism that matched her own. When she apologized for bumping into him, he growled what might have been an acceptance. Then he said, "Nice try, taking on Cazzine like that."

"What was the use? I let him make a fool of me."

"If you ask me, Cazzine's got more bullshit than the rest of us put together!"

She felt greatly cheered. The marathoners weren't all brainwashed Ernies idolizing the coach. Her interviews with individual marathoners would bring a range of responses to SUM's authoritarian tactics.

At the ballroom door, Tom darted ahead of her. A sign outside pointed the way to the restrooms down a narrow corridor. Men's room first. No line there. Around the corner snaked the queue for the Ladies' room.

She would write a light piece on the advantages of male anatomy. Men didn't get PMS. They didn't have to wear Jogbras. They could pee fast.

Ten minutes of shuffling brought her to the Ladies' room where facilities designed to handle no more than six at a time were in demand by a hundred women. Doors banged open and shut, and toilets flushed in chorus. If she hadn't been almost in pain by this time, Louisa would have walked out. At last a woman flung open the door of the next available stall. Louisa locked the door, put the seat down, and surrendered to relief.

The toilets were momentarily silent. Above the noise Louisa heard Deirdre's irritating whine. "Anybody got a trank? I'll buy whatever you got!"

A chorus of protests broke out. Marathoners were required to sign a contract agreeing not to use drugs or alcohol for the entire two weeks. "The contract, Deirdre!" "You signed it, same as the rest of us!" "You wanna get someone else in trouble?"

"Gimme a break, will ya?" Deirdre cried. "I got problems!"

Louisa did not hear if anyone volunteered to break the marathon contract and supply Deirdre with a tranquilizer.

When she came out of the stall, she did not see Deirdre. The washbasins were all taken. A brown-haired woman in the corner was applying a fresh layer of makeup. Another was combing her mane of frizzed hair. "Excuse me," Louisa said, reaching between them to wash her hands. Two pairs of eyes looked at her in the mirror. The looks were interested, assessing. Louisa had lost her anonymity. Confronting Cazzine had made her a marathon personality like Ernie and Deirdre.

Louisa, who had chosen pants and a sweater for the hours of sitting through the marathon, marveled at the women, like the plain brunette at the last basin, in her soft, expensive suit and pearls, who dressed as if the marathon was a party.

Deirdre was the only one, however, who had come dressed for a costume ball.

Louisa dried her hands and pushed past the women still in line and grumbling that they would be late getting back into the ballroom. In the lobby, marathoners grouped around chrome and leather couches under a forest of potted ficus trees were already getting up and stubbing out cigarettes as assistant coaches urged them to start moving. Louisa decided to forego conversation for coffee. She raced to the coffee shop and gulped a cup at the counter. When she finished it, the wall clock said one fifty-seven. She was cutting it close.

Hustled in with the latecomers, she dropped her bag on the table again and went to the seat an assistant coach sent her to. Deirdre clomped into the row and flopped down on the chair on Louisa's left. Her black tights stretched to the tops of a pair of boots, thick-soled and laced up to Day-glo orange legwarmers that bunched around her ankles.

"Shit!" Deirdre muttered. "I shouldn't of come back!" She had reapplied the purple lipstick. It stood out greasily against her face, which was gray, not only from smeared makeup, but from a sick pallor. Her forehead was shiny with perspiration, and the spikes of her green coxcomb were wilting.

"Are you all right?" Louisa asked. All she needed now was proximity to a person whose self-analysis induced nausea. It had already happened. Sickness bags were available.

Deirdre shivered. "I'm not going to barf, if that's what you mean, but I sure feel like shit. I tried to keep their fucking contract, didn't take a trank this morning. Now I'm strung out."

"Do you still think someone wants to...?" Louisa stopped. There was no way to ask the question tactfully.

"Dunno. Maybe I am full of shit, like Tony says. This marathon sucks. I'm like totally grossed out, I mean totally. First thing this morning they're on my case 'cause I'm five fucking minutes late. Now they're hassling me to get back in here. I mean, get a grip!"

"Did you get ...?" Another question that was hard to ask.

Deirdre whispered, "I never shoulda signed that fucking contract!" She turned up her right fist on her knee. Her fingers opened and shut quickly. Louisa caught a glimpse of a pink and gray capsule.

Deirdre would be an interesting person to interview for her article. What attracted a girl like this to the marathon? She must have known she would be asked to go without any drugs she used habitually. She would use Deirdre's story if she could get the girl to tell it.

The marathon contract, which she too had signed, required her to raise her hand and inform the coach that Deirdre had a controlled substance on her person. Her struggle with her conscience in the matter was no contest. Another thing she had against SUM was its insistence that everyone mind his *and* her neighbor's business.

Deirdre leaned closer to Louisa. "I gotta take this pretty quick. I didn't know I'd be so totally spaced. Someone tried to grab my purse last night. Pulled so hard on the strap I got marks on my neck."

"Where did this happen?"

"Subway platform. It was kinda late, you know? And like, the platform was empty. The train was coming, and I thought he was gonna push me onta the track. This morning I was so totally freaked with that and no tranks I was ready to drop out of the marathon, but my friend said I had to keep my contract."

"Did you see who attacked you?"

"No. Whoever it was come up from behind. I musta been totally bombed. Maybe I am, like—paranoid, you know?"

"Did you tell the police?"

"What good would that do? I didn't see the sucker."

Deirdre had dropped her voice to a confidential whisper. Louisa did the same. "I'd like to talk to you outside the marathon," Louisa said.

"No kidding?" Deirdre sounded pleased. "I don't know why not." She fumbled in her pockets, drew out a stiff slip of paper. She squinted at it. "What the fuck's this? Shit, I don't need this any longer, I got it by heart. You gotta pen?"

Louisa's pocket yielded a pencil. On the paper Deirdre thrust into her hand, she wrote the number the girl dictated. "Seventh Street—between Avenues C and D," Deirdre added. "Third floor—the back apartment. Name's Doyle."

"Shh!" The man in front of Louisa turned around and glared. Simultaneously an elbow poked her from the right. Kevin, the chief assistant coach, was standing on the platform and anxiously trying to compel silence by making eye contact with two hundred people. Louisa shoved pencil and paper into her back pocket.

Applause burst out as Tony bounded down the aisle, and it continued for some time, encouraged by stamping and whistling from the assistant coaches in the back of the ballroom. After the noise died down, Cazzine said, "I'm going to tell you what my life was like before I did the marathon."

The room became tense and expectant. One hundred and ninety-nine faces looked at the coach with trust verging on reverence. On her face, Louisa hoped, was a healthy skepticism.

"Ten years after I got out of the service, Vietnam was still running me," he said.

The silence became absolute.

"I couldn't get it out of my mind. The Vietnamese poet who wrote 'In my country it rains blood and hails bones' knew what it was like inside my head. Bodies. Burned houses. Screaming women and children. The faces of the men who were wasted when I had to lead them into what turned out to be an ambush."

In the row behind Louisa, someone made a short, harsh sound like a sob quickly suppressed. Male voices murmured or grunted from the other areas of the room.

"Twenty-three men died in that ambush. I was the only survivor. I lived because I was the first to be hit, and the dead fell on top of me. Their bodies saved me. The 'Cong came with bayonets to make sure."

Cazzine's face was white now, and the lines stood out on it. The energy that had sustained him seemed to be draining away. Against her will, Louisa felt moved.

"I raved for three days after they pulled the bodies off me. Why them and not me? Then I figured it out—God was saving me for something worse. After I got out of the hospital, I couldn't wait. Every day remaining in my tour, I ran out to meet it. I prayed for a quick end—a mine, a booby trap, a bullet in the brain from a sniper—anything but what God had saved me for. I called God a motherfucker, and I begged him to kill me. But I still lived.

"When I came home, I was like a grenade with the pin pulled out. My life was nothing but guilt that they had died and I didn't, and anger that God was still keeping me in suspense. I didn't have the guts to kill myself outright, so I went for the slow suicide of drugs and alcohol. They blotted out the horror—for a little while.

"From time to time I pulled myself together and tried to act like a real human being instead of a walking grenade. I went back to UCLA. Dropped out in four months. I got married. Divorced within two years. Three good jobs slipped away from me.

"My ex-wife did the marathon in L.A. She talked me into doing it. That's where I saw what was running me. I was obsessed with death. At the marathon I turned my back on it. The marathon saved my life and my sanity. I learned to let go of Vietnam and to accept myself for what I was—a lucky son-of-a-bitch—and I did what I had to do to get on with the life God had saved me for.

"You can do that too—wake up each morning and run out to meet life the way I used to run out to meet death. But first you have to take a good hard look at your life. You have to tell the truth about it. What's running you?"

He made it sound so easy. Take a look at your life, accept yourself, change what you don't like. All around her people seemed to be lapping up these simplistic formulas for self-improvement as if Tony Cazzine was a prophet from the Almighty.

He was either a consummate con artist or he was still psychotic. He could not have recovered from such a trauma, let alone addiction to drugs, so miraculously. He'd substituted one obsession for another. SUM was his tranquilizer, and he was handing it out to these people who were hungry for the easy way to assuage guilt and grief. His story was an insult to the memory of the men who had died or who still suffered from what they'd experienced in Vietnam.

Her anger faded, giving way to sadness and depression. The long hours in this room, and Cazzine's morbid story had taken their toll.

"You're going to look at what's running your life," Tony said. "Get ready for programming."

Programming required the marathoners to close their eyes, relax their bodies, and follow a series of suggestions designed to bring forgotten experiences and repressed feelings to the "screen" of consciousness. On command, Louisa let her eyelids fall and her muscles go limp. A drowsy numbness took hold. The sleep she craved was very near.

"Take a look at yourself," said Cazzine. "What are you most afraid to see?"

In the half-doze she quickly fell into, Louisa found her mind roaming the fears of her childhood. Dark. She'd been afraid of the dark and ashamed to ask for a nightlight. Deirdre's story had awakened another fear—the onrushing subway train. On the platform, she usually hugged the tile wall and waited till the train stopped before she moved toward its doors.

"What are you afraid of? Bring it to the screen. That's the way you'll delete it from your life."

She didn't want to look, but sleep had fled.

I'm afraid of failure. I've climbed so high, I'm afraid I'll fall. One error of judgement, one careless piece of research, and I'm through. There's nowhere else for me to go. I'm at the top of the ladder.

"What are you afraid of? What's running you?"

The noise began. A sob here, a sigh there. Then a groan. Another one. More. The sound was barely audible at first, but it grew. It gathered volume and intensity as one after another added cries to the keening chorus until the room rang with sounds of souls crying out of their hidden and most private hells.

On Louisa's right a man sobbed. Behind her she heard strangled, piping cries. Deirdre made no sound, but when the girl's upper arm touched hers, Louisa could feel her trembling.

On went Cazzine's voice, pushing questions that reached the depths. Louisa's dreads hovered. Her throat began to ache. She struggled to keep from feeling the panic that suddenly welled up.

I'm alone. I'm behind an armor of success and confidence, and I'm afraid to let anyone see behind it.

"What are you afraid of? What's standing between you and what you really want in life?"

The break-up of her marriage had hurt so much she still couldn't think of it without pain. She and Glen had had such good intentions. He was starting out in law as a junior partner in a big firm. He put in long hours and came home with his head full of cases. Often she felt she had to shout across a long distance to get his attention. He would never abandon himself fully to her, to just being with her. Work was always in the back of his mind, and she could feel its intrusion by his sudden silences and inattentions.

She felt rejected, unloved, and in her hurt she had pulled away into her own work, her writing. She found a voice, a point of view, and miraculously, an audience. She began to put in hours as long as Glen's, traveling, interviewing, writing. One day they had looked at each other and seen strangers. Neither of them was willing to take the time for counseling. They both simply wanted out. Nothing was left but the legalities.

Tears stung her eyes. She had a career she loved, but she had no one to love, no one to see her real self. She was afraid to risk another failure. She dated, but she kept her relationships light. Whenever a man seemed on the verge of admitting he was interested in a deeper commitment, she backed off.

"Fuck this!" Deirdre hissed. She shifted suddenly in her seat.

Louisa came to with a start and opened her eyes. She did not know how long she had been wallowing in the pit of regret and self-recrimination. She felt Deirdre move again, and she glanced over. Deirdre lifted her arm. Her hand went to her mouth. Deirdre gulped and choked a little as if the dry capsule stuck in her throat. Then she swallowed audibly. She had not held out. The tranquilizer was on its way into her blood-stream.

Fuck this! Louisa echoed fervently. She would not close her eyes again, be seduced by Cazzine's voice, and descend a second time into self-pity. How dare Cazzine force such emotions from her!

Where was he, anyway? The platform was empty. She looked around the room. He was over on the far left. He was roaming around, directing questions first from one side, then from the other.

Louisa felt a violent movement beside her and shot a quick look at Deirdre. The girl jerked upright. Her face was bright pink. Her hands fluttered in the air, then groped for her throat.

Deirdre opened her mouth. Sounds came out—strangled, agonized gasps that topped even the terrible chorus of grief all about them. Frothy saliva bubbled from Deirdre's mouth. Her upper body rocked back and forth. Then she gave a convulsive shudder. Her feet drummed on the floor and her arms flailed. With another violent convulsion, she pitched forward. Her forehead hit the back of the chair in front of her. She collapsed back into herself, flopping spasmodically like a beached fish. Her chin fell onto her chest. Her body twitched. Then she was still.

Louisa heard her own voice cry out. She jumped to her feet. Without thinking about what she was doing, she grabbed the girl's green locks and pulled up her head. She tried not to look into the staring eyes. She brought her mouth down to Deirdre's lips.

Then she stopped in horror. That odor! It was like peach pits—or almonds.

Almonds? Bitter almonds?

She had never smelled cyanide before, but she knew it had to be.

Footsteps pounded behind her. Cazzine was in the aisle, leaning urgently into the row where Deirdre slumped. Heads began to come up. Faces turned. Screams erupted.

Cazzine's eyes met Louisa's. "What's the matter with her?"

Louisa shook her head. Finally, choking a little, she said, "She swallowed something . . . a capsule . . . I think she just—

died.'' Her eyes filled with tears, and she stared helplessly at Tony.

His confidence was wiped away. His eyes were stricken. The look he gave her was almost beseeching. This was not bullshit. Someone *had* wanted to kill Deirdre.

TWO

DEIRDRE'S AGONY quickly brought half the people in the room out of their private nightmares and into the real one in their midst. Screams multiplied when those closest to Deirdre saw her terrible, slumped stillness. Within minutes everyone was up. People in the last three rows, Louisa among them, overturned their chairs in their scramble to get away. On the edges of the ballroom, people climbed up on their chairs for a better look. The room rang with cries. Panic was close.

Cazzine raced back to the platform. He began to give orders. The SUM organization, which had already imposed its structure on the two hundred people in the room, now kept them in control.

A doctor rushed to the back table for his bag and shoved his way toward Deirdre.

Cazzine's orders brought assistant coaches running in with more chairs. The last three rows were quickly reseated along one side of the room. Deirdre was alone with the doctor bending over her. Her face was still suffused with color, and her agonized gaze was on the ceiling. The doctor plunged in a needle. He eased her limp weight to the floor and began the rituals of resuscitation. Within minutes he stopped and shook his head.

For a moment the room was utterly still.

Louisa leaned over and put her head between her knees. She felt sick, and her whole body was shaking. Martin, on her right, leaned over and whispered, "I'll ask an assistant coach to get you a brandy or something. They can break the rules for something like this."

She shook her head. Deirdre had broken the rules.

"Water?"

The faintness was passing. She sat up. "Water—yes, please."

When the water came, she held the glass in both hands to get it to her lips without it spilling. She drank in small sips and took deep breaths. She knew people were looking at her, and she struggled to get herself under control. Finally she was able to look at the sprawled, pathetic figure on the floor. Deirdre's vulgar vitality had been snuffed out. Tangled green spikes of hair fell over her distorted, half-hidden face.

Louisa put the empty glass on the floor under her chair and forced herself to take in a terrible truth. She might be the only person in the room who knew that Deirdre had swallowed a capsule minutes before she died.

Or she might be the second person who knew that fact.

It had looked like a Darvon. Tampered with? The drug poured out and cyanide poured in? Someone had learned the lesson of recurring deaths from adulterated Tylenol and Excedrin—how to kill at safe remove from one's victim.

How would the police go about finding a killer among two hundred suspects? More, counting Cazzine, the eight assistant coaches, and quite possibly all the people in the hotel. Or the city, for that matter. Anyone could have come into the lobby, made contact with Deirdre on the shutdown, and given or sold her the fatal capsule.

Deirdre's death changed everything. Louisa was no longer a writer researching an article, she was an eyewitness to a murder. Sudden death at the marathon could put SUM out of business instantly, and with it, Tony Cazzine. She felt almost sorry for him. There was no point in writing the article the way she had planned. As soon as she'd talked to the police, she needed to call her agent. Hal would have ideas about how to seize the opportunity.

An assistant coach came in with a blanket, which the doctor draped gently over Deirdre's body. The noise level in the room rose higher and higher. A few marathoners tried to leave, and were firmly sent back to their seats by assistant coaches, who were soon reinforced by police.

The officers went through their rituals. The blanket was taken away while a photographer circled the silent, grotesque form on the gray carpet.

Louisa guessed that forty-five minutes to an hour had passed since Deirdre collapsed beside her. She looked around and began to match faces with name tags. The man in front of her,

Chet, had turned around to glare her into silence. On her right, Martin had sobbed like a child during the programming. Behind Louisa was Sylvia. On Deirdre's right was Arthur. Over the empty space now between them, he and Louisa looked at each other in silent commiseration. His face was still ashen. In front of Deirdre's chair, a fiftyish woman named Hazel was still occasionally wiping her eyes. The crack of Deirdre's head against the back of her chair had been a shock she seemed still to be reliving. Behind Deirdre's empty chair was Tom, dour and silent.

These three closest to Louisa might have overheard some of her conversation with Deirdre. She would surely be questioned first, then Hazel, Arthur, and Tom. Then what would the police do? Search all those bags and briefcases for cyanide disguised as Darvon?

Cazzine was on the platform with a heavy-set man who, apparently, was a detective. Cazzine's mike was off; he and the policeman were not audible. It was obvious that the detective was asking questions. As Tony answered, the detective's eyes roamed out over the ballroom. On his face was an angry frown. Louisa could imagine the conversation that was going on as Cazzine tried to explain to the policeman what the marathon was all about. Marathoners, shock wearing off, were now buzzing with alarm, speculation, and rising anger.

Cazzine pointed to the now reseated participants in the last three rows. The detective's look focused on the empty space beside Louisa. He spoke. Something was decided, for Cazzine motioned to Kevin, who eagerly listened to his orders, and all but saluted.

Kevin came over to the reseated rows and began to jot on a clipboard, consulting name tags. More police came and went. The detective left the room.

Cazzine came to the edge of the platform. The noise in the room slackened and died. All eyes were on the coach. He would tell them what to do.

He looked drawn, almost haggard. "A terrible thing has happened here," he said. "We have to handle our shock and grief." Nods and groans acknowledged him. "We'll do it together as soon as the police have finished with what they have to do in this room. You've been patient, and I thank you. So does Detective Malone of the New York City police.

"Some of you will be asked to leave for short periods to help the police by answering questions. If you do, treat that interruption exactly like a shutdown. Come back to the marathon as soon as the police let you go. Detective Malone has asked me to tell you how important it is that you stay here until they have finished their preliminary investigation. I remind you to keep your contract with the marathon."

The buzz of voices broke out again. Louisa had to admire the way he'd managed the old cliché, "Don't anybody leave the room."

Kevin was there, clipboard in hand. "Louisa, Hazel, Arthur, Tom—Detective Malone wants to see you first. Come with me, please. We're going to the SUM office on the mezzanine."

"I want to get my bag," said Louisa.

"You're not to take personal belongings at this time. You'll be coming right back to the marathon. I will escort you."

Hazel stood up. "I've got to have a cigarette!" Her hair was in untidy wisps around her tear-stained face.

Kevin looked pained. Clearly he was not ready to deal with counterproposals.

"Cut out the crap!" said Tom in a low, furious voice. "Let the ladies get their pocketbooks!"

Kevin looked toward the platform. No help there. Cazzine was again in conference, this time with a uniformed cop. Louisa walked boldly to the table at the back and picked up her bag, which was near the top of the pile. Hazel did the same.

"The marathon will resume in five minutes." Cazzine's voice was the last thing she heard as she left the ballroom. Just before she stepped onto the carpeted stairs to the mezzanine, she saw two men in white uniforms carrying a stretcher through the lobby.

A door of a room on the mezzanine had a taped on sign—SUM OFFICE. SUM's main office was in a building on lower Third Avenue. The furnishings of this room, which SUM apparently rented for marathon weekends, was limited to the basics—a desk, several chairs, a table with piles of SUM literature.

Detective James Malone was a big man. His bulk filled the chair behind the desk. He had a broad face, ruddy and weather-beaten, sandy hair that was going white, and pale blue eyes that met hers briefly and then looked away. Baffled irritation was on his face. Louisa was right about Detective Malone. He didn't know what SUM was all about, and he was angry.

She knew the rules about cooperating with the police; she'd learned them as a reporter. Keep on the good side of the cops if you want information. After she gave him her name and address, she was quick and concise with the details of Deirdre's collapse.

Malone was looking off somewhere over her shoulder while she talked. When she stopped, he grunted. "Pretty observant, aren't you?"

"It's my business to be that way. I'm a writer."

"Writer, are you? You work for a newspaper or what?"

"I'm free-lance. I do articles for magazines and newspapers."

He looked at the notebook in which he'd written her name. "Louisa Evans?" Then he looked at her. Recognition came. "You the one who wrote that story about cops and gays in the Village?"

"Yes, I wrote that." The article on the improving but still tense and uneasy relationships between the police and the gay community had come out in the *Village Voice* two months ago. She thought it was one of the best articles she'd ever written.

A sour look had come into the detective's face. "Controversial stuff like that does more harm than good if you ask me," he said. "Cops are no more prejudiced than the next guy. People read stuff like that, they get the wrong impression."

"I tried to be fair." She'd gotten good candid quotes from cops, both gay and straight, and from the gay men and women who came in contact with them. She thought she'd presented both sides, and she'd let her readers know that they'd come a long way toward trust and tolerance.

"You're better off ignoring situations like that. Gays read about other gays thinking cops persecute them, they start feeling sorry for themselves. That's what leads to incidents. Leave things alone, they work out. That's my opinion."

Obviously it was not the time for her to state her opinion about the public's right to know. She was used to accusations that she'd disturbed the status quo. What was disturbing in this situation was that she was already off on the wrong foot with Detective James Malone.

"You were sure she was dead. Why?"

He'd resumed his questioning so abruptly that for a few seconds she was caught off guard. "I . . . I . . . smelled cyanide, or what I thought was cyanide when I leaned over to try mouth-to-mouth."

"You ever see anyone die of cyanide poisoning?"

"No, but I've read about it. I knew about the odor and the suddenness. She died so quickly, so painfully . . ." To her horror, her voice broke, and tears came into her eyes again. She put her hand up to her mouth to hide the trembling of her lips.

"You said you leaned over to try mouth-to-mouth, but you didn't go on with it. Why was that?"

"From what I knew about cyanide, I thought there was no use—that is, if I thought at all—I was so shocked I certainly wasn't acting logically."

"How long between the time you thought she swallowed the capsule and the first sign of its effect?"

"Three minutes, four maybe."

"You ever see Deirdre Doyle before this thing—this marathon?"

"No."

"Prior contact with her during the marathon?"

"When I was in the restroom, I heard her voice. She was asking for a tranquilizer, almost begging for it, in fact. She offered to pay for it."

"You heard all this but didn't see her?"

"I was in a toilet booth with the door closed."

He nodded and avoided her eyes. "You get the impression she was asking one person?"

"No, I thought she was addressing everyone who was in there. The Ladies' room was very crowded. And a lot of women responded to her, reminding her we'd signed a contract not to use drugs of any kind during the marathon."

"Can you identify any of the women who answered her?"

"I didn't see them."

"But you recognized Deirdre by her voice."

"She has—had—a distinctive nasal whine. You have to remember, Detective Malone, that most of us in the marathon are still strangers to one another. We've been together only half a day."

"I know that, Miss Evans," he said dryly.

A mistake. He didn't like being told.

"When you came out of the uh, toilet, did you see Deirdre with anyone, like close enough to be getting something from her?"

"I didn't see Deirdre at all. She'd gone into a toilet."

"Do you remember the names of any of the women in the restroom?"

Louisa tried to visualize the line-up in the mirror. Surely the woman at the last basin was the one who had come out of the toilet Louisa had gone into. She hadn't seen that woman's name tag, but the one on the other side who'd been combing her hair—that was Cassie. She thought women named Amy and Marge were the next ones in line when she left the room. She told Malone the names she could remember. He jotted them down.

"Did you see Deirdre in the lobby after you came out of the restroom?"

"No, I went to the coffee shop and I had to hurry to get back into the ballroom on time."

"This capsule you say you saw in her hand—what did it look like?"

"A Darvon compound."

His eyebrows went up. "You're sure it was a compound, not a straight Darvon?"

"I've done research on drugs for articles I've written."

"Yeah?"

"I'm not a user myself, if that's what you're thinking!"

"I'm not thinking anything, Miss Evans, just trying to get a picture. How did Deirdre act when she sat down beside you before the marathon started up again?"

"She was very upset. 'Strung out' is what she said she felt. She was pale, her face was sweaty, and she was shaking."

"What did you think was the matter with her?"

"I thought she was having withdrawal symptoms. She told me she hadn't taken a tranquilizer today. When she showed me the capsule, she said, 'I can't hold out much longer.'"

"Anything else?"

"She seemed frightened. She told the whole marathon she thought someone wanted to kill her. She told me someone had tried to snatch her purse last night on the subway platform and she was almost pushed onto the tracks."

"Where did this occur?"

"She didn't say."

"She seemed to think the attack was aimed at her? Not a random purse snatching?"

"Frankly, Detective Malone, I thought she was paranoid. Abrupt withdrawal from tranquilizers can bring about delusions."

"But you were pretty upset with Mr. Cazzine for not paying enough attention to Deirdre when she said someone wanted to kill her."

So Tony Cazzine had told the detective about their exchange! "My quarrel with Mr. Cazzine was about SUM's methods—getting people to talk and then cutting them off before they're through."

The sandy eyebrows lifted again. "Is that so? Then what are you doing in the marathon if you don't like the way Cazzine is running the show?"

"I signed up for it to write an article about SUM."

"You going to give it the same treatment you gave the cops in Greenwich Village?"

"I'll try to be fair."

He shrugged. "You'll write about this girl's death?"

"I'll have to. This tragedy will have a big influence on the way the public perceives SUM."

He looked off over her shoulder without speaking for so long that she grew uneasy. Finally he said, "Whatever way you write it, you'll get big bucks for it, won't you?"

It was hard to keep her temper checked. "Writers don't get rich on magazine sales. I'll be lucky if I make—"

He interrupted. "What do you think of SUM?"

"I think the marathon at best is misleading and at worst is psychologically harmful to participants who aren't very strong emotionally. Deirdre obviously wasn't."

"What happened today kinda proves your point, doesn't it?"

"What do you mean?"

"Deirdre was murdered, or she committed suicide, or her death was an accident. Whatever it is, you'll give SUM the rap, won't you?"

"If they're to blame for not weeding out applicants who aren't emotionally stable, they need to be 'rapped,' don't you agree?"

"What I think of SUM is neither here nor there. Tell me, if you hadn't heard what you heard in the Ladies' room, would you have thought Deirdre killed herself?"

"Suicide was certainly possible, given her emotional state. God knows what was going on in her mind during that program. But I don't think Deirdre would have inflicted such terrible pain on herself. I think she was experienced enough with drugs to know easier ways to commit suicide."

He tore a sheet from his notebook and scribbled on it. "I'll want to talk to you again. If you come up with anything more, call me. Leave a message if I'm not at my desk."

As she took the paper with his number, she was very conscious of her dissatisfaction with the way the interview had gone. Detective Malone should have been grateful for having an observant witness, so near to the victim, of a particularly horrible crime. Instead, his objection to her article seemed to have made him dislike her and look for ways to question her observations and her motives.

What she was about to do next would only compound the problem. Malone would call her an ambulance-chaser, or worse. She had to talk to Hal and map out the new direction this story should take. She wanted to see Deirdre's apartment before the police got there. She had no intention of going back to the marathon. Her defection would make her a dropout in the eyes of SUM, and she was sure the group would pursue her aggressively. How her actions would affect Detective Malone's opinion of her would be a situation she would have to risk.

Kevin was waiting for her when she left the office. He grinned. "I'm to take you back to the marathon, Louisa."

"Kevin, I've *got* to go to the Ladies' room. I'll go right back to the ballroom afterward."

"I have to go with you, Louisa," he said seriously. Then he blushed. "Escort you there—I mean—wait outside."

"I'm a big girl. I can go all by myself." She smiled into his troubled young face.

Two minutes later the revolving door whirled her out onto the sidewalk in front of the hotel.

THREE

No one followed her. She was so relieved at her getaway that at first she didn't feel the cold. Shut into the hotel ballroom for so many hours, she had almost forgotten it was December.

She unpinned her marathon name tag and dropped it into her bag. Her down jacket was still in the ballroom. Away from the hotel entrance on Sixth Avenue, she found a clothing store where she quickly bought a fiber-filled jacket and a nondescript hat and glove set. Ignoring the raised eyebrows of the cashier, she asked for scissors to cut off the price tags and wore her purchases out onto the avenue that was thronged with holiday shoppers.

Her next stop was a pay phone. "Murder at the marathon?" Hal cried. "Sacrilege! Unbelievable!" When he had recovered, he spoke rapidly. "There's a book in this. You're an eyewitness. Start researching her life. I'll contact some publishers right away."

"I have her address. She lived in the East Village. I'm on my way there now."

"For God's sake, be careful!"

When she hung up, she pulled out the slip of paper Deirdre had given her. Seventh Street between Avenues C and D. That was the no man's land east of Manhattan's numbered avenues, an area called Alphabet City by its hipper residents. She'd done an article on its flourishing drug traffic. Prudence prompted her to put cash, credit cards, and apartment keys into the pockets of her pants. She tucked the paper with Deirdre's address into the palm of her glove.

A book. Hal thought she could write a book. She could see it now, almost feel it in her hand. She would follow the police investigation of the murder, and she would look into Deirdre's life for what had led up to it. They'd sell the film rights before the book even came out. Though the article exposing SUM had been a good idea, this was infinitely more exciting. This was the opportunity of her career.

"Big bucks," the detective had said. She'd recoiled at his cynicism. But the truth was that she could make more money than she'd ever made, and she needed it. Her income from freelancing was uncertain. She'd left a safe job on a newspaper while she was still married to Glen in order to take a chance on her own talent. She had to supplement her earnings by parttime teaching. A book would mean security.

But what would it mean to Deirdre's family, if the girl even had one? Could she write an honest book without feeling that she was capitalizing on the girl's horrible death?

At Columbus Circle the fountains were flinging scarves of water high into the cold, windy night. A crowd of families—light-hearted parents and children holding silver balloons—was emerging from the circus at the Coliseum and pushing toward the entrance to the subway in such numbers that Louisa hesitated. Then she reminded herself that one did not go into Deirdre's turf by cab, even if she could find a driver willing to take her to that neighborhood.

She took the train to Times Square, crossed over on the shuttle, and took the Number 6 train downtown. The crowds on the subway had thinned by the time she got off at Bleecker Street. She walked east. The handful of people who got off with her quickly dispersed. The few remaining hurried, with faces down against the wind. The new jacket was thinner than her other one, and it gave poor protection from the cold. She felt different in it, as if by putting on the cheap garment she had ceased to be Louisa Evans. Her errand here made her feel furtive, like the figures she glimpsed huddled in doorways of burned-out buildings.

Her excitement had died, and in its place was a deepening dread. A woman had died beside her. She was on her way to look into that young life that was so violently cut off. Detective Malone wasn't the only one to question her motives. Only the most careful research and the best writing she was capable of would make this book all right with her. She had to give some meaning to Deirdre's life and death.

The cold and squalor of Alphabet City weighed on her. She clutched her bag under her arm, the sharp corner of her notebook reminding her that she was a writer and she needed objectivity, not emotional involvement, when researching a story. Her job now was to find out what she could about Deirdre Doyle.

No names were on the bell plates of the doorway at the address Deirdre had given her. The front door had no lock. When she opened it and went into the front hall, the sound and stench nearly knocked her down. The sound, coming from the second floor, was the sounds of a bass, drums, and guitar being played so loud she could not even hear her footsteps on the wooden stairs. The smell was a mixture of pot, urine, stale cooking oil, and urban decay.

"Third floor back," Deirdre had said. That door was ajar. It was useless to knock or call out. No one would hear with the music blasting below. Louisa pushed open Deirdre's door.

The room had been ransacked. Its meager contents had been tossed with an abandon that suggested haste, or violence, or both. A woman's clothes—gaudy, cheap, and far from new—tumbled from an overturned cardboard wardrobe. Records were thrown helter-skelter with the jackets they'd been pulled from. Cushions, sheets, and blankets trailed on the floor, ripped from a daybed with a stained ticking. A rickety card table lay on its side. Papers had flown in and around it.

The search could not have taken long. There was so little here. Deirdre's strewn belongings were as pathetic as the sprawled corpse of their owner. A life and all its accoutrements had been tossed and abandoned.

In the midst of the shambles, photographs cascaded from a torn brown portfolio. Louisa took off her gloves. She knelt beside the pile of pictures. The room was so cold that her breath came in frosty puffs as she picked up each picture by its edges.

Seagulls off the bow of the Staten Island Ferry. Children on the carousel in Central Park. The towers of the World Trade Center askew against a mackerel sky. The Statue of Liberty shrouded in scaffolding for its renovations. The most banal and predictable New York City scenes, badly photographed. If the pictures were Deirdre's, they showed her as an utterly incompetent amateur.

At the first sight of the photographs, Louisa felt a rush of excitement. Letdown came quickly. She had not known what to expect, but nothing in this trite collection hinted at a motive for murder. And if there had been anything that looked incriminating, whoever had searched the apartment had surely found it. She was certain of one thing. Deirdre's apartment had not been searched by the police. Even in a hurry, they would not have thrown the girl's possessions about with such abandon.

She suddenly felt a sharp sense of the cold, the bleakness of the place, and the futility of her errand. She was so cold that her hands were shaking as she gathered the photographs together and stacked them to return them to the portfolio. She forgot that her back was toward the door, and that the music below drowned out all other sounds. The pad of a footstep right behind her was all she knew before an iron-hard arm in a khaki sleeve clamped around her neck.

Her air was cut off. She was suffocating. She flailed and tugged violently at the arm.

"Don't move!" A harsh whisper. The arm tightened. His other arm came from behind and into her line of vision. She saw a hand scrabbling in her bag, coming out empty, and turning the bag upside down. She also saw a flattened, misshapen thumbnail. The hand disappeared from her sight. Something hit the side of her head so hard she fell with a thud into the dark.

FOUR

TONY CAZZINE dropped down into the desk chair in SUM's weekend office. Midnight. The marathon had shut down. Marathoners were on their way to their homes or their hotels, the timid and the suburban by car pool and cab, the city-wise by subway. They would be back tomorrow morning at nine o'clock for the second day of the marathon.

Some of them.

The end of a marathon's first day usually left him on a high, his brain teeming with ways to turn the day's experiences into future insights. But instead he was leaden, with an exhaustion born not only of the hours of interfacing with people who were in the grip of shock, anger, fear, and denial—all the emotional by-products of proximity to sudden death—but from his fight to keep himself available to them and not overwhelmed by the same emotions himself.

SUM was as good as dead. And he had killed it.

The horror was still with him. It had receded for a few years, allowing him to think he was okay, to think that he had recreated himself after the ravages of Vietnam to become a person who had something to give to others. Now the horror had come back. It had struck into the heart of the place where he'd found life again. He'd had to watch Deirdre die in the midst of the marathon, now he would see SUM die.

The door opened. Alex Meigs, manager of the New York office of SUM, walked in carrying a manila envelope. His lean, usually benign face drooped like that of a tired beagle's. Tony roused himself from what he recognized as morbid self-pity and made a motion to get up from the desk chair.

"Stay there. You look like hell." Alex lowered himself into the chair across from the desk and put the envelope on the desk. "Detective Malone is herding the last of the reporters out the revolving door."

"All heading for their typewriters to write SUM's obituary."

"Maybe not, Tony. The marathon didn't crash. You did a hell of a job of holding it together."

"What's the damage?"

"Twenty people said flatly they weren't coming back. Others didn't say, but probably won't. A few muttered darkly about lawsuits. We lost some at the shutdown for dinner. One person didn't come back from police questioning."

"Louisa Evans."

"Who's she? I heard you had a powerful interface."

"Confrontation."

"Get out the data sheets—Malone wants them. He's coming up here to talk to you once he gets rid of the press."

Tony opened a drawer and brought out a cardboard file folder. "Did you tell him we don't keep personal files on marathoners? That we shred these data sheets as soon as the marathon is over?"

"I told him that. He wants to see them anyway. He hopes someone has answered our question. 'What do you want to get out of the marathon' by saying 'I want to kill Deirdre Doyle.'"

Tony leafed through the pile of data sheets until he came to the one Louisa Evans had sent in with her registration and check. Under "Occupation" she had entered "Free-lance writer."

"Oh, Christ, I thought so!" Tony said. "She writes for *New York* magazine and the *Village Voice*. She was hostile from the moment she came in. If the reporters are writing SUM's obit, she's warming up to a requiem."

"Est survived a bad press," Alex said. He did not sound convinced.

"No one was murdered at est." Tony closed the file folder and thrust it at Alex. "Too bad we didn't copy these."

"Way ahead of you, friend. I sent them over to our copy machine as soon as I heard the detective wanted them." He held out the manila envelope. "Copies."

By the time Detective Malone tapped on the door, the copies of the marathon's data sheets were in the file, and the manila envelope with the originals was on Alex's desk. The detective walked in slowly, moving almost reluctantly, Tony thought. Malone's face was tired, and a shadowy stubble showed on his cheeks. He still wore his look of puzzled resentment. Malone didn't want this case. Tony was sure of that. He'd had enough difficulty trying to explain the purpose of the marathon to know that the detective was not impressed with SUM.

When Alex handed the envelope to him, Malone said, "You need these? You could make copies."

Tony and Alex refrained from exchanging glances. "No problem," said Alex. "Is there anything more you need from me?"

"A couple of things. My partner and I, plus another team, will be here tomorrow. You still going to go on with this thing?"

"We can't abort even if we lose some."

"Get me the names of everyone who doesn't come back and a print-out of the whole roster. First thing tomorrow."

"We'll have them," said Alex. "We telephone the no-shows and try to bring them in. I'm putting extra people on the phones tomorrow."

"How do you take attendance?"

"We use the name tags. They're all like this one." Alex unpinned the tag from his lapel. "Alex" was printed boldly in green, "Meigs" in small letters under it. The tag was enclosed in a plastic shield. "We lay the tags out on a table by the door to the ballroom. They're in alphabetical order. Marathoners pick them up before they enter. No one can get in without a tag. Assistant coaches are posted by the door to see that everyone has a tag pinned on. When the doors are closed, we know who's missing because their name tag is still on the table. Then we get busy on the phones."

"What happens at the end of the day?"

"They drop their tags into a basket at the door. For the bathroom breaks, they keep their tags. But for the two-hour dinner shutdown and the overnight shutdown, no one leaves without turning in a tag, or re-enters without wearing one."

When Alex left, the detective took the chair across from Tony and sank into it with a slight groan. They'd already had two conversations, both brief, the first on the platform immediately after the police had arrived on the scene, and one later while Tony was on the dinner shutdown. Now, Tony supposed, he was in for a full-scale grilling. He braced himself to deal with the detective's irritation. SUM was outside Malone's experience.

"I'll try to be quick, Mr. Cazzine." Malone took out a notebook. When Tony gave his address, the detective said, "A long commute."

"Los Angeles is my home base. I go wherever SUM sends me. SUM holds marathons in twenty cities. I come to New York about eight times a year, and I stay in the hotel. Room eleven sixty-five."

"Tell me what you did between one-thirty and two o'clock this afternoon."

"I stayed in the ballroom on the platform until one-fifty, interfacing with individual marathoners. Then I went to the Men's room."

"The one outside the ballroom?"

"No, I came up here."

"Did you go through the lobby?"

"Not on my way out. A private stairway behind the platform leads from the ballroom directly to the mezzanine. When I came back to the marathon a few minutes after two, I came down the main stairs, through the lobby, and entered the ballroom by the door at the back. I make an entrance, you might say."

Malone closed the notebook and sat back in the chair. He sighed again, heavily this time. "What's this marathon thing all about? Tell me again. A cult, is it?"

Tony counseled himself to patience. "It's not a cult. SUM stands for Self Utilization Marathon. It's a series of planned group experiences taking place over two weekends. It's designed to help people let go of the past and discover their resources for living happier and more productive lives. Here." He pulled himself out of the chair, went over to the table, and took a pamphlet from a pile. "You can read about it."

The detective took the pamphlet, but he did not open it. "I want to hear you tell it so I can get it. What do you people believe in?"

"SUM doesn't have a belief system. There are no rules to live by."

"Then what the hell is it? Meigs tells me it costs five hundred dollars. What would I get for putting out that much money?"

"You'd find out you can make your life what you want it to be if you're willing to tell the truth about it. SUM helps people see the truth about what they want and about what's stopping them from getting it."

Malone gave a dry little grunt. "SUM, huh? Like—it all adds up?"

Tony only nodded. What did this cop know? There was no point explaining that sum also meant "I am" in Latin.

"On the other hand," the detective said, "it could be a play on words. My Latin is rusty, but sum means 'I am,' doesn't it?"

For a moment Tony felt a lightening of the weight that had settled on him when Deirdre died. He had let his picture of Malone as the stereotypical New York cop get in the way of his seeing what was behind the man. Malone's irritation with SUM was real, his density was not.

A tightening at the corners of the detective's mouth showed that this assessment had not gone unnoticed. "I'm old enough to remember when Mass was in Latin," Malone said.

Tony smiled. "So am I."

For a second the tension lessened. Then the detective asked, "Why do you do this work—this leading marathons? Is it the money? Or do you get off on having people applaud when you come into the room and hang on your words like you were the Almighty Lord God?"

Tony flinched. The small moment of fellow feeling had not dented Malone's skepticism. He was sure Malone would not believe him. "SUM saved my life," he said. "It wasn't until I told myself the truth about my experiences in combat in Vietnam that I was able to let go of them and stop fucking up my life."

He was right. Malone made a noise that unmistakably expressed disbelief and opened his notebook again. "I've questioned everyone in the last three rows. They all said Deirdre Doyle said someone wanted to kill her. Did you think she meant someone in the marathon?''

"That never occurred to me. Murder is the last thing I would expect in a marathon. But for Deirdre's sake, and for the sake of the confidentiality we try to maintain, I cut off her input as soon as she mentioned an angry ex-lover. I thought she was on the verge of blurting out his name."

"When she told you she was afraid, you said, and I quote from a witness, 'Are you ready to get rid of that bullshit?'" He closed the notebook and put it back into his pocket. He looked at Tony. "Wasn't that pretty hard-nosed?"

"Any coach in any marathon would have said the same thing."

Malone took the pamphlet off the desk where he had laid it. He opened it to the first page and scanned the introduction. Then he looked at Tony. "Do you mean to tell me that your attacking people like that, talking tough like that . . ." He began to read from the pamphlet, "'helps people let go of the past, learn how to utilize their inner and outer resources, and begin to lead more productive lives . . . ?'" His skepticism was now, clearly, verging on outrage.

"We talk tough because that's what people listen to. People come to the marathon with fears and delusions. Sometimes all they need is a shock to make them take a different look at themselves. Deirdre needed to look at that fear and see if it was based on a real threat to her life. If it was, she had to get help. If it wasn't, she had to get off it. Yes, we use rough language. Yes, we're often accused of being hard-nosed. But the marathon works."

The detective shook his head. He was silent for a few seconds. He closed the pamphlet and put it back on the desk. Then he said, "Are you full of shit, Mr. Cazzine?"

"I don't think so!" cried Tony with a startled laugh. "Why?"

"You'd say this marathon works for everyone who does it?"

"Now and then we have a holdout," Tony admitted. "Someone who shouldn't be in the marathon in the first place. Or someone who came looking for something to bitch about."

Louisa Evans. In every marathon he could spot the skeptics and the unbelievers, but he'd never seen anyone whose body language gave away as much as Louisa Evans. He'd seen her scorn long before she got up to confront him on the way he'd handled Deirdre. Her willingness to confront him was a good sign. He wished he'd handled her more tactfully.

Now that he knew who she was, he remembered an article she'd written for *New York*, a brilliant analysis of the media hype that whipped up the popularity of androgynous performers like Prince, Michael Jackson, and Boy George. If she'd come without her prejudices, she could have been a tremendous boost to SUM.

The detective's cold voice brought him back. "Your marathon didn't work for Deirdre Doyle."

"No, it didn't."

"And you don't feel responsible?"

"I *am* responsible."

Malone shifted his bulk in the chair. "Hold it right there, Mr. Cazzine! I don't want any legal screw-ups. If you're about to confess to the murder of Deirdre Doyle, I'll read you your rights. We'll stop right here, go over to the station, and wait for your lawyer."

"I'm not confessing that I killed her. I didn't. I'm saying that I'm responsible for the context in which her death occurred."

The detective sat back again. "That sounds like marathon bullshit to me. Alex Meigs has given me a pretty good idea of how you operate. You don't screen or interview marathoners, so you've no way to tell when you've got a person on the edge or one who's in a life-threatening jam."

"I should have seen that Deirdre was emotionally unstable, and I should have believed her when she said someone wanted to kill her."

"What did she tell you in your private—what do you call it—interface?"

"She apologized for getting hysterical. She told me she was still freaked out by something that happened last night. Someone tried to snatch her purse on a subway platform and almost pushed her onto the track just as a train was coming in."

"Did she tell you who she thought it was?"

"No. She started to tell me that there was a guy real 'pissed-off' at her, she thought maybe it was him, but I stopped her again."

"Why was that? She wasn't telling the whole world, only you."

"I'm not a priest, private interface isn't the confessional."

The detective grunted. "Too bad. You might have saved us a lot of trouble. She tell you what station the attack occurred in?"

"No."

"Anyone else hear your conversation with Deirdre?"

"I doubt it. Amy, one of the assistant coaches, was there to see that private interface is really private. She kept the others well out of earshot."

Malone, who had taken out his notebook and was jotting in it again, now closed it with finality. "This case is a bitch because of the sheer number of witnesses. We have to piece together Deirdre Doyle's movements on the shutdown. In the Ladies' room she begged for a tranquilizer. Louisa Evans says she actually saw a capsule in her hand some minutes before she apparently swallowed it. A Darvon from the description. Not exactly the tranquilizer she wanted, but apparently she was willing to settle for what she could get."

"A woman in the restroom gave it to her?"

"Not necessarily. But her asking for one does suggest that she didn't bring any with her. One person who talked with her said Deirdre told her she'd tried to keep to your no-drug contract. Maybe after so many hours off them she needed a fix so bad she didn't care if she broke it."

"And you think someone in the marathon gave it to her? And that it was poisoned?"

"It's certainly possible that her death is not connected with the marathon. Whoever gave her the capsule could have come into the hotel from the outside and met her in the lobby during the shutdown. That's why we have to find out where she went and who was with her. We have to question everyone in the marathon and everyone who's running it. I've questioned Alex Meigs. My partner is questioning your helpers down there in the ballroom. Now you tell me, aside from two conversations you had with her, one public and the other semi-private, what do you know about Deirdre Doyle?''

"Nothing. I never saw her until she came into the ballroom this morning."

"Do you know of anyone with a grudge against you?''

"What!" Tony could not conceal his astonishment.

"A person who might want to get even with you by discrediting you or the organization you work for? Witnesses tell me that you spoke of drug use, a divorce, lost jobs."

Tony shook his head. "I know I've done a lot of damage in thirty-five years, but I can't think of anyone angry enough at me to get even by killing an innocent person."

"A few years ago six people died at random from cyanide they swallowed in capsules they thought were Tylenol. The motive has never been established, and that killer has not been caught. It happened again with Tylenol and then with Excedrin. The second Tylenol incident was an attempt to set up an extortion. The copycat situations suggest that people got ideas about how to make a private homicide look like something else. If you can't think of anyone with something against you, how about someone with an ax to grind against SUM? You had a public argument with a writer."

Tony sat up in astonishment. "Can you see Louisa Evans as a poisoner?''

"I've seen poisoners even less likely-looking than Louisa Evans. An honor student in a fancy high-rise who murdered her whole family with roach killer, for instance."

Tony grimaced but said nothing.

"How much longer does the marathon run?''

"All day tomorrow, starting at nine. Next Saturday, and Sunday, and as far into Sunday night as it takes for everyone to get on-line."

"Get on-line? What does that mean?''

"Know that he or she is free of the past and able to utilize..." Tony saw the look on the detective's face and stopped.

"Christ, more jargon!" said Malone. "At least most of our witnesses will be here. Anyone who's thinking of not coming back tomorrow may think again—that's just what we'd expect of the murderer. First thing tomorrow we'll question the rest of your marathoners. Let them out a few at a time like you did the last three rows today."

"Anything we can do."

"Don't let any more get away like Louisa Evans did!" The detective took the envelope of Marathon data sheets under his arm and left the office.

Tony stayed where he was. He should go upstairs, but he knew he would not sleep. Deirdre's death in the midst of the marathon had been a terrible blow. In the months he'd been in rehabilitation, he'd found out how to make his life worth living. He hadn't realized how fragile his hold on it had been. He had to get hold of it again the only way he knew how. He had to take action.

He would find out where Deirdre's family lived, and he would visit them. In his brief encounter with her, he'd seen that she was a user. She seemed more unpleasant than dangerous, but she'd been a threat to someone, a big enough threat for that person to take an enormous risk. Yet she had seemed oddly childlike in that sleazy outfit. She'd needed life as the marathon could have opened it for her, but she had gotten death—sudden, hideous, and painful. He was angry at whoever had made Deirdre die in such agony. Someone had brought pain and death into the life-enriching space of the marathon.

Louisa Evans had come to find a fatal flaw in SUM, and before he could break through her hostility, she'd found what she was looking for. He'd made two mistakes today. He had not believed Deirdre when she said someone wanted to kill her, and he had made an enemy of Louisa Evans.

Deirdre's horrible death had dealt Louisa a blow too. He could see it in her face when she looked at him over the girl's dead body. She'd been shocked and sickened. Whatever she'd expected of the marathon, she couldn't have dreamed anything so terrible would happen. Unless she was a skilled con artist, Tony thought, she was passionate about truth and fairness; her writing showed it. It wasn't too late to get her to look at SUM again. He would stop wasting time feeling sorry for himself and try to get through to Louisa. If she didn't come back to the marathon tomorrow, he would go to her.

He took the file folder from the drawer. He pulled out the copies of the data sheets and leafed through them again until he came to the Es.

Predictably, she had left unanswered the two questions, "What do you hope to get out of the Marathon?" and "In what areas of your life would you like to experience improvement?" She was thirty-two years old. She lived on East Eighty-first Street. Under Relationship Status she listed herself as Single.

A knock at the door. It was Kevin, very tired and subdued, with circles under his eyes and a hang-dog look. "You said you wanted to see me, Tony?"

This was Kevin's first full assistantship. Tony had had doubts about the young man's readiness for the responsibility. The chief assistant coach had to be a juggler, in full control of the logistics of the operation that made the marathon run smoothly. He had to be ready to adjust quickly to the unexpected. Tony knew he had to give Kevin another chance. Violent death was an event SUM had not rehearsed for.

"I guess I fucked up today, didn't I, Tony?" Kevin said miserably. He remained standing in front of the desk and shuffled his feet on the carpet.

"The marathon won't work for people who walk out on it."

"Right, Tony."

"Louisa Evans walked out. Whose responsibility was that?"

Kevin swallowed hard. "Mine. I let her get away. It's my fault. I'm sorry."

"You don't need to apologize. All you have to do is take responsibility."

"I do! And I won't fuck up tomorrow. I promise!"

"Don't make promises. Just do your job."

"I will, Tony! I'll do my job. If Louisa Evans doesn't come back tomorrow morning, I'll call her. And I'll be sure no one else leaves the marathon. Thanks, Tony!"

"You can handle it. Goodnight, Kevin."

"Goodnight, Tony." In the corridor outside the office, Kevin pulled out his handkerchief and wiped his eyes. Tony was the best of SUM's coaches. It was an honor to work with him. Tony hadn't chewed him out. Tony hadn't said he was replacing him with someone more experienced. He'd be on the job early tomorrow, and he'd prove he could do it without fucking up. He was whistling as he descended the broad carpeted stairs into the lobby, now silent and deserted except for the night clerk.

Halfway down he stopped. He hadn't told Tony about the blank name tag that had turned up in the basket when the marathoners went out on the dinner shutdown. Louisa Evans had left the marathon with her tag on. He remembered seeing it pinned to her sweater when she told him she had to go to the Ladies' room. Deirdre's tag had gone to the morgue with her. The rest of the marathoners had dropped theirs into the basket at the door when they went out for dinner. When he sorted them and put them out on the table in alphabetical order, he found one blank tag in a plastic shield.

He'd pocketed it quickly, before anyone else saw it, and later he checked the tags against the roster. Every tag was there except Louisa's and Deirdre's. Two hundred names on the roster. One hundred and ninety-eight tags with names. And one blank. It didn't make sense.

Should he go back upstairs and tell Tony about it? No, he'd done what he was supposed to do. No tag was missing that wasn't accounted for. An extra one had gotten into the basket somehow, that was all. It couldn't be important. He could go home and sleep. He hadn't fucked up on this.

FIVE

WATER WAS FALLING on her face. She was cold, so cold, and her head ached fiercely. From a great distance a voice was calling. The voice came nearer. Now it was close to her, urgent and rough. "Wake up—you can't be dead!"

Louisa opened her eyes. She was lying on a bare, very hard floor. Her face was wet, and water from an unknown source was dripping into her hair. She half turned her head to avoid the icy drops, and her eyes fell on the photographs and the ripped portfolio.

With recognition came full consciousness. And chagrin. She was in Deirdre Doyle's ransacked apartment. Her street smarts had deserted her. She had allowed herself to be mugged.

"You're okay." It was a statement, not a question. Louisa raised her head. The young woman kneeling over her had a wet washcloth in her hand. Her fair hair was clipped as short as a GI's haircut, and she was wearing a severe slate blue jumpsuit of some thick, flannel-like material. Her eyes were not friendly.

Louisa sat up carefully. Her head rang, and the sharp pain behind her left ear made her feel nauseated. "Who are you?" she asked.

"You first."

"I'm Louisa Evans, and—oh, God!" She clutched at her pockets. Wallet, cash, and cards were gone. So were the keys to her apartment. Her bag, its contents scattered, lay empty on the floor. "Someone mugged me. I didn't see him. He came up behind me."

"What the fuck are you doing here? You a cop?"

"I'm not a cop, I'm a writer. I came here to talk to someone who knew Deirdre Doyle. Did you?"

"What do you mean, 'did'? Something happen to her?"

"I'm sorry—if she was a friend. She's dead."

There was no change in the hard young face. "How?"

"She was poisoned."

"Shit."

"Look, I've got to phone my super. Whoever mugged me has my wallet and the keys to my apartment."

"Jack," said the woman almost casually.

"Jack?"

"Deirdre's relationship. A scuz, totally. Everything Deirdre got, he ripped off—TV, stereo. Once he even took the phone. She had to take her camera to bed with her, sleep with it under her pillow."

"You think he's the one who mugged me?"

"Could be. Who knows?" She shrugged. "This place is rip-off heaven."

It took only a few seconds to ascertain that Jack had once again taken Deirdre's phone.

"Jack would sell his mother for coke," the woman said. "You can come down and use my phone." She didn't offer to help Louisa gather up the contents of her bag, nor did she reach out when Louisa staggered slightly getting to her feet. But her manner was less hostile. "My name's Clare," she said. "You look like you could use a drink or something."

On the second floor, where music still pounded from the front apartment, Clare unlocked her door with three separate keys. Her apartment was a twin of Deirdre's, but Clare had been luckier in keeping her modest possessions in place. "There's the phone. What do you want? Wine? A joint?"

Louisa's teeth were chattering. "Something hot if it isn't too much trouble. How can you stand it in here?"

"Landlord's a scumbag. I'm getting out next week. Instant coffee?"

"Fine."

Louisa called her super. "What does Jack look like?" she asked Clare, who was rattling about in the rudimentary kitchen.

"Short. Real light eyes that stare. When he isn't stoned, he twitches a lot. Last time I saw him, he was a skinhead."

Louisa remembered the hand that had reached into her bag. "Does he have a deformed thumb? Flattened as if he'd caught it in a heavy door?"

"I dunno. I never noticed his thumbs. I've only seen him a couple of times, hanging out with Deirdre."

"Is he likely to be armed?"

"A knife, probably. He might have a gun, but then again, he might've sold it to buy cocaine."

Louisa relayed to her shocked and disbelieving super the news that a drug addict with a shaved head might try to enter the building. She sensed that his esteem for her dropped considerably.

Clare brought over a steaming, chipped mug. Louisa took grateful sips. When the hot liquid began to warm her insides, she felt better. Her interest in Deirdre revived.

Clare's hostility had lessened, but not her suspicion. "If you're not a cop, who are you? A writer, you said? What do you write?"

"I was researching for a magazine article on SUM. I was there when Deirdre died. I came here to find out what I could about her."

"You said poison—you mean, like an OD?"

"She took what was apparently cyanide in a capsule she thought was a Darvon."

"Horrible."

"Yes." Louisa looked away from Clare's stare. A spasm of nausea hit her again. When the threat passed, she saw that Clare's look alternated between distrust and curiosity. Curiosity finally prevailed. Clare gestured toward the couch and said, "Sit down, will you? Sorry, I've been really on it since I found you in Deirdre's apartment. I wasn't a close friend of Deirdre, you know. To tell the truth, I thought she was an opportunistic bitch. But we talked sometimes, and she told me a lot of things when she was high, just kinda rattled on like she needed someone to listen to her. I got kinda fascinated. She was asking for trouble, no way she wasn't going to get it, but..." Clare shook her head, "Poison! That's a hell of a way to cash it in."

"She said something about a 'pissed-off' ex-lover. Would Jack have been angry enough to kill her?"

"You *sure* you're not a cop?"

"I'm not a cop."

"Then give me your word you won't tell anyone you even know me. You never saw me, here, or anywhere else."

"You have my word."

"Jack might have been crazy enough to kill when he was off his bird for coke. He's done time, she said, for assault, and he was kinda rough. I got the creeps just looking at him the couple times I saw him here. But it would have been stupid for him to kill Deirdre unless she had something on him, something big. She helped him buy coke by stealing stuff from the school for him to sell. Cameras, mainly. The only camera she wouldn't let him have was her own."

"What school?"

"She was taking a photography workshop at the School for Visual Arts. Had a fantasy about being a great photojournalist. You saw her pictures? Then you know it was all she could do to point the camera in the right direction."

"Is Jack a student too?"

"No, he's lead guitar in a rock band. Call themselves Heloise and the Abelards. Dumb name for a group. Jack wears a dress and a blond wig. The other three dress like monks—they wear black robes and dildos."

"Dildos?"

"On a leather thong around their necks. Like a monk wears a cross, you know?"

Louisa concealed her distaste. "If Jack needs money so badly he would steal Deirdre's phone, the band must not be very successful."

"They're not. Their music sucks. They hardly ever practice. Someone's always late or stoned or just had his guitar ripped off. Besides, they're a little—you know—kinky, so they don't get a lot of gigs. But they had one last night. I saw Deirdre going out about eleven, and she told me she was going to hear him play."

"How did Deirdre pay for the marathon? She didn't have that kind of money, did she? It wasn't Jack, was it?"

"If Jack had five hundred bucks all at once, he'd be in coke heaven, dealing up a storm. Last time Deirdre cornered me and starting telling me about the marathon, I told her it was a rip-off, but she said the guy who was paying for it said it might help her get her shit together. Get off drugs for openers.''

"Do you know who he is?''

"I think he's a teacher at SVA. I told her she was making a big mistake letting this guy give her five hundred dollars' worth of mind-fucking, but she said mind-fucking was all she was going to get from him. The relationship was over.''

"I thought Jack was her relationship.''

"They were off and on. Jack didn't care who Deirdre screwed as long as she brought home things he could trade for coke.''

"Did this teacher pay for anything else? The rent, for instance?''

"No, but I think this guy gave her the stereo and the records. She had a TV too, and the camera. Look at this place! Would anyone live here who didn't have to? The money her folks send barely covers the rent. How could she buy a stereo and a camera? To say nothing of a five-hundred-dollar mind-fuck for a good-bye present. And when I told her I'm moving, she said she was gonna get out soon herself. So maybe she'd got the guy to put up rent on something better.''

"Maybe he's married and she was blackmailing him.''

"She'd do that. Or maybe she and this guy were into something else. I think she and Jack made money sometimes working as a team, you know, going into bars and picking up guys who like a little variety. Some of them just want to watch. Others like to mix it up a little, know what I mean? One night I met Deirdre coming home. She was high and pretty excited, and said she and Jack had each made a hundred bucks from a guy who took them to his hotel room. She said something about doing it for money was almost as great as doing it for kicks with her two guys.''

This time Louisa didn't try to hide her revulsion. Clare, watching closely for her reaction, said, "I know. Me neither.''

"The marathon seems the last thing Deirdre would want to do.''

"She thought it would be like a great big singles bar.''

"Did Deirdre use cocaine?''

"Once in awhile. But most of the time she just mellowed out on pills. She drank a lot, too."

"How about last night? You saw her about eleven, you said?"

"I was just coming home. I waitress at a place in Soho. Deirdre was going to Jack's gig. She was loose, but no higher than usual."

"Did you see her when she came in?"

"No."

"Do you know her pictures well enough to tell if any are missing?"

"Not really, but I'll look at them if you want me to."

Clare triple-locked her door again, and they went back up the stairs. Clare looked at the pictures and shook her head. "I told her she should've stayed in Scranton and married her high school boy friend, but she just laughed and said he and her folks hoped she'd never come back."

"Any pictures missing that you know of?"

"The only thing I know is that she had an assignment to go around the city and take pictures of people's faces. She told me about it a couple of days ago. She thought it would be a blast."

"There are no people in these pictures, except for the children on the carousel, and they're not close-ups."

"So maybe she hadn't taken them yet. She was always doing her work at the last minute."

"Or she could have started the assignment and not finished it. In that case, the film would still be in her camera."

"Which Jack must've gotten this time. But it's not like Deirdre to have left it here. She takes it with her everywhere. She had it with her last night. She was putting on her coat. She had her purse and her camera. She was carrying both of them around her neck."

"She said something in the marathon about somebody getting her thrown out of someplace—"

"Honestly, I don't know anything more about Deirdre. I tried to avoid her, to tell you the truth."

Louisa got up to leave. She groped in her pockets. Clare caught the gesture. "I can lend you cab fare."

"All I need is a token. Thanks. And thanks for the coffee and for what you told me."

"Don't forget."

"I won't forget. I never saw you."

SIX

WHEN HE'D BEEN ASSIGNED a black woman partner, James Malone had gone straight to the captain and complained, bitterly and in vain. The precinct needed a highly visible male/female team that paired a white detective with a black one. Too many accused criminals and their lawyers were flinging charges of racism at the police. There had been media criticism about how slowly women were moving into detective ranks.

He'd felt safer with the old ways. Police work was hard and dangerous. He'd gotten to where he was by toeing the line. Rhonda Lord was a type of female James Malone felt uncomfortable with. She was tough, aggressive and cocky. As a black female, she bristled at any remark or situation that smacked of racism or sexism. She was one of the new breed of cops, too— bored with routine, eager to follow hunches, and raised on TV cop shows which glamorized the maverick and laughed at the plodder.

He was a plodder. He wanted to plod through the five years that remained before his retirement and be alive at the end of them. His relationship with Rhonda was more of an armed truce than a partnership. He was stuck with her, at least unless his worst fear was realized—that she would do something stupid to get one of them killed.

This fear was constant. He and other cops his age could voice it safely only in the Men's room, and even there only in sly jokes. He did not voice his other feeling about Rhonda. She made him uneasy. She looked, dressed, and smelled like a high-priced whore. He suspected that she was smarter than he was, and worse, that she knew it.

Not that she threw it in his face. Her deference to him fell just short of mockery. She let him take the lead in their investigations; she followed orders scrupulously. If she was bored with procedure, she didn't show it. She wrote up reports in admirably succinct English, better than his own. When she reported to him in that brisk, smart-ass voice of hers, in the depths of his mind he called her "tough bitch cop."

It made him nervous that she talked so freely about going out on dates. She seemed to be able to carry on a rich social life despite the long hours they often had to put in. He'd found out early in his career that, for him, going into the force was like going into the priesthood. Not that he was exactly celibate. But he didn't like being with women much. He always seemed to say the wrong thing.

He still smarted when he remembered their first day of partnership. Determined not to let her know how much this forced association bothered him, he'd prepared a little speech with a joking reference to his counting on her "woman's intuition" being an asset in their work.

Instantly she'd turned on him, so angry that she'd risked a reprimand for abusive language to a higher-ranking officer. "I'm a cop! Like you. Between my legs I have different equipment, but up here, it's called brains, man, you hear? Don't give me any of that 'woman's intuition' shit!"

A reprimand would have made a bad beginning worse. He'd tried to be conciliatory. "Okay, okay! No offense! I only meant I can count on your smarts, right?"

"Like I can count on yours."

She continued to irk him.

Their assignment to this case irked him too. With all the vile crimes committed in the city, he had no patience for trying to solve murders of people who would pay five hundred dollars to spend two weekends lapping up crap. SUM looked like a very lucrative con game to him. And these yuppies with more money than brains were buying. They would buy anything if it was disguised with enough "with it" terms like "input" and "interface" and "utilization of inner resources." This investigation did not need him. It needed a couple of those John Jay College boys in their gray suits and white shirts who spoke the same phony language.

He left the office on the mezzanine and went down the stairs to the lobby. He'd given Rhonda the job of interviewing the assistant coaches who were setting up the ballroom for tomorrow's session of the marathon. As he entered the ballroom, he saw the rug had been vacuumed and the chairs lined up again in precise rows. Each row had been widened to accommodate more chairs. The spot where Deirdre Doyle had died was now an empty space behind the last row. SUM thought of everything.

Rhonda was excited about something. He knew she wouldn't tell him right away, she'd make him wait while she went through her tough cop routine. "Identification and a home address in Scranton. Notification of the family completed."

"Good." Notifying the family was the most painful of duties; he was relieved that she had done it. More tactfully, no doubt, than he would have.

"I got her local address from the marathon roster. It's a grungy walkup in the East Village between C and D. Door was open, the place had been tossed. Everything in the bathroom cabinet thrown into the sink, so it looks like drug-related. But I found one thing that might be important—this was under the edge of the couch."

She held out a plastic bag. In it was a marathon name tag. He read the name, and his lips formed a silent whistle. Maybe his suspicion wasn't off the mark. "Anything from the other apartments?"

"Negative response from all of them. The place was as quiet as the grave. I had the feeling some of them were only playing dead."

"How did you get her family's address?"

"Among the papers on the floor was an envelope with a Scranton return address. I got the number and called it. Deirdre's father answered. His name is William—Bill—Doyle. I gave him time to break the news to the family and asked him to call me back. What he told me about Deirdre isn't much. She was twenty years old, a part-time student at the School for Visual Arts. She'd been in the city five months. Her parents have no idea who might have wanted her dead. They know nothing about her friends and acquaintances in New York. Her father's chief concern is how soon the body will be released. He wants Deirdre to have a proper funeral so, quote, 'people will know she was a decent girl in spite of her being killed by some maniac,' unquote.''

"What about that?"

"The medical examiner's office says Monday. I told Mr. Doyle to go ahead and make arrangements. When do you want me to go to Scranton?"

"Monday or Tuesday. Tomorrow we question the one hundred and fifty marathoners we didn't get to today. That means contacting the ones who don't show up." He could not bring himself to acknowledge how thoroughly she'd carried out her part of their assignment. All he could do was say, "What have you found out here?"

"Inside job," she said. She pointed to the table at the back of the ballroom. "There's the proof."

A tired, but still alert, young assistant coach, whose name tag identified her as Mickey, was standing by the table on which there was a collection of forlorn objects. Several brown paper bags torn open to show garbage and unfinished snacks. A thermos bottle. Two briefcases. A camera. A pile of hats, scarves, and odd gloves. A smart, expensive, down jacket and a moth-ridden, ancient fur coat.

"What's all this?"

"Items marathoners forgot to pick up when they left to-night," Mickey said promptly. "They'll be taken down to our main office and put into the Lost and Found. All except the food, of course. We throw that out."

"I don't get it. What does it prove?"

Rhonda said, "The briefcases have ID inside. Both belong to males. No name on the camera, no film in it. The down jacket belongs to Louisa Evans. The ratty fur is Deirdre's."

"Go on."

"Every woman who came into this room with a handbag had to leave it on this table. They're not allowed to have them at their seats. No watches either. That's so nothing will be on hand to distract them from the marathon, Kevin says. He also told me that Louisa Evans picked up her bag before she went up-stairs to talk to you. Presumably she took it with her when she left the hotel."

"So?" He was getting hot. He wished she'd get to the point. She was trying to make him feel stupid.

"Mickey was in charge of the table when the marathon came back from the bathroom break. Deirdre was one of the last ones to come in. Mickey remembers distinctly that Deirdre threw her bag on top of the pile."

"I remember the bag too," said Mickey brightly. "It was a tacky little plastic bag with a Scottie dog on it."

He was still frowning when he looked at the table. What the fuck? Then he got it. Where was Deirdre Doyle's handbag?

SEVEN

ON SUNDAY MORNING between nine o'clock and noon, Louisa's phone rang twenty-seven times.

She had notified the Credit Card Bureau of the theft of her cards. She talked with her building super and the doorman. Both were relieved that no bald, twitchy stranger had tried to enter, but they were furious at the tactics of the reporters who wanted to get in to interview Louisa for an eyewitness account of Deirdre's death. She had no cash with which to tip the super and the doorman until she could get to the bank on Monday. She had to assure them that as soon as she could, she would show her gratitude if they let her slip in and out by the service door that had an exit to Eighty-second Street.

Behind her door's new lock, installed Saturday night by an emergency locksmith, Louisa sat at her typewriter and struggled to write a coherent account of the tragedy she had been so close to.

From time to time she listened to the taped messages on her answering machine. Reporters from three networks and two newspapers begged for interviews. Hal had a tentative go-ahead for a book he and the papers were calling *Murder at the Marathon*. SUM wanted her to come back.

"Louisa, this is Kevin. I'm real sad that you didn't go back to the marathon when you left me yesterday. We need you. Come back and log-on."

"Louisa, this is Janet from SUM. What happened here yesterday was a bummer. Come in right now, please? We need you to help us get on-line."

"This is Tony." He sounded angry. She sat up to listen, compelled in spite of herself. SUM took her truancy seriously indeed, if it had set the coach on her. "Is this the way you run your life, Louisa? You don't seem like a person who drops out when things get rough. I want you back in the marathon."

If she'd been taking the call on the phone, instead of the tape, she would have hung up on him. She snapped off the machine. Then she turned it on again.

At noon she pulled a sheet of paper out of her typewriter and sat back, drained. Writing down what she had seen and how she had felt when Deirdre died had been cathartic. Now she needed to think. She needed to do much more work before she could even settle on her point of view. She needed background on Deirdre, which she would get in Scranton. She would interview the SUM manager, Alex Meigs, and get his view of the impact of the tragedy on his organization and his plans for preventing similar incidents.

Most of all, she needed to talk with Tony Cazzine. She wanted to know why he had so abruptly cut off the girl's input and what he had learned from that interface on the platform. More than facts, she needed to know how he felt. Had he been able to fit this ugly death into his system of truisms, or did he too feel the horror?

These would be tough questions to ask. His tone on the message tape suggested it might be tough to get him to answer them. He would force her to be defensive about leaving the marathon. He would ask her confrontational questions like the one he'd asked on the phone. Somehow she would have to make his aggressiveness work to her advantage. If he really wanted her back in the marathon, he'd have to agree to a no-holds-barred interview.

Her apartment, a legacy of her marriage—she had bought out Glen's half—seemed claustrophobic in spite of the nine-foot ceilings and windows offering a view of Central Park to anyone willing to lean out a little. She longed to go over to the park, and walk to clear her mind. Her head still throbbed from the mugger's knockout punch.

She felt isolated and strangely cut off. She wanted to know how many people had been frightened away from the marathon. She already knew it was still going on—she had called this morning without giving her name. She wanted to ask marathoners how Tony had handled the emotional tumult that had surely broken out when the marathon resumed after Deirdre's body was taken away.

For a few seconds she reconsidered her decision not to return to the marathon. Going back would seem an admission that she needed SUM or that she acknowledged its usefulness. She did not want to appear to have conceded. No, she wouldn't go back. She'd get what she wanted from other sources.

She'd go to Scranton tomorrow and get a motel room from which she could do her investigation of Deirdre's background. After she returned, she would try to track down the violent and elusive Jack. Before her phone could ring again, she called the newspaper in Scranton and got the information she needed about funeral services for Deirdre Doyle. The funeral home had visiting hours. That would be her contact with the family.

She hoped that the weather, which had turned mild, would stay that way. Her down jacket was still in the marathon. She would not risk going back to the hotel to get it. She would surely have to face Tony Cazzine or one of his minions. She wasn't ready for that.

Her phone rang again. She unplugged it. She went into her bedroom and unplugged that phone too.

EIGHT

By Tuesday afternoon, Malone had a trail of three-by-five cards across his desk. Ladies' room on the right, ballroom on the left, lobby in the middle. It was typical of his plodding ways, he thought, that he hadn't come up with a quicker way to plot Deirdre's movements from the time she left the ballroom during the shutdown until the moment of her death.

What he'd done with the cards was reduce the information he'd been given (by an almost unworkable number of witnesses) to a picture he could almost see of the last hour of Deirdre's life. Unfortunately, the picture was blank at the crucial spot—he could not see where Deirdre had been handed the fatal capsule.

He could work in his slow way without having to put up with Rhonda. He'd sent her to do the legwork in Scranton. Seniority did have a few advantages. He remained at his desk, taking reports from other detectives who were combing the East Village with Deirdre's picture, trying to find someone who knew her. Malone's questioning of people in Deirdre's building had drawn a blank. Now he was going over the information he already had, hoping that something would come together.

"When you find out *how*, *who* and *why* will come to you on a silver platter." He'd run across that axiom of detecting somewhere. He'd forget the silver platter and take *why* on a tin tray if it showed up with facts to prove it.

On a second set of cards he'd written what Deirdre had said, and who she said it to, during the roughly thirty-five minutes from the beginning of the shutdown until Kevin quieted down the marathoners for Tony Cazzine's entrance.

Louisa Evans headed the list of marathon defectors. She had left after he questioned her, and she had not returned on Sunday. Ten people had abandoned ship during the dinner shutdown on Saturday. Forty more did not show up for the second day of the marathon.

All but one of the fifty-one had been reached by phone by SUM's people. Twenty-five had been persuaded to come back to the marathon and had straggled in, one by one, throughout the day. Rhonda had phoned the remaining dropouts and taken their stories. Anxious not to be suspected of leaving the scene of a crime, they had answered questions eagerly. Unfortunately, their information was of no help.

Neither SUM nor Rhonda had been able to reach Louisa. She had disconnected her phone. It looked like she had gone straight from the marathon to Deirdre's apartment and searched it, dropping her marathon name tag in the process. He'd send Rhonda to track Louisa down as soon as she came back from Scranton. Maybe she'd get more from Louisa than he had. They were two of a kind in a way, smart, pushy—and young.

The medical examiner's report was in. Deirdre had died of acute respiratory arrest caused by the ingestion of a compound of cyanide. Traces of gelatine indicated that the poison had been introduced into the stomach in a capsule. When the capsule dissolved in the stomach, three to five minutes after its ingestion, the deadly dose had been released. The effect was swiftly fatal. No surprises there.

The contents of Deirdre's pockets were in a plastic bag on his desk. No surprises there either, except for an odd item that could be important, or give them hours of legwork and lead nowhere at all. The pockets of the fur coat yielded nothing but a couple of subway tokens. The jacket pockets were stuffed with tissues smeared with mascara and eye shadow, a half-empty pack of Camel Lights, a book of matches, and a narrow slip of white paper with an Upper East Side address on it. The address turned out to be a big, fancy apartment building on Sutton Place. Not a clue as to why Deirdre was carrying that address in her pocket when she died. He hoped the silver platter would show up before he had to assign additional detectives to door-to-door questioning of Deirdre Doyle's neighbors. The case had attracted a lot of attention in the media, and there was pressure for a quick arrest.

His phone rang. It was tough bitch cop reporting from Scranton. "I found a very talkative lady, Deirdre's Aunt Pegeen. She rattled off the story like she couldn't wait to tell it. Deirdre was the black sheep of a good Catholic family, bored in high school, and a trouble maker. Suspected of drug use, which the family tried to ignore. The aunt says Deirdre was disgraced in high school when she accused her guidance counselor of making sexual advances. So when she saw a story in *Life,* and she decided on a career in photojournalism, her parents were glad to see her go. They paid her tuition at SVA and sent her what money they could."

"Did they hear from her?"

"Hardly ever. She didn't write letters. Called once in a while, collect, to ask for more money. She had a boy friend in high school, but he's out of the picture, engaged to another girl. Deirdre's graduation picture, which the family gave to the newspapers, shows Deirdre with long brown hair. I've also talked with Bill Doyle. I asked him how much money he sent Deirdre every month. He told me a hundred dollars was all he could afford, and I got that he begrudged that.

"Then I asked him if he'd sent her the money for the marathon," Rhonda went on. "His answer was, and I quote, 'No, I wouldn't give a kid of mine money for that kind of claptrap. If she wanted five hundred dollars for letting people meddle with her mind, she got it from someone else!' "

Malone cursed himself in soft but very explicit tones. He had forgotten to ask something so elementary that he ought to be sent back to walking a beat in Far Rockaway. After Rhonda hung up, he dialed a number. Alex Meigs was not in his office. Would detective Malone care to leave a message? He would. Have Alex call him as soon as he came in.

They had a lead, however slender. Deirdre had been a photography student at SVA. A photographer had to have a camera. The camera on the table at the back of the ballroom—forgotten by a weary marathoner, or unclaimed because its owner was in the morgue?

He'd ask Alex about SUM's Lost and Found. He'd get the camera and send it to the lab for prints.

The rest of Rhonda's information about Deirdre was a cliché. Young woman from Scranton—or Iowa or Minnesota—comes to the city for an exciting career and ends up on a slab where a medical officer, with little difficulty, finds that she'd died of a beating, or an overdose, or stab wounds. She wasn't the only girl from a good Catholic family to come to such an end.

The difference was that Deirdre had died, not in her bare apartment, nor in a rat-infested vacant lot. She had died in a room with more than two hundred other people, the victim of someone savvy enough to have gone unnoticed among them, smart enough to have substituted cyanide for the powder in the capsule, and familiar enough with Deirdre's habits to know that, sooner or later, she would take the fatal dose.

The cards might yet show him how and where.

On Sunday, he, Rhonda, and two other detectives had questioned the marathoners. Their questions had been brief and pointed: "Did you see Deirdre Doyle during the shutdown?" "Where?" "With or near whom?" "What did you see her do?" "Hear her say?" And last, "Did you know or had you ever seen her prior to the beginning of the marathon on Saturday?"

The answer to the last question was consistently "No."

To the others they had a range of answers. A few had merely noted her in passing. Others, notably Tony Cazzine and Louisa Evans, had actually talked with her.

The more than two hundred witnesses were reduced to thirty-five whose stories supplied pieces of the mosaic of Deirdre's last hour. The thirty-five were further reduced to fourteen—fifteen counting Louisa—who admitted having been in the Ladies' room, or entering or leaving it when Deirdre pleaded for a tranquilizer.

It was certain that someone was not telling the truth, and the picture was unclear in some important details. None of the marathoners was wearing a watch. Time was only a guess. The marathoners had been together only for the morning stretch, and they'd had little interaction. Although each was pinned with a name tag, only the remarkable, like Deirdre, or the contentious, like Louisa, were remembered by name.

Even he was having trouble matching witnesses' faces with their stories. He picked up a card. Marge Lindskey. Amy was the washed-out blonde with the big tits, so Marge was the girl with glasses and bad skin.

"Yeah, I heard Deirdre," Marge had said. "She was about three people behind me on line. She said 'Anybody got a trank? I'll buy it from you'—or something like that. Then a whole bunch of us started telling her to remember the contract we all had to sign. Then she said, really whinylike, 'I got problems!' and lotsa people said they had problems too, who didn't, but they didn't have to take tranquilizers to handle them, and did she want to get someone else in trouble. Stuff like that."

"Did you see Deirdre during this?"

"Yeah. She didn't look too good."

"Did you see anyone give her anything?"

"No, I'm sure of that."

"Could someone have given her a capsule without being seen?"

Marge thought for a moment. "I guess someone could've dropped it into her pocket. We were all standing pretty close together."

Risky, but possible. A woman standing close to Deirdre on line or at the sinks could have slipped a hand into her pocket. She could have signaled by eye contact. None of the witnesses, however, had seen this happen.

"Do you remember the names of any of the women who were on line with you, or at the wash basins, or entering or leaving the toilets while you were in the restroom?"

"Well, there was that good-looking woman named Louisa who told Tony off. She came out of a booth when I was next on line, and she went over to wash her hands. There was Amy who was behind me. We talked while we were waiting. At the basins? Let me think. A woman at the last one was doing her face, a complete makeup job. Why she bothered I don't know, she looked okay to start with. Next to her a woman was combing her hair—one of those wild, frizzy hairdos. She finished and left. I don't really remember any names."

"Did you see Deirdre when you came out of the toilet?"

"No, she was close enough behind me that she must've gotten into one while I was...."

"When did you next see Deirdre Doyle?"

"Not until I stood on a chair and saw her laying there dead on the floor. I was way up front and didn't see what happened to her."

"Had you ever seen or had any contact with her before the marathon?"

"No."

He looked through each of the fifteen statements he'd taken from the women in the Ladies' room. After she'd come out of the toilet, Deirdre had said nothing. Five women remembered that she had splashed water on her face, completing the ruin of her makeup. She had put on more purple lipstick and raked her fingers through her spikes of green hair. Eleven women still in line remembered that she had passed them on her way out. Two leaving the restroom at the same time had walked behind her on the way to the lobby. Everyone who had seen her said she looked shaky and sick.

Next he read the information given by people in the lobby. Twenty remembered seeing Deirdre smoking a cigarette and pacing about. She had spoken to no one. When the movement back to the ballroom began, Deirdre ignored it. She lighted another cigarette from the stub of the one she'd been smoking. Four witnesses saw her disappear behind a stand of potted trees. Between the time she was last seen moving behind the ficus trees with her cigarette, and the time Gary, an assistant coach, had come out to the lobby to round up stragglers, Deirdre had apparently been invisible to everyone in the marathon. But not to the rest of the lobby. Her position by the trees had hidden her from the ballroom entrance, but it put her in full view of the bell captain, who, attracted by her hair and costume, claimed that he had not taken his eyes off her for the two or three minutes she was in his sight.

He had watched her stub out her cigarette in the roots of a ficus tree, even though there were large cylindrical ashtrays full of sand arranged throughout the lobby. Deirdre had moved very slowly, in fact, sullenly, according to the bell captain, when Gary came around the trees and spoke to her.

"Did you see anyone else speak to her?" Malone had asked the bell captain.

"Nope."

"Anyone pass close enough to hand her something?"

"No one went anywhere near her."

He had seen at least one other person, a woman, also put out a cigarette in the planter, as well as several hotel guests who stopped to do a double take when they saw Deirdre. The lobby had been busy. The hotel was full, and there was constant movement in and out. He could not recall anyone specifically but Deirdre, whose looks had so compelled his attention.

Malone described Louisa Evans.

"Oh, that lady! Yeah, now I remember her. She came through the lobby in a big hurry."

"From the Ladies' room?"

"No, from the opposite side of the lobby, from the Coffee Shop."

"Did you see Louisa Evans on her way *to* the Coffee Shop?"

The bell captain had not.

The assistant coaches had reported that Deirdre had come into the ballroom so closely behind Louisa that she had been seated beside her. Marathoners did not pick their own seats. They were sent to fill in rows as they entered the room. Louisa and Deirdre first would have been directed to the table at the back to put down their bags and then to their chairs.

Detective Malone shuffled the cards in his hand. For all the hours they'd put in, nothing was certain except that the bell captain's story ruled out a contact in the lobby from someone outside the marathon. That narrowed the field from the entire population of New York City, permanent and transient, to what was, by comparison, a mere handful. He picked up his second pile of cards, which recorded various peoples' conversations with Deirdre.

The top card was Louisa's. What she'd told him about—what happened in the Ladies' room—was confirmed by the other witnesses. He also had Louisa's version of the conversation between Louisa and Deirdre as they waited for Tony to enter the ballroom. What others may have overheard of that conversation was ambiguous.

He picked up Hazel's card. She'd been sitting in front of Deirdre. "I heard that poor child say 'I'm strung out' or some such phrase. A little later she used the word 'freaked.' I really couldn't hear a lot of what they said, they were talking softly, and other voices around me drowned them out. But I'm sure one of them said 'Here' just as the room quieted down."

"Which one?"

"I don't know."

Martin, on Louisa's right, and Arthur, on Deirdre's left, had heard even less than Hazel. Tom, a sour bastard seated behind Deirdre, had snarled "I mind my own business" to Rhonda, but when pressed, he admitted he saw a gesture which looked like something had passed between the two women. He thought that Deirdre had given and Louisa received. Yes, he supposed it could have been the other way around. Deirdre could have reached out, not *with* something, but *for* something that Louisa had in her hand.

Louisa alone had seen the fatal capsule. She had not told him that she knew where Deirdre lived, and she had gone directly from the marathon to the girl's apartment and searched it. She'd told a convincing story when he'd questioned her, but she was a writer, and accustomed to putting facts together and making them seem logical and plausible. She knew a lot about drugs. Cyanide as a murder weapon was infallible. Its effects were so quick and so painful that the victim hardly had time to realize what was happening, let alone choke out the name of the person who had administered the dose.

Given the state of the traffic in pharmaceuticals in New York City, both legal and illegal, getting enough cyanide to kill a human being was merely a matter of making the proper arrangements. Anyone familiar with the city who knew about drugs would know the places to buy anything—with no questions asked.

He was guessing ahead of his facts. He had a lot of suspicions, but he needed far more than that to make a case. The next card was Tony's conversation with Deirdre. Unless the girl had been hallucinating, she was attacked on a subway platform the night—actually the early morning—before the marathon. Tony and Louisa had both heard the story, which was apparently the source of Deirdre's belief that someone wanted to kill her.

The last puzzle was Deirdre's handbag. Seventeen people swore they'd seen the bag with the Scottie dog. She'd carried it dangling from a strap around her neck. She'd taken the purple lipstick from it in the Ladies' room, and the cigarettes from it in the lobby. She had not put the cigarettes back into it, for they were found in her pocket.

Louisa and Deirdre had been among the last to come into the ballroom; their bags would have been close together on the top of the pile. Kevin Mulroy, who was still in disgrace for letting Louisa escape from the marathon, told Rhonda that Louisa had insisted on having her bag when she went for questioning. Caught off guard and with no instructions, Kevin had given in when the other woman, Hazel, also demanded hers. Kevin did not actually see Louisa take her bag, nor did he see her with two bags. But Deirdre's bag was small enough to be slipped inside a larger one. Hazel, who had been rummaging in the pile for her own, did not see any sleight-of-handbag on Louisa's part.

His phone rang again. Rhonda. "Louisa Evans is here," she said. "I just saw her go into the funeral home. Our paths will cross at the service tomorrow."

He hunched forward. "Okay. Cross her before that. Question her. Find out what she was doing in Deirdre's apartment. Push her hard. If she's got her own agenda on this thing, I want to know what it is."

"Yes, boss! You putting your money on Louisa Evans?"

"Don't know enough. But you know what they say about poison"—He bit off the words. He'd been about to put his foot in his mouth again. Damn the bitch!

"What's that?"

"Not important." When he hung up, he wiped his forehead.

The phone rang again. Alex. He asked about the camera, and then he asked the question he should have asked on Saturday: "How did Deirdre pay the tuition for the marathon—cash or check?"

Alex hung up to consult the computer. Within minutes he called back. Deirdre's tuition had been paid by credit card—an American Express card belonging to someone named Harvey Wardleigh. No, Harvey Wardleigh was not in the marathon.

NINE

DEIRDRE DOYLE was buried on a December day so warm that it seemed like late summer. But the sun hung low and pale in a milky sky, and the shadows were long behind the ranked gravestones and leafless trees.

Louisa stood in the outer ring of mourners while Father Doyle, an uncle of the deceased, sent his niece's soul to its equivocal fate. Behind the family and friends, newspeople, with cameras, jostled and angled or muttered into microphones.

The murder continued to be a sensation. No media story was complete without reference to Deirdre's green hair and punk clothing, the attack on the subway platform, and the rifled apartment. Last night the police had announced the discovery of a new clue—a camera identified by fingerprints as Deirdre's, but emptied of its film and abandoned at the marathon.

From the moment Louisa stepped into the funeral home, she was treated with deference. She was ushered into a side room where the family was receiving only a select few mourners.

Deirdre's mother had the girl's round face, sagging with grief. Her eyes, staring and blue like Deirdre's, were bloodshot. "Did she say anything, Miss Evans?" she begged.

Louisa then understood her special treatment. She had been beside Deirdre when she died. She could not tell this anguished mother that her daughter's last words were "Fuck this!"

She had to fall back on the banalities. "She suffered very little, Mrs. Doyle, you can be sure of that," she said gently.

Deirdre's father seemed caught between anger at his daughter's death and awe at the attention it had brought him. "The cops told us you tried to give her mouth-to-mouth."

"I leaned over her—I was going to try—but I could see it was too late."

Mary Doyle began to sob. Louisa eased her way out as soon as she could. This was not the place to ask questions. The family had been through so much—hounded by reporters and probably badgered by police. She would find someone less grieved to interview. She needed to know what had brought Deirdre Doyle from this working class Catholic background to the East Village, and from there to her death in the midst of one of New York's trendiest self-help groups.

A fresh ordeal was ahead. The same attendant who had brought her in to see the family, bade her enter the flower-banked parlor, and motioned toward the casket. Louisa steeled herself to look for the last time on Deirdre Doyle.

The mortician had tried to recreate the image of the girl who had been confirmed at St. Joseph's altar, even to a virginally white dress and a wig of brown hair. The painted dead face was a lie, less honest than the painted living one had been. Deirdre's punk image had been, at least, a form of self-expression. This dead face was someone else's expression, and its look of sleeping innocence was horrible. No cosmetician's art could deny the violence and ambiguity of her death. The pale pink lips seemed curved in irony, as if from beyond the grave Deirdre still had the last word—"This sucks!"

Once Louisa had shaken off the reporters, she had no trouble finding people who were willing to talk about Deirdre. The story was drearily familiar, a drug-ridden adolescence and the sudden decision to go to New York to pursue a career for which she had neither talent nor self-discipline. Her family, plainly, had been relieved that she left home.

The rest of the story Louisa could piece together from what Clare had told her. Deirdre had dabbled with drugs and prostitution. Her extreme selfishness had probably saved her from falling prey to a pimp, but her involvement in supplying Jack's drug needs by stealing was just as perilous, given Jack's inclination toward violence. Even more problematical was her relationship with the man who had paid for the marathon. A blackmail victim? A sex slave? More than one person might have wanted Deirdre dead.

Louisa could only hope that the family would be strong enough to bear the fresh revelations when they came out. Her point of view for the story was developing slowly. She would try to show that Deirdre's death was a consequence of the violent, exploitative subculture she lived in, which was itself spawned by lawlessness and exploitation on a larger scale. Suddenly she could almost understand why people were attracted to SUM. It seemed to offer a cure for society's malaise.

Absorbed in these gloomy visions, she was leafing through the newspapers on Tuesday morning in the restaurant of her motel and having her second cup of coffee. She had one more obligation to the Doyles, the funeral mass at St. Joseph's, and the interment in the city's largest Catholic cemetery. Then she would get a cab to the railroad station and head thankfully for New York.

The story in the *Daily News* quoted Alex Meigs, who claimed that SUM had not been affected by the bad publicity. Enrollments in SUM events had fallen off slightly, true, and a few people had declined to return to the marathon. But the enrollments were expected to increase as more and more people became aware of SUM. Alex gave Tony Cazzine credit for handling the participants in the marathon in a supportive manner that did much to calm them. A marathoner was also quoted, saying, "No, I'm certainly not afraid to go back to the marathon next weekend. In spite of the tragedy, it's one of the best things I ever did."

"Ms. Evans?" Louisa looked up. A young black woman with enviable cheekbones was standing by the table. She looked like a model from the pages of *elle*. Incredibly, she was holding out a badge. "I'm Detective Rhonda Lord of the New York Police Department—got a few questions to ask you, okay?"

Louisa concealed her astonishment. "Of course! Sit down."

On a rich wave of Halston cologne, Detective Lord sat down and ordered coffee from the hovering waitress. Louisa could not imagine anyone less like the stereotype of the New York City detective, than Rhonda Lord. She had to be near Louisa's age. She was wearing a smart black cowl-neck tunic with a gray skirt and sleek fitted black boots. Nowhere on that slender figure could she have been wearing a gun. It must have been in the outsize leather handbag she dropped on the bench beside her.

"You make it kinda hard to get in touch with you, Ms. Evans!" She sounded only faintly reproving, as if Louisa's unanswered phone had been amusing rather than inconvenient.

Louisa explained hastily. "I was writing—didn't want to be disturbed—reporters were calling, people from SUM...."

Rhonda nodded sympathetically. "I get it. No harm. Here we are." She sounded cheerful, even chatty. Her coffee came. She added sugar and cream and stirred it. "We've had some developments that make it look like we need a little more information from you," she said. "For example," she took a sip of coffee and set the cup down in the saucer, "where did you go on Saturday after you left the marathon?"

Louisa's heart gave a thump. They'd found out. She'd keep nothing back except her encounter with Clare. She tried to speak in an ordinary voice. "I went to Deirdre Doyle's apartment."

"Why?"

"I'd talked to her briefly at the marathon, and I wanted to use her experience in an article I was writing on SUM. After she was killed, I went there to find out what I could about her background."

"How did you know where she lived?"

"She gave me her address while we were sitting together."

"You didn't tell Detective Malone that."

"It didn't seem important." Obviously it was. She'd made a mistake in not telling Malone she had Deirdre's address. Now the police saw her defection from the marathon in suspicious light.

"All the time he was questioning you, you knew you were going to skip out of the marathon and go to Deirdre's place to search it?"

"Not to search it. Just to look around, get a feel for the kind of life the girl led. I knew they wouldn't let me out of the marathon to call my agent until the next break, and I needed to talk to him—Deirdre's death made a new situation for me. I reacted like a reporter."

"What time did you get there?"

"About five. I took the subway."

"And what did you find out—as a reporter?" Rhonda's lovely, almond-shaped eyes were wide and ingenuous, and her tone was casual, but Louisa suddenly became wary. The jaws of a trap were opening. This cozy kaffee klatsch setup did not deceive her. Within this policewoman's shapely head, with its sleek, high-fashion haircut, was a mind like a computer. She had to walk a careful path. She would have to cooperate with the police to free herself of suspicion, but keep Clare out of it.

"The apartment door was open. Everything in it had been tossed on the floor. I'd say that someone had searched it with desperate thoroughness."

"Did you find what you were looking for?"

The implication was too much. Louisa clenched her teeth. Rhonda Lord had forced her on the defensive. "Someone who was there before me searched the apartment! And someone who came in after I did mugged me."

Perfect eyebrows went upward. "Really? Did you see this assailant?"

"I saw his arm in a khaki sleeve and his hand reaching into my bag. Then he hit me so hard I blacked out." Almost unconsciously her fingers went to the lump behind her ear. "When I came to, my wallet was gone. I also lost my keys and my credit cards."

"And your marathon name tag."

So that's how they knew! The tag had fallen out of her bag when the mugger emptied it. In her scramble to retrieve the scattered contents, she'd missed it. Rhonda was taking sips of coffee. A slight frown now drew her brows together. Louisa waited with some apprehension.

"Was your assailant white or black?"

"White."

"Male?"

"Yes, I'm certain, although I didn't see his face. He was very strong." She remembered the grip of that arm around her neck. "And he had a deformed thumbnail."

"Deformed how?"

"You think I'm making this up, don't you!"

Rhonda Lord smiled. For a fleeting moment Louisa marveled at the variety in the NYPD. The differences between Detective Malone and Detective Lord were stark. "Don't take it personally, Ms. Evans," Rhonda said. "What you say has to fit with our other information. Someone else tells us a man in khaki with a deformed thumb went into that apartment on Saturday, your story will have more clout. All I know is what you tell me. You haven't told me what you were looking for or what you found."

"I did tell you! I was looking for background on Deirdre— what her tastes were, her income level, her interests...."

"And?"

"She lived in poverty, and she was an inept photographer. On the floor was a collection of very bad photographs of scenes in New York City. Whoever searched the place must have looked through them and thrown them aside with the rest of her things."

"Among these pictures—did you find any with identifiable faces?"

"No."

"Did you take anything from the apartment?"

"No!"

"Deirdre brought a camera to the marathon."

"I read that in the paper. No film, the story said. Is that true?"

Rhonda Lord nodded. "It's true."

In silence they finished their coffee. Louisa motioned to the waitress for her check. Under the cover of paying and folding up her newspapers, her mind was working frantically. The police should have Clare's information. To tell it now was to ask for trouble.

"Ms. Evans, did Deirdre say anything else that you didn't tell Detective Malone about? Or maybe there's something you've remembered since then?"

That was putting it tactfully. And inescapably. She did not want to withhold information that could help the police find Deirdre's killer. "Let's go outside," she said, "I do have some things to tell you."

They walked around the outside of the chain link fence that surrounded the motel's empty swimming pool. Louisa stopped at the diving board. She looked at Rhonda and said, "I can't tell you my source. This is what I know about Deirdre. She was involved with a musician named Jack. He leads an unsuccessful rock group called Heloise and the Abelards. She stole things for him to sell to keep himself in cocaine. Another man in her life gave her things Jack sold—a stereo and a TV. He gave her her camera, too, and he may have paid for her to take the marathon. This last relationship, my source said, was over. The marathon was a parting gift to help her get herself together."

"Last names of these men?"

"I don't know. Heloise and the Abelards shouldn't be impossible to locate. The other man may be a teacher at SVA. He assigned a series of close-up shots of people typical of New York City, or some such theme. My source said Deirdre went out Friday night about eleven to see Jack's group play. She was carrying her camera around her neck."

Rhonda was very still. Her eyes held Louisa's. "That's mighty important information, Ms. Evans."

"I know it is. I hope it will help you find the killer."

"Your source isn't Deirdre herself?"

"No."

"And you won't tell me who it is?"

"No. This person is protecting . . ." She started to say "herself" and realized just in time that she did not want to reveal even that much about Clare. "This person, naturally, is fearful and demanded anonymity."

"We could guarantee it."

Louisa shook her head.

"Refusing to name a source can mean trouble for you."

"I know that."

"It could impede our investigation."

"I've told you all I know—except the source's name."

Rhonda's steely look revealed absolutely nothing about what was going on in her mind. With unspoken consent, they resumed their walk. "There's my car," Rhonda said as they approached the parking lot.

She took her keys out of her bag and unlocked the car. With her hand on the handle, ready to open the door, she said, "Oh, just one more question, Ms. Evans. What time was it when you left Deirdre's apartment?"

The trap was set. If she told Rhonda the truth, the jaws would snap. Rhonda would guess that her source was inside Deirdre's building. She lied without hesitation. "Allowing for the ten minutes or so that I was unconscious, I was there probably about half an hour."

"Did you see anyone besides your assailant?"

"No."

"On the street as you were going or coming?"

"No."

"Where did you go after you left the apartment?"

"Directly home. I had to report the loss of my cards and get a new lock for my door."

"How did you get home?"

"By subway. I walked back to Bleecker Street."

"He'd taken all your cash, you said."

"He overlooked a token in my back pocket." Lies came so glibly that she was frightened. If the police had managed to locate Clare and persuaded her to talk, she was making a fool of herself. Or worse.

"Sometime after you left the marathon on Saturday, you talked with someone who gave you this information about Deirdre."

"Yes." Louisa did her best to summon up the professionalism that had been the strongest element in her armor until she met Rhonda Lord. Professional had met professional. Her respect for this woman cop was as great as her fear of what she could find out. She continued to look steadily at Rhonda. "I could have denied I knew anything about Deirdre except what I observed in her apartment. I didn't do that because I don't want to hold back facts that might help your investigation. But I have an obligation to my source, and I have the right to protect it."

Louisa thought she saw in Rhonda's eyes a gleam of respect. "As a reporter you do. But reporters can go to jail when their refusal to name a source impedes a criminal investigation. And, like it or not Ms. Evans, you're a witness, an important one. You're a smart lady. You act like you know what you're doing. But lying or withholding from the police is a one-way ticket to trouble, trouble you walked into when you walked into Deirdre's place. You compounded that when you didn't tell us you were going there, or that you'd been there. And in protecting your source, you're doing yourself no favor.''

"Thank you," Louisa said.

"For what?"

"The warning."

Rhonda shrugged. "So if you change your mind, or if you find out anything more, from that source or any other—"

"I will! I'll call you or Detective Malone."

Louisa went back into her motel room thoroughly shaken. She had never had a reason to lie to the police, and she had never felt the way she did now—guilty and alarmed. Rhonda clearly suspected her of taking evidence from Deirdre's apartment. Rhonda might even suspect that the real source was not an unnamed person, but Louisa herself, and that she had lied to Detective Malone about having no acquaintance with Deirdre prior to the marathon. They couldn't prove that because it wasn't true, but if they speculated along those lines, they might think that she was saving material to use in her book—material that would cause a sensation when it came out.

She gathered up her things from the motel room and stuffed them into the shoulder tote that served as both overnight case and pocketbook. The same gray dress she'd been wearing for two days would do for the funeral.

Two hours later she stood with the overflow congregation from St. Joseph's which now circled the Doyle family plot. Her position in the back of the mourners let her look around during the interminable prayers.

Clare was not there. Neither was anyone who looked like Clare's description of Jack, who, if he were the one who had contrived to slip Deirdre the poisoned capsule, was not pushing his luck by attending the funeral. No one in this congregation had so much as passed through St. Mark's Place. Or probably even heard of the East Village except what they now knew from the newspapers about Deirdre's apartment in Alphabet City.

Except one.

The man who caught her eye also stood on the outer edge of the circle. He had sandy hair, expensively styled to conceal a receding hairline, a tan in December which meant either money for a winter vacation or a sunlamp, and light-adjusting glasses that had darkened so she could not see his eyes. A superbly fitting suit and a light raincoat draped over his shoulders completed the picture. This man, clearly, was not one of Deirdre's kinfolks.

During a pause in the innumerable prayers, Louisa heard shuffling and whispering behind her and a flurry among the reporters. Someone had walked across the grass to stand right behind her. She looked over her shoulder.

Tony Cazzine.

They were face to face, and once again they seemed to be sizing each other up. One part of her mind noted how utterly different and very good-looking he was in a dark suit with a white shirt and a discreetly somber tie. She understood why the clothes he wore at the marathon were so neutral. What the coach was wearing should not distract the marathoners.

Another part of her mind registered dismay that became alarm when he whispered, "We've got to talk. Now." He put a hand on her arm and drew her away from the congregation to a grassy space beyond which were the media and the police.

"Why didn't you return my call?" he demanded. "I want to know why you walked out on the marathon." He looked less haggard than he had after Deirdre's death, but he still looked tired. She could imagine the pressure he'd been under, not only from the press and the police, but from shocked and angry marathoners.

"A girl died beside me! Isn't that reason enough?"

"Don't you mean you came to do a hatchet job on SUM, and when you got material that proved your point, you left?"

He didn't mince words. She'd gotten her no-holds-barred interview without even asking for it. "Deirdre's death proved that the marathon does psychological damage. Your programs raise feelings people can't handle, and the high-handed way you cut her off upset her so much she turned to the only consolation she had—drugs."

"That's—" He stopped so abruptly that she knew he'd been about to say "bullshit." He went on with "far-fetched nonsense and you know it!"

"Then why did you stop her from telling her story?"

"She was about to give the whole marathon the name of the person who might have tried to kill her. She tried to tell me again when we talked at the shutdown. I told her to go to the police. I should have seen that she did. But she chose to swallow that capsule. I didn't drive her to it. And I certainly didn't put cyanide into it. So now—tell me the truth—why did you leave the marathon?"

"I was shocked and upset from being so close to her when she died so horribly."

"That I understand." Somehow she knew he did.

"I knew your assistant coaches wouldn't let me out to use the phone. I had to talk to my agent, and . . ."

"Your agent—now we get a little closer to the truth, don't we? If you'd stayed you might have gotten something that would let you write a really honest article about SUM. A lot of people learned about themselves on Saturday—how they act in a crisis, and how they handle grief and shock and fear. Your article can do damage to something that's helped thousands of people live better lives. Why are you doing it? Because you're paid better when you're smart and cynical? Or did you leave because you were afraid you'd find out you were wrong about SUM?"

"Oh!" She was so angry she was speechless. When she found her voice she had to force herself to keep it down. She was aware that this face-to-face was not going unrecorded. She could hear the click of cameras. Sarcasm came easily. "If you'd look around, you'd notice that we are at a funeral. And you're trying to tell me it's all right Deirdre died because her death provided a learning experience for the one hundred and ninety-nine who didn't die! I think that's perverted, and I'm going to say so."

"And part of your mission is to expose me as a peddler of a modern form of snake oil?"

"Something like that, yes!"

"Has it occurred to you that you have a responsibility in Deirdre's death?"

"What do you mean?"

"Didn't you sign the marathon contract?"

An inkling of what was coming made the blood drain from her face. She tried to resist it, but she could feel herself going pale, and her limbs felt suddenly heavy. Tony Cazzine was a ruthless bastard. She dropped her eyes. "Yes, I signed it."

"And?"

She looked up again and said angrily, "It wasn't a contract, it was manipulation! We were given no choice. If I didn't sign it, I couldn't be in the marathon."

"When you signed your name to that contract, you agreed to stay in the marathon until its completion, maintain confidentiality, and follow the rules, one of which was not to use drugs or alcohol while you were a marathoner. What else did the contract say about drugs, Louisa?"

She turned her back on him. Under pretense of bowing her head for Father Doyle's prayers, she fought to get herself under control. No resistance and no rationalization would hold off that damning truth. If she had raised her hand when Deirdre showed her the capsule, the girl might not be there in that casket now being lowered into a grave. It was a stark and terrible fact. In one part of her mind she'd known it all along, and she hated Tony Cazzine for bringing it to her full consciousness.

He was standing very close behind her now, and to her surprise she felt the pressure of his arm around her. It was strangely comforting. "Come back to the marathon, please, Louisa?" He was speaking very quietly now. "You interrupted the program you were in. First we look at ourselves and tell the truth. Then we see what we can do about it."

She moved away from his arm and looked at him. "No one walks away from two weekends of mass hysteria cured of guilt and grief!" she said bitterly. "You make it sound easy. It's not!"

"If we didn't make it sound easy, no one would take the first step. SUM doesn't claim to be a miracle cure or instant therapy, but everyone who does the marathon can walk out knowing what to do next—some go to therapists, some to rehabilitation centers, some to Alcoholics Anonymous. Some quit jobs they hate and let themselves do the work they've always wanted. Some need to go to people they've hurt to try to clean up what's between them. That's what I did about my shit in Vietnam. You're right. It wasn't easy."

"What did you do?"

"After I got off drugs, I located the families of the men who were killed in that ambush. Took me a year and a half to find and visit them all—parents, wives, girlfriends."

"I suppose they all forgave you for surviving when their men died!"

"Some did, some didn't. Some couldn't care less. Some had found their peace, and they gave me some of it."

Members of Deirdre Doyle's immediate family were stepping forward now to drop flowers into the grave. The service was nearly over. Louisa thought briefly about all the things she'd wanted to ask Tony Cazzine. Now they seemed irrelevant.

He took her arm again. She almost shrank from the urgency she felt in him. "All the marathon does is give people a place to look at themselves and see if they're satisfied with their lives. Is that perverted?"

"No," she said reluctantly.

"If they're not satisfied, they can see what they really want and what's stopping them from getting it. You, Louisa—you're beautiful, and you're successful—do you have what you really want?"

She shook her head, not in answer to his question, but to try to ward off the thoughts crowding in on her. She was being forced to take an honest look at what she did not want to admit. *I want a relationship—a committed, permanent relationship with a man. In spite of everything, I want—marriage. And children.* She stood, her lips tight. She would die rather than say these things to Tony Cazzine.

"What's stopping you from getting it?"

Fear of failure. It was that simple. I failed at marriage because I forced a situation in which I thought I was choosing between my marriage and my career. All I did was run away. Work was safe. I could count on succeeding there. I was afraid to risk the hard work of saving my relationship.

She felt dull now, and sad. "Your marathon is nothing but a magic wand. Wave it and get what you want!"

"People who think they want magic wands get magic wands. They won't learn to live fully, they'll just keep on waving their wands and getting pissed-off when things don't get better. Some people make SUM into their religion. Coaches become priests, and the organization becomes a hierarchy. They start at the bottom as assistant coaches, like acolytes, and they think they're going to work their way up. We don't ask them to do that. SUM has never passed itself off as the way to the Holy Grail. All it is, is a place for you to see that you're responsible for your own life. Not your parents for not loving you enough, not your husband for not understanding you, not your President for the wrong policy in Vietnam—you, all by yourself. You can accept it, overcome your fears, and work through your barriers instead of running away from them. Your ninety-dollar an hour shrink will tell you exactly the same thing. So, probably in a slightly different form, will the good father over there."

Father Doyle was intoning what sounded like the final prayer. Louisa half-turned from Tony and bowed her head again. She felt confused. Many times she'd thought of calling Glen, asking him to have lunch with her, and telling him—what? That she finally took responsibility for what happened to their marriage?

The last amen was said. The mourners began to stir. "Come back to the marathon, Louisa," Tony said.

"No." She faced him again and hoped he would not hear the uncertainty she was feeling. "If you'll excuse me, I came here to do a job, a hatchet job as you called it, and I'm going to get on with it."

He looked over her head at the gravesite. "I have a job here, too. I've got to see Deirdre's parents."

"I suppose you're going to confess to them the way you did to your gold-star families."

"I already have. I phoned them Sunday morning."

"And admitted your responsibility for her death?"

"I told them I should have taken her fear much more seriously and much sooner. I should have seen personally that she went to the police." When Louisa gave a small shrug and hitched her bag up over her shoulder, he reached out. "There's a reason for this, Louisa. For SUM, for you, for me, for whoever killed Deirdre.''

''I never heard anything so absurd! I suppose you know why I was the person with the bad luck to be sitting beside her!''

''No, I don't know. But there's something you want that you're not getting, isn't there?'' When she did not answer, he looked at her in silence for a few seconds. His nearness was disturbing. Then he smiled. She had never seen him smile. In the marathon he'd been forceful, serious, angry, but never like this. The smile was as disturbing as his nearness. He said, ''If you come back to the marathon, you might find it!''

''Not on your life!'' she said with what she hoped was cutting finality. She turned her back on him for good.

First Rhonda. Now Tony. Two intense confrontations in one morning. She was tired and angry and very upset. She needed the train ride back to New York to be alone with her feelings, to sort them out. But before she could make her escape from Scranton, she had one more person to face. Her quarry was the sandy-haired man of the impeccable suit, who was now shaking hands with Bill Doyle. He was the only person here who could possibly be the SVA teacher Clare thought Deirdre had been involved with. She could not pass up this opportunity.

He seemed to be talking interminably. Then she saw another handshake. The sandy-haired man turned and began to walk rapidly, his steps quickening as if he were as relieved as she was to be getting away.

She stationed herself near the gates so he would have to pass her on his way out, and suddenly she found herself surrounded by reporters. A microphone was thrust into her face.

TEN

"WHAT DID YOU SAY to the Doyles about their daughter's death?"

"I have nothing to say about Deirdre Doyle's death!" Louisa walked rapidly ahead of the reporters, her heels clicking on the sidewalk.

"Would you comment, Ms. Evans...?"

"No comment!"

Behind her she heard a polite voice. "Excuse me, Ms. Evans. Will you allow me to help you get out of this godforsaken—oops—I guess that's wildly inappropriate under the circumstances. My name is Harvey Wardleigh, and my car is just outside the gates."

The reporters closed in. "What was your connection with the deceased, Mr. Wardleigh?

"Ms. Evans, is it true that you're writing a book about this tragedy?"

Though hampered by her high heels, Louisa began to run. She reached the gate with her rescuer before she even got a good look at him. The reporters scrambled behind them shouting questions. Harvey Wardleigh unlocked the passenger side of a gray Toyota and opened the door for her. Seconds later he slammed the door on his side and turned on the ignition. Before the car had even left the curb, the media pack had turned to hunt down more cooperative sources.

"Forgive my casting aspersions on your profession, Ms. Evans," Harvey Wardleigh said, "but really, they are too much!"

"Thank you for getting me out of that. It's disconcerting to be on the other side after all the years I had 'no comment' flung in my face."

Harvey Wardleigh laughed, a musical sound that seemed oddly studied and at variance with his face. Louisa, taking covert looks at him as he concentrated on threading the Toyota through the traffic, guessed that he was in his early forties. The eyes behind the glasses were light with pale lashes and brows sandy-colored like his hair. Standing beside him while he opened the car, she'd noticed that she was a few inches taller than he in her high heels. Parallel creases between his brows and a set of lines circling his mouth gave his face a look of permanent peevishness.

He spoke pleasantly, however. If he was peeved, it was not because he'd rescued her. "I'm at your service, Ms. Evans. Where can I take you?" he asked.

"Are you going back to New York?"

"I am. My pleasure to give you a ride."

When he had found his way through the city streets and onto the expressway, Harvey looked over. On his face was undisguised eagerness. She was about to be pumped for information. She was just as curious as he seemed to be, but she hoped her eagerness was less obvious.

"I'm honored to have such a well-known writer willing to ride with me. Tell me, are you here out of respect for the dear departed, or are you working? Is it true there's a book in the offing?"

This day's ordeals were not yet over. She thought longingly of that solitary train ride. "I started out to write an article about SUM," she said, "but the murder shifted my interest to Deirdre. What about you?" If she had to go through with this, she was going to get all she could from Harvey Wardleigh.

He made a little grimace of distaste. "I had the misfortune to be Deirdre's faculty advisor," he said, "also her photography teacher. The administration thought that as I was known to be friendly with her, I should represent SVA at the obsequies."

She wanted to ask "how friendly," but she held back. That sort of information would be far better if it came naturally. Harvey's face and tone had already shown his feelings about Deirdre. The facts might not be far behind.

She was right. Harvey went on as if she'd asked the question. "It's no secret that I was—shall we say—somewhat avuncular. As a matter of fact, I tried to get her to give up photography. She was hopeless."

He seemed so willing to explain his relationship with Deirdre that she decided to take the risk. He would probably warm to a mixture of coyness and frankness similar to his own. "So tell me, how avuncular were you, really? Did you encourage her to take the marathon?"

Harvey laughed delightedly. "Was that tidbit on today's news? Yes, I encouraged her. To the point of putting her tuition on my American Express card, a mistake that's earned me top billing on Detective Malone's prime suspect list!"

Louisa laughed too, with the first genuine amusement she'd experienced since Deirdre's death. "Welcome to the club!"

Harvey looked over. "You too? Of course. You were sitting right beside her. Our quick-witted sleuth thinks you fed her the cyanide. Your motive? Don't tell me, let me guess. You wanted to create a scandal that would bring SUM crashing down and win you a Pulitzer Prize for a daring exposé!"

Louisa laughed again. The situation was absurd, but it had its macabre humor. She was almost enjoying herself. Harvey actually seemed more eager to give information than to get it. Maybe she could use that eagerness.

Harvey laughed too. "It'll take more than murder to bring down SUM, I'm afraid. I see by today's papers that its popularity has scarcely been diminished. Didn't I see you in a tête-á-tête with Tony Cazzine? Who was trying to straighten out whom? You both looked a bit miffed, I thought."

"Call it ideological warfare," she said lightly. "Tell me, did you give Deirdre the marathon as a gift or a loan?"

Harvey's look became almost sly. "A gift, actually. I did the marathon a few years ago. When Deirdre mentioned it was something she wanted to do, I agreed to pay for it. Actually I hoped it would do the little bitch some good."

"Very generous of you."

Harvey chuckled. "Detective Malone's exact words! And in just that tone of voice—dry—a bit prim. He so obviously disapproved of me. He's an absolute stereotype. Can't you just see him in 'Hill Street Blues'?"

"He questioned you?"

"Tediously. At length. As soon as SUM's computer spit out my name, he was on my doorstep, eager to find something naughty in my willingness to front five hundred dollars for what he thinks is a communist-backed conspiracy to brainwash America's yuppies. Which brainwashing he thinks they deserve for being both rich and gullible."

"I agree."

"That SUM is brainwashing, or that my altruism is perverse?"

"Both."

Again the peal of laughter that did not match his face. "I know why you write so well, Louisa! You don't mind if I call you Louisa, do you? And please call me Harvey."

"All right, Harvey, tell me the truth. Was it altruism?"

"You'll ferret it out, so I might as well be candid. Can I count on you to be kind?"

"That depends on what the truth is."

His voice dropped as if he suspected an eavesdropper in the back seat of the Toyota. Louisa wondered if Harvey Wardleigh was trying out his story on her. She also wondered if he had told the same story to Detective Malone. "I made several mistakes with Deirdre," he said. "The biggest one was sleeping with her. It was the green hair—irresistible. Do you know, she even dyed her—but never mind."

"Harvey, are you sure you want to tell me all this?"

The look he turned on her was mock reproachful. "I trust you, Louisa. The number one suspects club is awfully exclusive. We've only got each other!"

"So far as we know."

"You are *so* right! There may be hordes of prospective members out there the police haven't turned up yet. Knowing Deirdre as I do—did—it's more than likely. But to get back to my story, by the time Deirdre's novelty staled, which was quite soon, she'd gotten it into her fuddled little head that she could bring charges of sexual harassment. She was so bitchy in public, so totally disliked, and so permanently in a fog induced by various chemicals, that she could not have made the charges stick. Besides which, she was about to be thrown out of the school for pilfering, which had gone beyond petty. But there would have been publicity, embarrassment—you get the picture. So I negotiated. In return for dropping the idea of charges and doing without favors, I offered a few trifles which she eagerly snapped up—a stereo, a TV, a camera—and finally, the marathon. That was it, I told her. I hoped SUM would make her see the truth about herself—that she was a stupid, conniving slut.''

"Harvey, you've been more than candid. You've incriminated yourself.''

"I have, haven't I? Now you see how far I'm willing to trust you. I freely admit my misdeeds. I make appropriate *mea culpas*. But frankly, I'm relieved she's dead. Except to those miserable people in Scranton, and maybe not even to them, she's no loss. And I didn't kill her.''

"And you have an impeccable alibi for Saturday afternoon?''

"I was with my mother at Lenox Hill Hospital,'' he said promptly. "She's recovering from the cancer surgery she had on Friday. Actually, she's recovering from surgery, but not from the cancer. It's only a matter of time until it recurs. I'm her only child.''

"I'm sorry.''

"I'm sure that bumbling detective will be there asking stupid questions, wearing her out...'' After a short, brooding silence, he looked over again. "And what does Malone have against you—besides your unfortunate proximity to the deceased?''

"I walked out of the marathon.''

"Oh, dear, that *was* a boo-boo! SUM never forgives. So the police think you left the scene of your crime?''

"Apparently. Malone's partner, Rhonda Lord, cornered me this morning. After I left the marathon, I went to Deirdre's apartment. The police have found out, and now I'm afraid they suspect me of removing evidence.''

"You braved Alphabet City? All by yourself? What did you think you'd find? Or perhaps I should ask what evidence do they think you took?''

"I was looking for background on Deirdre. But the apartment had been ransacked before I got there, and all I got for my trouble was a mugging."

"In Deirdre's apartment?"

"Yes."

"Which I'm sure the police think you deserved. Did you see who did it?"

"Not enough to identify him. I saw only his hand and arm. He has a squashed left thumb."

"Really! How observant of you. And did you find useful background on Deirdre for your book?"

"Not much beyond proof that she was a really poor photographer. I'm not surprised you tried to discourage her."

"You saw her pictures?"

"Dreadful, boring, and totally nonincriminating pictures of New York City."

"Ah, city scenes in their glorious banality! How about city faces—did you see any of those?"

"No, was that one of your assignments?"

"I send my students out into the city to shoot close-ups of interesting faces. They have to ask the subject's permission, of course. Some of my students do outstanding work. But Deirdre would have settled for the drearily familiar—a cop with a beefy Irish visage, a black tot or two in a carriage, a seamy old bag lady perhaps."

"I saw nothing like that. Whoever searched must have taken them. Now I can guess why."

"Oh, do let me in on your hunch!"

"Suppose Deirdre didn't ask the subject's permission before she took a picture? If she was stoned all the time, as you say, she might not have bothered. Suppose she caught someone who had a good reason not to want to be photographed?"

"You mean someone committing a crime? Or just scratching himself in a naughty place? How about a man in a nightclub with his mistress when his wife thinks he's in Chicago on business? Really, Louisa, you are imaginative! Have you read this little scenario to Detective Malone?"

"Actually I just thought of it. And what would be the use? Anything I tell the police now will only look like an attempt to throw suspicion onto someone else."

Harvey was silent while he concentrated on maneuvering the Toyota around a truck. Then he said, "I have a suggestion, Louisa. I hope you won't think I'm paranoid."

"What is it?"

He glanced over. "All joking aside. With that vivid imagination of yours, I'm surprised you haven't seen that your adventures could arouse the suspicions of a person or persons other than the police. If there's any truth in your scenario, someone else may be wondering what you found in Deirdre's apartment. And come looking for it."

"Oh, Lord, I didn't think of that!"

"Well, think about it now."

By the time the Toyota entered the Lincoln Tunnel, Louisa was fantasizing another scenario she would not share with Detectives Lord and Malone. She wouldn't share it with Harvey either. His candor sounded, at times, like a well-rehearsed story. Although he seemed to her oddly sexless, his involvement with Deirdre may have included far more than he'd let on. In spite of what he said, Deirdre could have threatened some serious damage to his status or reputation. Knowing Deirdre and knowing the marathon, he could have seen an opportunity to commit an anonymous murder.

The flaw in the scenario was that Harvey had an alibi. He had not been at the marathon; he'd been visiting his mother at Lenox Hill. All day? Surely not. He could have slipped into the lobby during the shutdown and been ready to supply the trank he knew she'd be crawling for.

"When did you last see Deirdre?" she asked.

"I saw her a week ago Thursday, but I talked with her on Monday. She called to demand reassurances that the marathon wouldn't turn her into a Moonie."

"How about Saturday morning?"

"How did you know about that?"

"She told me she'd been about to drop out of the marathon, but a friend said she had to go through with it."

"Did she tell you why she wanted to drop out?"

"She said she'd been frightened by an attempted purse snatching on the subway on Friday night. And she was feeling the effects of going off tranquilizers."

"She phoned at the crack of dawn on Saturday, almost hysterical. I talked her back into it. SUM doesn't refund the money for last-minute dropouts."

"Do you know Jack?"

"Jack who?"

"I don't know his last name. He's a musician Deirdre was seeing. His rock group is called Heloise and the Abelards."

"She told you all this while you were sitting in the marathon? My, she was in a talkative mood!"

"Yes." She had no compunction about lying to Harvey. She didn't want him to know about Clare, either.

Harvey's face wore a smile of satisfaction. "I thought Deirdre's protests about my disenchantment had a hollow ring. Heloise and the Abelards—too tasteless! Where did they play?"

"She didn't tell me that."

"So she threw me over for Heloise, or was it Abelard? She probably didn't know—or care. One could never be sure with Deirdre. Did she tell you anything more about this Jack?"

"No, that was all."

By the time the car reached midtown, Louisa was thoroughly sick of Harvey Wardleigh. His affair with Deirdre had been "too tasteless," and his eagerness to tell her about it even more so. Not even the fact that the man's mother was dying of cancer could arouse much sympathy for him.

He insisted upon taking her to SUM's office on Third Avenue when she told him she wanted to pick up the jacket she had left at the marathon on Saturday. He lived in a co-op in Chelsea, he told her, and when she protested that he was going out of his way, he said, "I just want to be sure Detective Malone isn't hanging out there waiting to grill you again. If we spot him, I'll simply whisk you away!"

No detective was lurking outside the building where SUM had its office. Louisa thanked Harvey and opened the door of the car. When she got out, Harvey leaned over to say earnestly, "You will think about what I said, won't you? And be discreet?"

"I will, Harvey, thank you."

"And if anything comes up—remember, you and I are the charter members of the suspects' club—we have to help each other! I'm in the phone book. Eighteenth Street."

Louisa sincerely hoped that nothing would come up that required her to seek help from Harvey Wardleigh, but she nodded and smiled and shut the door of his car.

Since Tony was in Scranton, it was safe for her to walk boldly into the SUM office and up to the reception desk where an assistant labeled "Gloria" listened to her inquiry about her jacket. While Gloria went to the Lost and Found, she had time to look around. SUM's offices were not lavish, but they were furnished in sufficiently good taste to show that the organization was not operating on a low budget. The reception area had gray carpeting and paler gray walls with framed posters of SUM slogans. She saw the door marked, "Alex Meigs, Manager." She really needed to interview Alex. What she really wanted to do was go home.

Gloria brought the jacket with a cheery, "Here you are, Louisa! I hope you'll log back on with us on Saturday."

Louisa didn't know what prompted her to ask Gloria, "Does Tony Cazzine stay in the Park Summit?"

"Yes, he does, but he's not there right now. He went to that funeral, you know? Would you like us to take a communication? I can have him call you."

"No, thanks. But I would like to see Alex Meigs. Would you ask him if he has time to talk to me now?"

ELEVEN

HER TACTICS for avoiding the press had succeeded. They'd given up. No reporters were hanging around outside her building. It was safe to go in by the front door.

The first thing she did when she got home was kick off her shoes. Then she hung her coat and her down jacket in the closet. There was the cheap jacket she'd bought on Saturday. She didn't want it. Tomorrow she'd fold it and put it out on the top of her trash. Whoever collected the building's refuse would surely know someone who could use a new winter jacket. The hat and gloves could go with it.

She pulled them out of the pockets where she'd stuffed them. Something was in one of the gloves, something that crackled. She pulled it out. It was the slip of paper Deirdre had given her in the marathon, the one which she had scribbled the girl's address. She must have stuck it into her glove after she found Deirdre's building. She was about to throw it away, but she stopped. On Saturday she had looked only at the address. Now she unfolded and looked at the paper itself.

It was a strip about five inches long and a little over an inch wide. It was perforated all along one side, and it bore a long number printed in blue. It was stamped with Saturday's date. It looked familiar, like something she had used often. It was a claim slip of some sort.

She carried it into the living room and put it down on her desk. She pressed the listen button and the rewind on her answering machine. Hal had called twice. SUM five times. Reporters were still asking for information, but politely, and by phone. She had one invitation to lunch and two to dinner.

She was on her way into her bedroom to get out of the all-purpose gray dress and into jeans when the next voice stopped her in midstride. It was a stranger's voice—male, young, and slightly hoarse, as if the speaker were trying to disguise it. "Uh,

Louisa Evans? You know, I think you've got something I want. And like, maybe I've got something you want. We could, like, uh, get together, see what happens? If you're interested, call this number...."

An obscene call on an answering machine was a hazard of modern technology. At least he didn't breathe hard. And he didn't get specific about what he had that she might want.

She washed, changed into jeans and a sweater and made herself a pot of coffee. With cup in hand, she went to her desk. She had good notes from her interview with Alex Meigs, who had gone out of his way to be candid and cooperative. She'd been impressed with his manners, and with his enthusiasm for SUM. He liked his job, and he had no doubts that SUM was a worthwhile endeavor. He also liked Tony. Tony, he'd told her, was considered the best coach SUM had—dynamic, forceful, and "a hell of a guy." She had kept her reservations about both SUM and its supercoach to herself.

She wanted to fill in her notes from her talk with Alex and to write her impressions of Deirdre's funeral.

Her phone rang. "Louisa Evans?" It was the same voice as the tape. Less hesitant now. "I know you're there. Don't be stupid. I know what you've got. Call this number...."

She hung up. She sometimes got crank calls and occasionally they were obscene, but she did not want to be forced to get an unlisted number. Now she felt a touch of fear. "I know you're there." He could be out there watching. He'd seen her go in, and he'd seen the lights go on in her windows. Even now he could be at a pay phone.

Her eyes fell on the paper Deirdre had pulled out of her pocket. An entirely new possibility made the flesh crawl on the back of her neck.

That wasn't an obscene caller. That was Jack. But if he was her attacker, what did he want from her? He had her credit cards and her keys. He must know she had stopped charges on the first and replaced the second. He'd been in Deirdre's apartment and knew she had taken nothing from it.

She had nothing of Deirdre's but this piece of paper. It had to be that.

For a few seconds she fingered it. Then it all fell into place. Her hunch had been right. This piece of paper was a torn-off claim slip from an envelope into which someone had put a roll of film.

TWELVE

LIGHTS STILL BURNED in the SUM office on Third Avenue when Tony got back from Scranton at ten o'clock. Alex and Detective Malone were sifting through a pile of papers on Alex's desk. Both men looked tired. The detective's fleshy face was sagging, and his eyes were red-rimmed. Alex looked up when Tony came in. "How did it go?"

Tony took off his jacket and loosened his tie. "Grim. The friends and relatives tried to say the right thing, but all they did was confirm their belief that her death was divine retribution. Or divine providence."

"She brought shame on the Doyles, did she?"

"She did, poor kid. And according to them, God's judgment on herself. I think the Doyles are more angry about the way she lived than the way she died. They'd never seen her green hair until they brought her body home. What have you got here?"

"So far not a fucking thing," said Malone. "I pulled out a pile of data sheets on people who answered your questions in a way that might mean they weren't totally in control. Or that they had an ax to grind. Alex has been looking them over, helping me with this SUM double talk. Here—what do you make of this one?"

Tony pulled an extra chair up to the desk and took the sheet the detective handed him. The marathoner's name was Ernie Grimes. He remembered Ernie well. After a long and tedious build-up, Ernie had admitted his homosexuality and had experienced a release bordering on euphoria. To the question "What do you hope to get out of doing the marathon?" Ernie had written, "I want to log-on to the truth about myself."

"What's the problem?" Tony asked Malone.

"What does the guy mean, 'log-on to the truth about myself'? What the hell is he talking about?"

"Ernie wanted to be able to admit that he's gay."

"Did he?"

"He did."

The detective's grunt could have meant disbelief, disgust, or both. "What about this one?"

The name on the sheet was Vic. Vic wrote, "Peace of mind is all I want. I get so depressed sometimes I think I might do something terrible."

"I don't know Vic," Tony said. "He hasn't spoken up. Do you think the man's homicidal because sometimes he feels down? If that means he's out of control, your suspect list is going to get out of hand."

"Don't you get a lot of kooks in this thing?"

"Very few," said Alex. "Most of the people who do the marathon are pretty solid citizens. We get a lot of lawyers, doctors sometimes, lots of people in the media and the performing arts, advertising. Look, right here on Vic's data—he's an accountant. Over half of them are college-educated, a lot of them make over twenty-five thousand a year—"

"I get the point. But impressive statistics aside, you've got a bad apple in this barrel."

Alex's face fell into the sad lines nature had carved in it. "You're absolutely sure then, that the killer is one of the marathoners?"

"I'm absolutely sure of nothing. But if the bell captain is telling the truth, no one made contact with Deirdre in the lobby during the shutdown."

"How about the corridor from the restroom to the lobby?"

"Two women who left the restroom right after she did said she was in their sight all the way to the lobby and alone the whole way. She's totally accounted for in the lobby. It's ballroom or Ladies' room. And no one in the Ladies' room saw anyone give her anything."

Tony picked up a sheaf of data sheets that were separated from the rest. Louisa's was on the top. "What are these?"

"Those people didn't answer the questions at all," said Malone. "Could be that one of them didn't want to risk writing something that sounded suspicious."

Tony leafed through the pile. Six people had left the answer spaces blank: Louisa Evans; Tom Karelsen; Muffy Barnes; Fernando Perez; Steve O'Rourke; and Irving Stein.

"Know anything about any of them?" Malone asked.

"Louisa would hardly have told us she was here to get material for an exposé of SUM."

Malone only grunted.

"She came to get her jacket late this afternoon," Alex said, "and came in to interview me about the effect of this thing on our organization. She wanted to know our ideas about better screening of registrants, our plans to allay the fears of prospective marathoners—she asked good questions."

"She wasn't hostile?" Tony asked.

"She pressed hard, made me think—but no, I wouldn't describe her as hostile. When I told her we hoped she'd reprogram on Saturday, she smiled enigmatically."

"That wasn't what she did to me. She snarled 'Not on your life!'"

Alex shrugged. "What can I say? Some of us have charm, some of us don't. She asked about you though, Gloria said. Asked if you were staying at the Park Summit."

Tony raised his eyebrows. "Why does she want to know that, I wonder?" He caught the detective's look and said, "I'm sorry, Malone. We got sidetracked." He held out the data sheets. "You questioned these people, didn't you? What do you know about them?"

"Nothing helpful. This Tom Karelsen is naturally close-mouthed. O'Rourke insists he didn't know Deirdre, didn't see her on the shutdown. Barnes was one of the women on line for the Ladies' room who saw Deirdre go out. Perez has a problem with English, speaks brokenly and no doubt writes worse. Stein said he just couldn't think of anything he wanted to get out of the marathon, and no, he didn't know Deirdre. Looks to me like Louisa Evans had the best reason for not answering your questions."

"What are you talking about? Louisa did not kill Deirdre Doyle!"

"Don't bet on it," said the detective.

"What have you got on her that I don't know yet?"

"Saturday after she walked out on your marathon, she went to Deirdre's place and searched it."

"How do you know?"

"She dropped her name tag. Detective Lord questioned her today in Scranton and got some story about her going there to get material for a book she's writing about Deirdre. Evans claims the place had already been tossed before she got there. She also claims she was mugged, lost her keys, cards, and money."

"And you don't believe her!"

"Let's say I'm skeptical. Looks to me like she's got something going on that's more research on this book or whatever she's writing. She asked a lot of questions in Scranton, and somewhere she got information we weren't able to dig up. She refused to name the source."

"What kind of information?"

"About Deirdre's relationships with two men."

Tony exploded. Malone's earlier hints about Louisa had seemed only a theory, to be discarded when the facts brought him closer to the real murderer. Now he seemed to be trying to make every new fact fit into that first theory. "Why the fuck aren't you out there looking for those two men instead of sitting on your ass and letting circumstantial evidence indict Louisa Evans?"

"We *are* looking, Mr. Cazzine! One of the men is Harvey Wardleigh, who paid for Deirdre's marathon. He says his motive for that was pure, which I don't altogether believe, but he has an alibi for Saturday. His mother is in Lenox Hill Hospital. He was there with her."

Tony tried to calm himself. Getting Malone hot under the collar was not going to get the detective off his obsession with Louisa. "What does Wardleigh look like?"

"Light hair. Forty-three. Well-dressed."

"I saw him at the cemetery this afternoon."

"That fits. He was Deirdre's faculty adviser at the art school."

"What kind of guy?"

"I thought he was a faggot."

Tony wondered what the detective would make of the fact that Louisa had left the funeral with Harvey Wardleigh. He had looked back and seen them get into a car. He did not know what to make of it himself. He decided not to risk it on Malone. "Wardleigh's covered for Saturday?"

"He was definitely at the hospital. But what you've got to face is that no one—*no one*, Mr. Cazzine—of Wardleigh's description or any other description came anywhere near Deirdre in the lobby. You see where that leaves us."

Tony saw only too clearly. He didn't like the implication. "You said men interested in Deirdre. Who besides Harvey?"

"A rock musician with a heavy habit. We haven't been able to locate him yet. His name is Jack, according to Evans' secret source, and he has a band called Heloise and the Abelards. Mean anything to you?"

"Kinky. Not my type. Look, Malone—if this guy is a heavy user, he's got to be in trouble. Deirdre had a habit too. Same for her. Any number of people could have wanted her dead."

"The question is not *who*, Mr. Cazzine, but *how*. No one but Louisa Evans saw the capsule that killed her."

Alex spoke up. "Maybe Deirdre hunted through her pockets and bag and found she had one on her after all. You said she didn't answer Louisa's question 'Did you get...' in words. She just opened her hand and showed her."

"And that could mean," said Tony, "that someone put the capsule into her supply days, even weeks ago, in the certainty that sooner or later she would take it."

"Maybe it wasn't even meant for Deirdre. She's an innocent victim of an attempt to kill someone else—like the poisoned Tylenol and Excedrin deaths," said Alex.

The detective heaved himself up out of the chair. "That's a possibility I don't even want to think about."

"Maybe you ought to!" Tony said. He was on his feet, too.

"You trying to tell me how to do my job?"

"I think you're so obsessed with Louisa Evans you won't even look for another possibility."

"Look what she gets out of this—a book contract."

"Oh, God, that's absurd! She came to find something wrong with SUM, and she found it, yes. But she did not create it by killing Deirdre Doyle!"

They were glaring at each other now, and both of them were breathing hard. Alex was looking from one of them to the other, eager, Tony knew, to step in and make them get off it. He was relieved when the detective broke the tension by turning away.

Malone walked to the door, picked up his coat from a chair, and opened the door. In the doorway he stopped. He turned back to Tony with a look of exasperation and pity. "I've known plenty of killers in my career. Enough to know that you don't pick them by the way they look. All I have to do to remind myself of that fact every day of my life is to look in the mirror. I've killed in self-defense, and I've killed in anger. Think about it, Mr. Cazzine—what do *you* see when you look in the mirror?"

THIRTEEN

ALEX WAS LOOKING at him, inviting him to talk. Tony didn't feel like it. He was too angry at Malone, too disturbed by Louisa's mission in Deirdre's apartment, too....

" 'Tell the truth about your experience.' " Alex smiled as he quoted from the SUM brochure.

"I don't know what the truth is yet," Tony told him. "When I find out I'll let you know. Thanks. See you tomorrow."

Four crosstown and ten uptown blocks were a long enough walk to work off some of his tension. He was edgy in a way he never experienced while he was coaching a marathon, no matter how many hours he'd been leading and interfacing with sometimes stubborn people. Normally he went back to California and stayed there doing his other work—counseling Vietnam vets—until he had to fly back for the second weekend of the marathon. Because of the murder, he'd had to stay in New York. He thought longingly of the beach.

His beach was very far away. Malone's question had brought a host of nagging doubts. "Nothing is but what is not" and "There's no art to find the mind's construction in the face." *Macbeth* was the one Shakespeare play he'd really understood. Louisa's face, white and anguished the way it was this afternoon in the cemetery, came into his mind.

She didn't look like a murderer. Neither did the man he saw in the mirror.

A very dark mood was on him. Not even the beach would help him through this one. He had to ride it out. He'd come back from Scranton saddened by what the Doyles were going through, but hopeful that he'd gotten through to Louisa. Her cordiality with Alex was a promising sign. Then what Malone told him skewed the whole picture.

Louisa knew more about Deirdre than the police had been able to find out. She wouldn't give her source. How long, really, had she known Deirdre? How long, for that matter, had she known Harvey Wardleigh?

Taken one way, the facts piled up damnably. The most damning of all was that no one had seen the capsule but Louisa. That sudden paling of her face this afternoon when he confronted her with her responsibility for Deirdre's death—it could have been remorse. Or it could have been fear.

He suddenly thought of Vietnam. He'd not seen the real face of the war until he got there. He'd seen an appeal to serve his country, a particular view of history, and a chance to show how macho he was. His country had betrayed him with lies, its administration's attempt to justify that view of history had been a political and military disaster, and the macho man had killed and killed and killed until the ambush had turned his loathing back onto himself.

By the time he reached the Park Summit and was in the elevator on his way up to his room, he was wondering if he was going to be able to sleep at all. The elevator door opened onto his floor. His footsteps were silent on the thick carpet. He went around the corner and opened the glass door that separated his section from the elevator corridor. He pulled out the plastic disk that unlocked his door.

The hall ahead of him was dark, blacked out completely as if all the bulbs that lighted it had burned out. The glass door swung softly shut behind him.

Something made him stop. He sensed, rather than heard, a soft footfall ahead of him where the closed doors stretched away into darkness. Remembering Vietnam had shaken his senses, and now memory jerked him into another time and place. He was back in the nights and days when death waited behind every ridge and clump of trees, where even a field open to the sun could conceal a deadly crop of mines.

"Who's there?" He knew no one would answer.

The light was behind him. He was silhouetted, a perfect target. In sudden terror he flattened himself against the wall. In that split second he heard a roar and a crash and felt a blow that knocked him sideways. A second bullet shattered the glass door behind him, showering him with flying shards. He knew he'd been hit; he knew the glass had cut him, but he felt no pain.

Behind the doors the hotel guests were stirring fearfully. He heard their cries. And he heard something else—the slide of fabric against nylon. And he caught a faint, elusive whiff of perfume before the third bullet hurled him into the dark.

He did not hear the running footsteps nor the soft click as the fire door at the far end of the hall was shut.

FOURTEEN

THE NUMBER did not answer. She let it ring and ring. Either the number he'd given her was incorrect, or he was trying to get on her nerves.

He was succeeding. She was ready to scream with frustration. She pulled the curtains across her front windows and went into her bedroom and did the same. She was hungry, but now she was too keyed up to eat. She had her notes to work on, but she was too worried to concentrate.

Tomorrow she would put an end to this. She would not let this man harass her. She would turn this slip over to Detective Malone, let the resources of the police department find the photo developer it came from. There must be a thousand places in Manhattan, dozens between Deirdre's apartment and....

And where? Deirdre had gone out Friday night with her camera to take pictures of Jack's band. On Saturday afternoon, when her camera was found on the table in the ballroom, it was empty. That narrowed both the time and the places. She had to have left it on Saturday morning somewhere between her apartment and the Park Summit. She'd gotten to her seat in the ballroom shortly after nine. "Five fucking minutes late!" she'd said to Louisa. That meant a place that opened at nine or before on Saturday. There would not be many of those.

Giving the claim slip to Malone would let her in for some very pointed questions. He would not believe how Deirdre casually gave it to her.

Why had Deirdre been so offhand with that claim slip? If she really knew someone was out to get her, and she was passing along something she knew could lead to her killer, surely she would have said something. Victims in crime plots did that just before they expired. It was a classic opening.

But it hadn't happened that way. Deirdre did not say, "Here—if anything happens to me, I want you to have this." She'd seemed pleased that Louisa wanted to talk to her, then she'd groped in her pockets for something for Louisa to write on. When she looked at the slip, she'd said something like "Guess I don't need this anymore, I got it by heart," and handed it over as if it were of no more importance than an old grocery list.

What had she meant by "got it by heart"? Surely not the claim number. Even if she had memorized the number, she would need the slip to get her pictures back. She remembered the girl peering at the paper. Was she nearsighted? Could she have been so upset and confused from drug withdrawal that she'd made a mistake? Had she more than one piece of paper in her pocket and given Louisa the wrong one?

The phone rang. Her heart thudded.

"Louisa Evans?" It was the voice from the tape. He was young and not altogether sure of himself. In his very hesitancy was menace. This was a man who could act without thinking.

"Yes?"

"You, uh, interested in like, you know, a deal?"

"That depends on what you're offering and what you want." She spoke crisply. She did not want to scare him off, but she wanted him to know she was in charge. He had nothing she wanted.

"Yeah, well, we gotta talk about that. I think maybe someone we both know gave you something more use to me than to you, if you know what I mean."

"I don't know what you mean."

"Look, lady, I know you're not stupid." The voice was no longer unsure. "Not smart enough not to get into trouble, maybe, but not that dumb. If you didn't get it from her, you got it someplace you shouldn't of been."

"Maybe I could say the same thing about you."

He giggled. It was a dreadful sound. He sounded as if he were drunk or high. This was the man who had hit her hard enough to knock her out. This was the man who had planned Deirdre's cruelly painful death. Clare had said that he was the type to carry a knife. She would make an arrangement with him, hang up, and call the police at once.

"We gonna meet?"

"Where?"

"You know Rivington Street?"

Rivington Street ran east off the Bowery; it was in the heart of a notorious drug district—dirty, run-down, and dangerous. She would not go there without knowing police were backing her up.

"And in case you're thinking of bringing along, like, the troops? I know where that person you were with the other day hangs out now."

"What person—who do you mean?"

"You know who I mean! You went into her apartment. You were there a long time. She moved out since then. I know where she went. Her building is real easy to get into. I already did."

He'd been somewhere watching after he mugged her. He knew she had gone upstairs with Clare. Now this creep was threatening her. If she had given Rhonda Lord Clare's name, this would not be happening. She didn't have many choices. Rivington Street was unsavory at any time, but at eight o'clock at night, surely there would be people about. Drunk or stoned, maybe, but the street would not be empty. "All right, I'll meet you," she said.

"Smart move. And bring what I want."

"I don't know what you want! You searched me and you searched my bag. You know I don't have—"

"Shove it! I know she told you something and gave you something, or she told you it was in her place and you found it. I want it. I want it tonight. You be on the southeast side of Rivington—in the park in the middle of Allen Street. At eleven-thirty. I'll be there, and I'll be watching to make sure you're alone. If you screw up, if I smell cops, you'll get pieces of our friend in the mail. I'll start with her tits. Got it?"

A wave of nausea swept over her. In the silence she desperately tried to think. There was no way out of meeting with this sick, violent man. "All right," she said finally, no longer even trying to sound confident. He knew how completely he had the upper hand. Allen Street—she wasn't even sure where it was.

"Didn't hear you. Say you got it!"

"I got it."

"Where?"

"Allen Street, in the park, south side of Rivington at eleven-thirty."

"Alone."

"Alone."

"And, like, if you got any ideas about not showing up, what I said before still goes for our friend. Got that?"

"Got it," she said wearily.

She hung up. She had no idea where Clare had moved. Could she dare hope that anyone so tough and streetwise could take care of herself? Jack could be bluffing when he said he'd already gotten inside her building. She could go down to Clare's old place and knock on doors, maybe find someone who had Clare's forwarding address. Get her phone number—if she had a phone yet. Warn her.

What she should do was give all her information, the claim slip, and Clare's name to Detective Malone. Her hand went out to her notebook. She opened it to the place she had stuck the page from Malone's book on which he had written his number. She reached for the phone, rehearsing what she would say. "I'd like to give you the name of my source now so you can protect her."

"Protect her from what?" Detective Malone would ask.

"From a homicidal maniac who's threatening to cut off her breasts." She could hear herself trying to explain that the piece of paper Deirdre had given her at the marathon to write her address on had suddenly become a claim slip for some film Deirdre had left somewhere to be developed, and that now someone wanted it desperately. Then she would try to explain her theory about Deirdre's picture taking on Friday night.

She was already under suspicion of taking evidence from Deirdre's apartment. Her story was so melodramatic that he might not believe her. Or he'd accuse her of trying to throw suspicion on someone else—just the scenario she'd discussed with Harvey.

He might not take her seriously enough to even start looking for Clare. But if by a miracle he did, how long would it take the police to locate her? What would they find when they did? If Louisa didn't show up for the meeting with Jack, would the police find Clare before Jack carried out his threat?

She didn't dare take the chance. Meeting Jack was a terrifying prospect. She had to go through with it. She had to see what he looked like. She had to be sure it really was the claim slip he was after.

She had to do that without actually giving it to him. No way was she going to let that out of her hands. Too much could depend on who or what Deirdre's pictures showed.

She got out her map of Manhattan. Allen Street ran parallel to Bowery, a block over. A park ran down the middle of it. That meant it would be empty, not a street where stores stayed open late and lights meant safety.

She would try Clare's old building first. If she got no response, she would go through with this meeting.

She made her preparations carefully. A facsimile of the slip would not do. She had an unfinished film in her camera; she rewound it and took it out. She walked over to Lexington Avenue to a Fotorush store and left it to be developed. As she walked back she thought, with sinking heart, that if Jack was watching, he might figure out what she was trying to do.

But if her trick worked, by the time he found out she'd given him the wrong claim slip, she might know enough about him to get Detective Malone to find out why Jack wanted Deirdre's pictures. She might even be able to help the police set a trap for him, using the real claim slip as bait. By that time the police would have located Clare, please God, and made sure she was safe from the maniac with the knife.

It could work out if she didn't let fear make her act stupidly. She put on a warmer sweater and her running shoes. She reached in the closet for her down jacket—and instead pulled out the jacket she'd bought on Saturday. It was poorer-looking, less conspicuous. She tied a scarf around her head. No bag— that was asking for trouble even if Jack never showed up. She took only a couple of bills in her pockets and some tokens for the subway. Like Deirdre's neighborhood, the intersection of Allen and Rivington was no place to go in a cab, but after she met with Jack, she would go to Houston Street and try to find one to come home in. She tucked a ten dollar bill into her shoe.

A transit cop patrolling on the train gave her some comfort, but when she left the dubious safety of the subway and got out on Bleecker Street, she had a moment of panic. There was no going back. Jack held power. If he'd killed Deirdre, he was quite capable of killing Clare.

She hurried to the building on Seventh Street, too preoccupied with her errand to even notice the ugliness that had so depressed her when she came here on Saturday. No windows were lighted in the front of the building. When she went inside, she was met with silence. Whoever had been playing the stereo at high volume was either out, or his amplifiers had been stolen. No one answered when she pounded on the doors on the first floor. Nor on the front apartment on the second floor. The door to Clare's vacated place was open, and the rooms were empty. On the third floor Deirdre's door had been padlocked by the police. A line of light appeared under the door of the front apartment on Deirdre's floor. As soon as she knocked, it went out.

She pleaded. "Please, do you have a forwarding address for Clare, the woman who moved out of the back apartment on the second floor? I need it urgently." Not a breath, not a footfall on the other side of that door. Silence was the only answer.

"I'm not a cop. I'm a friend of hers."

No answer. She knocked again. As futilely. That was that. She had time to kill before her rendezvous. She went back to the safety of Second Avenue and had coffee at a counter restaurant. She watched out the window as dozens of women costumed like Deirdre had been, as well as males similarly dressed and coiffed, hurried by. Uptown, Deirdre had been a freak. Here she would have gone unnoticed in the crowd.

Eleven-fifteen. It was time. She paid for her coffee and left, her heart thumping and fear radiating from the pit of her stomach.

Below Houston Street, Third Avenue became the Bowery. She walked rapidly, trying to ignore the bundles of clothing and blankets in doorways and on gratings, bundles that stirred and called as she passed, "Spare some change, Miss?" On Rivington Street her feet crunched on a sidewalk littered with the fragments of broken bottles. A block farther east was Allen Street. Dark, gated storefronts lined the north and south sides of the street. In the middle was the park, where the trees thrust their patchy trunks upward to naked branches sighing in the chilly wind. Dry, dead leaves and discarded papers and plastic rattled around the benches and the roots of the trees. The pale glare of the sodium lights illuminated a place empty of human life. To the north, traffic moved on Houston Street, and to the south it rumbled on the lighted elevated parkway to the entrance to the Williamsburg Bridge. But here in this isolated pocket, even the city's night noises seemed muffled and far away.

She crossed to the south side of Rivington. The sagging, vandalized park benches were empty. She was alone. She'd never felt so vulnerable.

After a few minutes of indecision, while the sighing of the trees, and the rustling of wind-blown trash sent waves of fear through her, she began to walk. Anything was better than standing still and waiting for Jack to show himself. She felt like the target of hidden, watchful eyes. She crossed Allen to the east, turned and crossed Rivington to the north and then she went to the park on the north side and across the west side of Allen. Rivington again. Allen again. Back to her starting point in the park.

Moving was better. It gave her something to do. She concentrated on putting one foot in front of the other. Her eyes darted from side to side, scanning the streets, the sidewalks, the shadows. Two cars passed, one from the north along Allen, one from the east on Rivington. According to her watch, she walked this circuit for fifteen minutes.

Then she stopped. A figure was moving along Rivington from the Bowery. The person was as muffled as she was against the wind. He looked neither right nor left. Ten minutes later another bundled, vaguely masculine figure approached from the other side. Her heart beat violently. The figure drew near, stopped, and just as she was about to take a hesitant step forward, veered off and walked rapidly in the opposite direction.

She was alone again in this bleak corner of the city. Even the dealers who usually hung out on these mean streets had been driven inside by the cold.

Allen. Rivington. The park. Across Allen again. Rivington again. She held her watch up to look at the illuminated digits. Eleven fifty-five. She had begun to shiver in spite of her walking.

Once more crossing Allen to her starting point in the park, she saw that she was no longer alone.

In her first fearful scrutiny of the dark fronts of the buildings and the shadowy doorways, she had seen no one. Nor had she seen anyone since then except for the two walkers who had passed by. Now someone was there—a motionless form that seemed barely human was slumped on the step in a deeply recessed doorway on Allen Street.

She had no idea how long he'd been there. Ever since she came? Or had he slipped into the scene when she was on the other side of the street? She'd sensed no movement, seen no change in the shapes of the shadows on that side. She would not cross over. If the watcher was Jack, he knew she was there.

Her heart was thudding in erratic jerks, and her breathing was shallow. She stood at the appointed spot on the south side of Rivington and waited. The silent watching went on. She was stiff, poised, her whole body ready to run. It took all her will power to stay there, waiting until Jack made his move.

She looked at her watch again. Twelve-ten.

On the other side of the street, the shadow stirred, lengthened slowly, and shrugged off something—an enveloping coat or blanket. Hard soled boots hit the sidewalk as the figure moved out of the doorway into the light.

Slender legs in black tights. A man's jacket with heavily padded shoulders, which hung on the slight form and weighed it down. The head was bowed, the face in shadow. But Louisa could see the hair. It was cropped to the skull on the sides and back, and it erupted over her forehead in a tangle of stiffened spikes. Even in that uncertain light she could see the color.

Louisa put her hands to her mouth to stop the scream that rose into her throat. Her mind went utterly blank. She was frozen, hypnotized, fixed where she stood, unable to do anything but stare at that silent figure moving toward her, each slow step punctuated by the crack of boot heels on concrete. Step by step, closer and closer....

In the middle of the street the figure lifted her head, and Louisa saw her pale face, black-rimmed eyes, and a slash of purple lipstick.

A car was coming along Allen Street from the west. Its headlights made the shadows of the tree trunks in the park lurch and veer. Louisa took her eyes off the figure advancing across the street and glanced toward the moving vehicle.

A police car!

It was traveling slowly. Cops, on a routine patrol. Now it was only half a block away. She looked back to where the figure had been.

The street was empty in the pale glare of its lamps.

The police car had stopped at the traffic light. That gave her a few seconds. Louisa ran.

She ran up a block. A glance over her shoulder showed the patrol car in the intersection, still traveling east. She slowed down. Whatever was behind her, she must not attract the attention of the police in that car. To be stopped and questioned in the middle of the night, and possibly taken in for loitering or whatever charge they could bring....

On the Bowery, a ragged figure lurched toward her. "Hey, lady, got any change?" He was in her path, so close that she could smell his fetid breath, the stench of his unwashed clothes. She fumbled in her jacket, thrust a dollar into his hand, and moved ahead of him. Another figure loomed up. And another. They were coming out of the shadows, up from the doorways. They'd seen her give money to one and now four more were coming at her, demanding their share.

She dodged them and ran. They were befuddled and feeble. She outran them. When she reached Houston Street, she looked back, not knowing what she most dreaded to see. A pack of filthy old men staggering behind her with their hands out? A policeman with his gun drawn, ready to shout "Freeze!"? Or that silently approaching figure in the huge jacket and the blaze of green hair?

The Bowery was empty. She reached Houston and crossed it, then turned toward Greenwich Village and safety.

At Lafayette Street a cab came by. She flagged it down.

FIFTEEN

LIKE TONY, Malone chose to walk. He would go over to Times Square to get his train to Queens. Since sundown the temperature had been dropping to a level closer to normal for December, and the wind had quickened. He hoped the fresh air would clear his mind.

Looking for clues in the marathon data sheets had been a fucking waste of time. It showed how desperate he was for a fresh lead. Nothing solid had shown up. The lead suggested by the camera had gone nowhere. Without film, it was useless.

Either Louisa Evans gave Deirdre the capsule, or it was slipped to her in the Ladies' room. There was no other place she could have gotten it unless he accepted Alex's idea that Deirdre had found it in her bag or pockets during a frantic search, probably while she was locked in the toilet booth. After she'd come out, there had been no more pleas and no contacts until she sat down beside Louisa Evans in the ballroom.

And he had only Louisa's version of their conversation.

Harvey Wardleigh. He'd gone to Harvey's place on Eighteenth Street to question him after his discovery that Harvey had paid Deirdre's marathon tuition. At first he was sure that Harvey was a queer. Then Harvey had reluctantly admitted to having had a relationship with Deirdre. He'd made no attempt to conceal his embarrassment about this affair, and his dislike for the girl. She had been a poor student and a bad photographer, and she was on drugs most of the time. Harvey had suspected that she was stealing from the photography lab. A couple of cameras, extra lenses, and piece by piece, the components of an enlarger had disappeared. Theft and vandalism were constant problems at the school. He had no way to prove Deirdre had done it unless he set a trap. Harvey had not been willing to do that; the girl was failing the course and would be leaving the school anyway when the term ended in two weeks.

Besides, Harvey had hemmed and hawed and finally admitted, the relationship had gone sour. Yes, he'd given her the marathon in the hope she'd let him alone. Yes, he'd given her a camera, a television set and a stereo. What she'd done with them he couldn't care less—he never wanted to see her again. No, he did not know any other men Deirdre had been involved with, though he suspected there had been some.

Deirdre's last assignment had been to photograph a series of faces in close-up. She had not turned in her work. Since her pictures were always late or not turned in at all, he did not know if she had even done the assignment.

"A five hundred dollar marathon is a pretty big payoff for a girl you'd gotten tired of. Sure she wasn't a bigger pain in the ass than you've let on? She threatened a counselor at her high school in Scranton—did you know that?"

Harvey had reddened to the roots of his carefully styled hair. His lips were tight. Finally he admitted Deirdre had threatened to charge him with sexual harassment unless he gave her credit for the course she was failing. "We thrashed it out, and we reached a compromise. I wouldn't accuse her of theft, she wouldn't accuse me of harassment. I couldn't give her credit for the course; that would have made me look ridiculous with the other students, and it would have lowered my credibility with the administration. The course had cost her parents almost the same amount as the tuition for the marathon. She would take the failure gracefully and accept my gift. She'd heard some students talking about SUM. She said the Marathon sounded like a blast. I warned her they'd insist she leave off the drugs—she said no problem, she could handle that. But obviously when her last dose wore off, and she went into withdrawal, she couldn't."

"Did she usually carry substances with her?"

"She always had pills in her bag and a supply in her apartment. No, I do *not* know where she got them. That aspect of Deirdre's life I did not inquire into."

Harvey was furious that the detective wanted to question his mother. "She's a very sick woman—dying, a fact she is not entirely able to face. You'll only get her upset and make her worse!"

At Lenox Hill a doctor had allowed him a few seconds to see Harvey's mother as she lay in bed with postoperative tubes and monitors which seemed to be her only precarious link to life. She had come through the operation well, but the surgery was only a measure taken to relieve pain. Its effects were temporary. The cancer had metastasized. Radiation therapy would help, but only for a short time. It was a matter of a month, two at the most.

Vivian Wardley, as she spelled the family name, was still asleep. He did not get confirmation of Harvey's alibi for Saturday from her.

Mrs. Wardley's nurses definitely remembered that Harvey had hovered outside the recovery room on Friday until his mother had been moved upstairs. He had left the hospital about eight on Friday night. He'd been there, off and on, most of Saturday. Both nurses commented favorably on Harvey's concern and his faithfulness. After Mrs. Wardley had been moved to a private room, the floor nurses also remembered that Harvey had been there on Saturday. None of them could swear that he'd been there all day. A nurse who had gone in to check on the patient late in the afternoon had found her alone and sleeping.

Security at Lenox Hill, where the administration evidently trusted that it had nothing to fear from the citizens of the affluent Upper East Side, was not what it was in hospitals in rougher neighborhoods. Visitors could go in unannounced, unaccounted for, and without passes. People like Harvey, whose mother had just come out of surgery, were not confined to the regular visiting hours.

Harvey's alibi, therefore, did not clear him completely of the opportunity to murder Deirdre. When Malone asked him about his absences from his mother's room, Harvey had exclaimed irritably, "I can't just sit there and watch her sleep! I do have to go to the Men's room occasionally! And I went to the cafeteria for coffee, and I went out a couple of times and I walked around the block. When the nurse said on Saturday evening that Mother was likely to sleep through until morning, I left. That was about seven. I went home and stayed there the rest of the night."

"When did you find out that Deirdre was dead?"

"Not until I watched the eleven o'clock news. I was shocked that she'd apparently been that serious a threat to someone, and I wished she'd died less agonizingly—and publicly. But I didn't kill her."

"Why did you change the spelling of your name?"

"A bit of vanity, of which I am now ashamed. When I set out on my career, I thought a photographer's name should simply reek of class."

Malone's gut had tightened when he questioned the woman who lived in Deirdre's apartment building. A dyke if he ever saw one. Clare Smithson had been throwing things into boxes. She was moving. She knew nothing, but nothing, about Deirdre Doyle. She minded her own business. No, she didn't know anyone named Louisa Evans. No, she had not seen or heard anyone in Deirdre's apartment on Saturday afternoon. She didn't know Harvey Wardleigh or a drug-addicted musician named Jack.

The door to the front apartment on Deirdre's floor was opened by a man wearing a sleeveless gray tank top. His pants looked like something out of a harem. Malone wondered, in all those pleats and folds, how the guy found his fly. His bleached hair stood up in pink spikes, and he wore a set of earphones with antennae that made him look like a creature from another planet.

He stood in the doorway bouncing and swaying to the sounds in his head until Malone shouted at him to remove the headset. No, the guy said, he had never talked with Deirdre. "Look man, it's like live and let live down here, know what I mean? We don't know nothin', we don't shit on each other."

Malone thought he understood why none of the people in this building wanted to know any of the others. Much of Alphabet City was still years away from gentrification. Relatively low rents in dilapidated buildings attracted a large population of Spanish-speaking immigrants, as well as a fringe of kooks—failed artists and performers, most of them heavy drug users. Some of them might be trying to make up for professional failure by flaunting their kinkiness.

He'd dealt with hundreds of the marginal people in the city, had scant sympathy for most of them, and none at all for these self-indulgent weirdos. Most of them could have a better life if they got up off their asses. Maybe a kid born in the South Bronx had little chance to be anything but a criminal and an addict, but Deirdre Doyle had come from a solid, middle class family. Clare Smithson talked tough, but she'd had an education. And the baggy-pants swish from Mars was clearly not starving.

At Times Square he stopped at a pay phone and dialed Louisa's number. With no surprise he listened to the first few words of her now familiar recording. He hung up. Tomorrow he'd confront her, come down heavier than Rhonda had. He'd make her give them the name of the person who'd told her about Deirdre. It looked like Louisa's source was their only lead.

SIXTEEN

HER PHONE WAS RINGING. She could hear it as she stood outside her apartment door turning the keys in the locks. It stopped as soon as she got in. Without taking off her jacket, she crossed the room and sank into her rocking chair.

She was numb. She knew what the numbness was keeping her from feeling.

Fear.

Fear so huge, so engulfing, so draining of hope and energy, she felt as if she were on the edge of a dark, bottomless whirlpool. If she let herself be sucked into it, she would never get out.

She must not feel. Think, not feel.

Her phone rang.

Thought flew. Panic grabbed her, made her heart pound, and her throat close. She got up and groped her way slowly, like an old woman, to her desk. She lifted the receiver. Swallowing hard, she made her mouth frame the word. She could hardly get it out—"Yes?"

"Bitch! I told you—no cops!"

"I didn't—they were patrolling—!"

"This is your last chance. Don't screw up. Carl Shurz Park."

She moaned. Not another park! Fear seized her. She felt herself going under on waves of panic which brought her close to fainting. Then from somewhere she found a thread of sanity. And her voice. "Not the park—I won't come to the park!"

She could hear his hoarse breathing, more obscene than any lewd call she'd ever gotten. Then a string of words so vile her mind simply would not take them in. "Okay," he said finally. "You fuck up this time, you get a package tomorrow. I got a sharp knife, and I get off on hearing women scream. Here's what you're gonna do...."

SEVENTEEN

SHE WAS THERE. The doorman had seen her go out at nine. He'd let her in again at twelve forty-five. She'd come home by cab. A few minutes later, she'd gone out again. She had just come back.

Louisa Evans was going to tell him where she was when Tony Cazzine was shot.

It was two o'clock. The phone call that had sent him back to Manhattan almost as soon as he'd gotten home had come from Roosevelt Hospital, where Tony Cazzine had been taken with gunshot wounds.

She couldn't be asleep, not after the night she'd had. On his fourth ring of her doorbell, he heard the faint click that meant she'd lifted the cover of the peephole.

"James Malone."

The bolt slid back. Locks grated. Louisa Evans opened the door. Her foyer light was dim, but even in that light he could see that she was deathly pale. She wore jeans and a sweater. She was clutching a red, fringed shawl around her shoulders as if she was cold. She was wearing running shoes.

"I have to ask you some questions, Ms. Evans."

She nodded without speaking, almost as if she had expected him, and led the way to the living room. When she sat down on the couch, he dropped his coat onto a chair and took a seat across from her in a surprisingly comfortable rocker. He had the feeling that's where she had been sitting, wrapped in her shawl. Rocking and thinking—of what? Her alibi? Her next move?

His glance took in the room. Too many antiques. He liked modern furniture and no clutter. Louisa's place was full of old stuff—a quilt in faded calicos on the wall behind the couch, paintings he supposed were good, books everywhere.

He began without pleasantries. "Where were you tonight at eleven-thirty?" If she said she'd been home all evening, he'd confront her with the doorman's story.

"I was out. Walking."

"Where?"

"Around the neighborhood. Up to Ninety-sixth Street, across to Fifth Avenue, down to Seventy-second. I did that circuit, oh, ten times maybe. I lost count."

"Why did you do it?"

"I was restless, and I needed the exercise." She sounded like she knew he wouldn't believe her.

"Do you often go out alone so late at night?"

"Only when I'm particularly tense. Deirdre's death, today the funeral—I've been under a strain."

"No doubt," he said drily. She was lying. "Did you stop anywhere?"

"No."

"Did you see anyone who could identify you?"

"Not that I know of." Her hands were clasped tightly in her lap. She was rigid as if she was trying to keep herself from trembling. She had not asked the first question put by the innocent and the guilty alike—"Why do you want to know?"

"Your doorman tells me you came in at twelve-forty-five. He saw you get out of a cab. You went out a second time, a few minutes later. You're wearing running shoes. A woman as young as you and in good shape could have walked from here to the Park Summit Hotel fairly easily in twenty minutes or so—it's only a little over a mile."

"I could, but why would I want to?" She looked surprised. This was not what she had expected to hear.

"You tell me."

"I didn't go to the Park Summit. Why do you want to know?"

"Do you own a gun?"

"No! What's this all about?"

"Have you had experience with firearms?"

"Some target practice years ago when I went to summer camp. That's all. Now you tell me why you're asking these questions!"

If she was bluffing, she was doing a hell of a job. He waited, deliberately, for a few moments before he said, "Someone shot Tony Cazzine tonight at eleven-thirty in the corridor outside his room at the Park Summit."

Louisa shook her head slightly. Her face had gone, unbelievably, whiter. Her eyes were open and dazed-looking. She opened her mouth, but at first nothing came out. Then her lips moved stiffly. "He's dead?"

"He's not dead. He has a scalp wound from a near-miss, some deep cuts in his face from flying glass, and two broken ribs from a bullet that missed his heart. He'll recover. His attacker was a poor shot."

Her reaction could not have astonished him more. She put her head down and covered her face with her hands. She was shaking. For a few seconds she sat that way. When she looked up again, her face was wet. "I'm sorry," she said. She wiped her eyes with her hands. "Excuse me, I'm going to get a handkerchief."

He watched her leave the room. He would play out her game. The news that Tony Cazzine was not dead seemed to have knocked her back to square one. He was so sure she was on the verge of saying something incriminating that he was tempted to take her down to the station for questioning. But that would mean she'd want her lawyer. While they waited for him, she would have figured out what she'd better not say.

She was back in the room now. Her face was still white, and there were dark smudges under her eyes. She wrapped the shawl around herself and sat down again.

"Do you own a gun, Ms. Evans?" he asked again.

"No, no." She made a gesture that seemed to brush away his question. "I've never owned a gun! I didn't shoot Tony. I don't know who did. But I was lying about where I was tonight, and I better tell you the truth now."

This put a different light on the situation. He didn't want any legal screw-ups with her, either. "I should warn you of your right to counsel."

"You're arresting me? For what?"

"I'm not arresting you. But I think you know you are under suspicion in both the death of Deirdre Doyle and the failed attempt against Tony Cazzine."

"I have no reason to want either of those people dead! I didn't know Deirdre. My being next to her in the marathon was pure chance. Why isn't the person who was sitting on the other side of her under suspicion?"

"How do you know he isn't? Besides, the person who shot Tony was female. He heard a skirt moving, and he smelled perfume just before the third shot was fired."

She stared at him without speaking. Then she she shook her head and said in a kind of moan, "Oh, no!" After a few seconds of silence, she said, "Tony's conscious then? He talked to you? Is he really going to be all right?"

"He'll be all right. Some scars here and there."

"What hospital?"

"Roosevelt."

"Will you let me see him?"

"When he's allowed visitors, I won't stop you."

"But I could be in jail by then, couldn't I?"

"Ms. Evans, I've said that I'm not here to arrest you. You said you lied about tonight. If you're going to tell the truth now, you have nothing to be afraid of."

She took a deep breath. "A man called me tonight. I think he's the one who mugged me in Deirdre's apartment. He said he had something of mine that I wanted. I thought he meant my keys and credit cards. He told me to meet him at the corner of Rivington and Allen Street at eleven-thirty. I went."

"You know better! If you live through a mugging, you change your locks, stop your cards, and kiss your money goodbye. Tell me why you really did it."

"I wanted to see what he looked like. I was so angry that someone would do that to me—I wanted to see what kind of man he is."

She was lying. No one as smart as she was would take such a risk without a better reason than that. "When this person called you, did he give his name?"

"No. He just told me where and when to meet him, and he said not to bring anyone or tell the police."

"This morning you told Detective Lord you had a source of information about Deirdre Doyle. Did you go out tonight to meet that source?"

"I went out to meet the man who mugged me!"

"Do you have any clue about his identity?"

"In the attack I saw only his arm and his hand. His thumb is misshapen. He's white, and his arm was very strong. He might be the musician Deirdre had a relationship with. His name is Jack."

"Did he show up for your appointment?"

"Not the way I expected him to." She stopped. Her face crumpled and tears were standing in her eyes again. Finally she said, "He's playing a game with me—trying to frighten me!"

It sounded like Deirdre's paranoia was contagious. "What makes you say that?" he asked. "Did you see him or didn't you, this musician with the thumb?"

She swallowed. Then she said, "I saw Deirdre."

"Deirdre." He spoke flatly.

"Oh, don't you see?" she cried. "Jack dresses up when he leads his band. He wears women's clothes. He put on clothes like Deirdre's and a wig! Or it wasn't Jack himself—he sent someone from his band while he went to the hotel dressed like a woman and shot Tony."

"Why would he do that?"

She was sitting up and leaning forward eagerly now. "He was afraid of what Tony might know about him. He knows Tony had a private conversation with Deirdre at the marathon. That was in all the newspaper stories the day after her death. He can't be sure the police told the reporters everything there was to tell about what Deirdre said to Tony. You might have good reasons to keep something back—"

"Ms. Evans—" He had to stop her.

"Oh, don't you see? I was set up! He lured me downtown so I wouldn't have an alibi for tonight when Tony was shot! Oh, can't you see what someone is trying to do to me?"

"I see a lot of things, Ms. Evans. One of which is that you are very upset. Do you want a glass of water? Something stronger? You tell me where things are in your kitchen, I'll...."

She put her hands over her face again. She sat that way for a couple of minutes. When she looked up, her eyes were dull and without hope.

"Did you see anyone on this expedition to Rivington Street who could identify you?" he asked.

"I gave money to one of those old men on the Bowery. At Lafayette I got the cab I came home in. Maybe you could locate the driver."

"Maybe."

"Maybe. But you won't bother, will you? Because you might find someone who could give me an alibi for the time Tony was shot! Did anyone see me at the Park Summit tonight?"

"This afternoon when you went to the SUM office to get your jacket, you asked the receptionist if Tony Cazzine had a room in the hotel. Why did you want to know that?"

She shrugged. "Only curiosity, though I suppose you won't believe that. In the marathon he mentioned California, as if he lives there. What about tonight—*did* anyone see me at the hotel?"

"The hotel is unusually crowded. A convention is meeting there. They were using the ballroom tonight for a dinner that didn't break up until eleven-thirty. At the time of the shooting, there were a lot of people milling about in the lobby, going in and out of the bar, using the elevators."

"And no one who saw me, isn't that so? You don't believe I was on Rivington Street, and you can't prove I was at the hotel. So what happens now?"

"You can tell me the name of your source without my having to arrest you."

"No. Not until I have to."

"You can tell me where you went the second time you left this building tonight."

"I was still restless. I went out to walk again."

"You can tell me what you and Harvey Wardleigh talked about on your way home from Scranton this afternoon."

"How did you know I rode home with him?"

"Detective Lord saw you get into his car."

"We talked about our mutual status as prime suspects in the murder of Deirdre Doyle!"

"Did you know Harvey Wardleigh, or had you ever seen him before you met him at the cemetery this afternoon?"

"No." Her lip curled a little. "We're not conspirators."

"What's your impression of his relationship with Deirdre?"

She hesitated a moment. "I know he disliked her. He told me that."

"Enough to kill her?"

"I don't know."

"Is there anything else she told you before she died that you didn't tell me? Besides the fact that she gave you her address?"

"Nothing. I told Detective Lord that this morning."

"I'm going to be frank with you, Ms. Evans. You had both the motive and the opportunity to give Deirdre the capsule. You're smart enough to know that what we have is still pretty circumstantial—but if you know anything you haven't told us, you better tell me right now."

"I can't believe this is happening! Please, what is supposed to be my motive for killing a perfect stranger?"

"You were writing an article, which has now turned into a book, to prove that the marathon was harmful to its participants mental health. You made an opportunity to prove that point. The capsule kills Deirdre, the publicity kills SUM. Only it didn't work out that way. SUM looked like it was going to bounce back. So you gunned down Tony Cazzine. SUM gets a reputation for potential violence."

"That's ridiculous! If I plotted Deirdre's death, why did I tell you she showed me the capsule? You would have thought she committed suicide, or that she'd been poisoned by accident. The case against SUM would be just as damning. From what Harvey told me about Deirdre, she probably had plenty of enemies. Someone who knew her and her habits came into the lobby and waited until the shutdown and gave her the capsule."

"Deirdre made no contact in the lobby."

She stared at him. Her face, which in anger had colored, now went so white he thought she might faint. She licked lips that had suddenly gone dry. "Oh, no!"

"No one came near her. She was alone from the time she left the restroom until she sat down beside you."

She had lost all animation. Even her voice sounded dead. Dead and bitter. "You think I killed her. And you think I tried to kill Tony. All because I was honest enough to admit I was critical of SUM and unfortunate enough to have been sitting in the wrong seat!"

"I'm not accusing. But if you know anything you haven't told me—like the name of your source or what you think Deirdre's boy friend really wanted from a meeting with you—you'd better tell me. If you're holding out something...."

"I have nothing more to tell you." Her face was stony.

"A witness sitting near you in the ballroom saw you hand something to Deirdre. What was it?"

"I gave her a pencil. She wrote down her address."

"On what?"

"On a scrap of paper she got from her pocket."

"Do you still have that paper?"

"No, I threw it away." She was not looking at him now.

He rose and picked up his coat. She followed him to the foyer, silently opened the door, and closed it behind him. As he punched the button for the elevator, he heard her locks click shut.

She knew where she stood. Her next move would be crucial. He would ask if any undercover people had seen her in the vicinity of Rivington and Allen tonight. He'd get a full report of whatever went on between her and Tony if she went to the hospital to visit him. He'd question Harvey again about that conversation in the car. If he could establish that Louisa had lied about not knowing Harvey until today, he could work on a conspiracy theory. Both Harvey and Louisa had reasons for wanting Deirdre dead, and Louisa had had the best opportunity. The trip from Scranton to New York was long enough for the most careful rehashing and rehearsing of alibis.

Malone decided to send Rhonda to the School of Visual Arts to smoke out what Harvey's colleagues really thought of him, who his friends were. Rhonda could talk to Mrs. Wardley too, confirm Harvey's alibi for Saturday afternoon, and find out more about Harvey's friends.

He'd gotten nowhere in the search for Jack. No one in Deirdre's neighborhood admitted to seeing him, alone or with Deirdre. The guy might not even exist. He could be entirely a creation of Louisa Evans, along with the source she could not reveal, and the Deirdre look-alike she tried to make him believe appeared to her at Allen and Rivington Streets.

But if it turned out Louisa Evans really was at Allen and Rivington at eleven-thirty, and not at the Park Summit, they had a whole new case on their hands.

EIGHTEEN

Tony groaned. His head still pounded, and he could not draw a breath without pain knifing his ribs. Stitches made shaving out of the question; his face itched abominably in the places where it did not hurt. But his anxiety and fury at being confined were far worse than his pain.

It was Friday. He could finally have visitors. Alex came bearing a floral tribute from the SUM staff.

"I didn't die, and I didn't win the Derby," Tony growled when Alex set the arrangement of roses and gladioli on the windowsill. "But I'm grateful for the flowers. The condition of my face will not permit me to smile."

Alex came near the bed. "How are you feeling?"

"Good. I can handle the marathon tomorrow."

"Are you kidding? You won't even be out of the hospital. I lined up Mark Mayer for the second weekend."

"After this, will anybody come to it?"

"We've had so many calls, I've had to get volunteers on the phones all day. Some twenty or so said no way were they coming back—this latest act of violence was the coup de grâce—but most have called to ask about you, to wish you a quick recovery, and to swear they'll never desert SUM."

"What's new on the police front?" I know Malone finds me a most unsatisfactory victim—I can't tell him who shot me. I didn't see the person Malone refers to as 'the perpetrator.'"

"I fear the Park Summit will not renew our lease. Cops swarmed all over the hotel, but they didn't find anything. She apparently got out by running down the fire stairs to the basement, then out one of the service doors without being seen. They don't have a clue."

"Malone has heated up his argument that Louisa was trying to put SUM out of business. As far as I'm concerned, that argument sucks."

"It might be her, Tony, you know?"

"I know, but I can't believe it." Tony sighed and rubbed at his face, producing a rasping sound. "Probably just as well I'm not coaching this weekend. I'd frighten the rest of them away."

Alex grinned. "You're definitely not living up to your image as SUM's sexiest coach. By the way, do you know there's a cop sitting outside your door?"

"Malone said he wouldn't take any chances. What did the cop do, frisk you?"

"Yes, she did. And subjected the flowers to a similar investigation. I doubt they enjoyed it as much as I did."

When Alex left, Tony closed his eyes. He was more tired than he liked to admit. Malone had asked him to think about the incident, to try to remember more clearly that the person who shot at him from the dark was a woman. Malone had also asked him to recall his interface with Deirdre. Could he remember Deirdre telling him anything he had not already reported to the police?

Someone had tried to kill him. This was not a random attack. He'd been the target. That had been an everyday matter in Vietnam; he'd gotten used to it along with the rest of the horrors—noise, filth, blood, corpses. But like Deirdre's murder, the attempt on his life in the context of the marathon seemed obscene. A soft footfall made him open his eyes.

"You awake? You have another visitor." This petite uniformed person was Sergeant Rose Casey, the guardian angel Malone had put at his door. He pulled himself up against the pillows.

The policewoman spoke over her shoulder to someone waiting outside the door. "It's okay. You can come in now."

Seargent Casey crossed the room at the foot of the bed and hoisted herself up onto the windowsill, beside the roses and gladioli. Her feet dangled. She looked like a kid dressed up in a cop suit. Only the gun looked real.

Louisa was in the doorway. She glanced at Tony, then at the policewoman on her perch. Tony got it. Alex had been allowed to come in alone. Louisa got it, too. Her face was bleak.

"I brought you some flowers," she said, her voice uncertain, "but I had to leave them outside."

He tried to smile. "If my mother brought me chicken soup, they'd send for a taster."

She took a couple of hesitant steps that brought her closer to the bed. They looked at each other. Her eyes widened when she took in his appearance—the bandage on his head, the criss-crossed stitches on his unshaven face. Her face was drawn, and her eyes had deep shadows under them. Coaching marathons had made him a good reader of people's states of mind. Louisa was frightened. She had lost her nerve. He cursed James Malone silently. He could hardly believe this was the same energetic, forthright woman who had stood up to him in the marathon.

Suddenly her eyes filled with tears. "I didn't do it."

"I know you didn't," he said promptly. He wished he could smile to reassure her. He wished he could put his arm around her the way he had done in the cemetery. She seemed so lost, so alone.

The policewoman's presence was not the only barrier. Their last meeting, at the funeral, had been tense and explosive, but each of them had had something to say to the other. Now they'd been thrust into a new relationship. Here they were tentative and uncertain. He wanted to know what she was thinking. He couldn't find the words to ask.

"I'm sorry. I mean, if anything I'm involved with caused someone to..." She looked at the policewoman who was now elaborately gazing out the window. "I really do have reservations about SUM—you know that—and I was going to write about what I experienced, but I never intended to hurt anyone, only to tell what I thought was the truth. I didn't give Deirdre that capsule, and I didn't shoot you. But I was sitting next to Deirdre when she died, and I have no witness to where I was Wednesday night." She bit her lips.

"You're in a hell of a spot. Any chance of getting off Malone's suspect list?"

Her eyes flicked again to the policewoman, then back to his. "Not much, I'm afraid," she said. "Tell me, are you really going to be okay? You look..."

"This look is frightening, but temporary. In a couple of weeks I'll be good as new, and only a little less beautiful than I was before. I want you to know that this fiendish grimace is meant to be a smile. And if you really came here to cheer me up, I'd like you to smile at me."

To his surprise, she did. For a second the whole room seemed brighter. He forgot he was in pain.

"Can I take that as a sign that hostilities are lessening? When I get out of here, can I get you to the peace table?"

Her eyes still held something of the smile. "For negotiations—maybe. For surrender—no."

He started to laugh. It changed to a groan as the pain knifed him. "Tough, aren't you?" As he saw the shadow come back to her face, he said, "But not tough enough. Look, I'm doing my best to persuade Malone that if he thinks you did this, he's crazy—desperate, in fact. He's got to find the real culprit. When I get out of here...."

She shook her head. "Don't worry about me. Just take care of yourself. Can I do anything for you?"

"Pour me a glass of water, will you?" he said, shifting around to indicate the carafe on the table beside the bed. "I can't reach."

Before Louisa could move close enough to pick up the glass, the policewoman was off the windowsill. "I'll handle that!"

Louisa jumped back as if she'd been struck. She glared at Rose Casey. "Do you think I came into this room to finish him off? Do you really think I'm stupid enough to put cyanide into his glass right in front of your eyes?"

Sergeant Casey poured the water and handed it to Tony. "Look, guys," she said, "two's company, three's a crowd. Neither of you wants me here. I'm sorry about that, I'm not crazy about it myself. But this is my job."

Tony drank and handed the glass back. The policewoman put it on the table beside the carafe and resumed her spot on the windowsill.

Louisa was still standing, frozen. When her eyes met his, her look appealed. He knew how desperately she needed someone to talk to. He wanted to hear what was going on, hear her tell him her side of the case Malone was building against her. There was no way they could talk with this policewoman in the room. He kept looking at her urgently, and when he knew she was

trying to read what was in his eyes, he nodded his head almost
imperceptibly toward the telephone.

He saw her relax. She understood. "I'll go now, Tony. I hope
you feel better." She smiled wanly at him again before she
turned and went out the door.

The policewoman followed. "I really am sorry about this,"
she said to Tony as she passed the foot of the bed.

"Bring me my flowers," he growled. "Or do you have to
clear them with the bomb squad?"

Louisa's bouquet was a fragrant mass of jonquils, tulips, and
Japanese iris—a touch of spring from a hothouse in December. He was touched by her taste.

The flowers came into the room, held gingerly by Detective
James Malone. "Sergeant Casey says these are okay. I passed
Louisa Evans at the elevator. She didn't speak to me."

"I'm not surprised."

"I don't think you realize how serious this situation is. You
act like you think you've got a charmed life. Is that some more
of your SUM bullshit?"

"Of all the people involved, I am probably the one most
painfully aware of how serious the situation is. But I know
Louisa didn't shoot me."

"Then did Deirdre tell you some jealous wife had it in for
her?"

"No, I've told you everything Deirdre said to me."

"I've arranged for a tap on your phone."

"What the hell for?"

"It's a precaution, like having Sergeant Casey out there. In
case someone tries to get you to leave this room and go where
you can be ambushed again."

"Damn!" cried Tony. "That's got to be a violation of my
civil rights!"

"It's not. Whoever wanted you dead still wants you dead.
She was very thorough. All the lightbulbs in the corridor outside your room had been unscrewed. Anything more you've
remembered? Anything that took place before the attack?"

Tony resisted an impulse to slide down in the bed and put the
covers over his head. "I told you everything I remember. I'd
been thinking about Vietnam and suddenly felt as if I was a

target. If I hadn't been scared shitless and flattened myself instinctively, I'd be in worse shape than I am. And what I am right now is fed up with your questions!''

"I'm sorry," said Malone with real contrition. He sighed. "I'll look in again tomorrow morning."

"What are you doing to find Deirdre's killer? How are you looking for the person who shot me?"

"We're questioning people who knew Deirdre at the school. We're still looking for Heloise and the Abelards. In your case, we're questioning marathoners again. It's a long, slow business."

Louisa's flowers were the only bearable thing in the room, Tony decided. Pain and anger had made him churlish. He closed his eyes. He heard the detective tiptoe away.

NINETEEN

LOUISA STOOD WAITING for the light to change on Columbus Avenue. Her lips were pressed together to keep them from trembling, and her eyes kept welling up with tears. The look on James Malone's face when she met him at the hospital elevator had told her everything. His lifted eyebrows had said more plainly than words what he thought she'd come for. She was sure he was congratulating himself on his foresight in putting a guard on Tony.

She thought of Tony and felt a sudden rage at whoever had so mercilessly gunned him down. Her anger against him had dissolved, how and when she did not quite know, and in its place was something new, tentative, and strangely sweet. He was different in his pain and helplessness. Not so arrogant, not so intimidating.

Maybe there in the cemetery, she'd finally let herself see that he was genuine. His belief in the power of SUM was genuine, too. She would never feel the way he did about it, but she could let herself hope that they could meet at the peace table and get to know each other. A fierce longing welled up—to have someone understand. To have someone on her side.

She didn't have time for such hopes. If she didn't clear herself of the suspicion of murder, the future had no promise.

It was only a matter of time until Malone decided he had enough evidence to risk arresting her. A good lawyer would get her off, but her career would be ended, her life in shreds. Unless the real murderer was found, she would never be able to live down the shadow of suspicion.

She'd never be able to rest, knowing that someone had gotten away with killing Deirdre so horribly. And the threat to Tony would not end.

Malone would never believe her. Tony might be on her side, but he was in no condition to help her establish her innocence.

Her only hope now was to help herself. She had to find Deirdre's pictures. That was the first step.

When the light changed, she crossed Columbus and walked across Fifty-ninth Street toward the subway. As she stepped onto the escalator to descend to the platform, she glanced over her shoulder. The feeling that she was being followed had persisted since the nightmare of Wednesday night. It had kept her a virtual prisoner in her apartment all day Thursday. For the first time, she had called New York University and cancelled her class. She'd never felt like this before, afraid to go out alone. She told herself that it was a natural consequence of anxiety, tension, and the threat of imminent arrest, but her fear for herself and Clare did not lessen.

The second time Jack had called, and she had refused to meet him at Carl Schurz Park, he'd insisted that she leave what she had for him at a phone booth three blocks from her apartment. That time he'd kept himself invisible, a watcher deep in the shadows. She wondered what her doorman thought when she went out the second time and came back twenty minutes later. She wondered if he was still under instructions to report her comings and goings to Detective Malone.

She had left an envelope in the phone booth. In it was the claim slip she'd gotten from Fotorush when she left her own roll of film. By this time he'd picked it up, and he knew she had tricked him. What this meant for Clare, she could only guess. Her only comfort was that no bloody package had arrived addressed to her. Jack had not called again.

She had to find Deirdre's pictures. They were the key. Whatever or whoever those pictures showed would explain Deirdre's death and the attack on Tony. She should have been looking for the pictures yesterday. Fear had immobilized her. She was ashamed of her cowardice.

She was close to the Park Summit. She should start at this end of Deirdre's trek from Alphabet City to the marathon. She would assume, to begin with, that Deirdre had come by subway. She descended into the Fifty-ninth Street station by the escalator and stopped to look at the map displayed against the blood-colored tile of the station wall. Deirdre could have walked from her place to the Broadway/Lafayette station and taken the D or the F train uptown. Or she could have gone to Bleecker Street and taken the Lexington Avenue line, changed at Grand Central to the Times Square shuttle, and from there gone uptown two stops on the Number 1 train. Or she could have taken the R train to Times Square. By any route she would have gotten off here at Columbus Circle and walked to the hotel on Sixth Avenue.

Beyond the turnstiles, Louisa could see the yellow and red displays of a film shop. This was where she would start. She wanted to be finished with the shops in the subways before rush hour.

TWENTY

TONY THRASHED. He tried to get up. He heard running feet. A light was shining in his face. He opened his eyes, then shut them against the glare. The hospital. He was in bed, in the hospital. This face bending down to his was the nurse's. He was having a nightmare.

"Hey, man, you okay? Lay back now. We don't want no ribs pokin' into your lungs."

Tony lay back. Sweat was running off his face. His whole body was wet with it. The nurse poured a glass of water and helped him raise his head to drink it. He drank with great thirst.

"Thanks," he said. He noted that this ministering angel was male.

"I can get you medication for pain, it says so on your chart."

"No painkillers. I'm a former addict."

"I hear you, man. Better pain than that shit again. The supper trays are coming. You feel like eatin'?"

"Not really, but I'll try. Help me up." The nurse took back the glass, put the bed up, and helped Tony ease into a sitting position.

The nightmare was losing its power, although he still felt weak in its aftermath. With the tray of unappetizing food picked at and pushed aside, Tony let his mind go back to it. He no longer felt the helplessness and panic. His close call the other night had brought up to his consciousness the memories of Vietnam. He always dreamed about it after he told the marathon his story. Telling Louisa about the families of his men had alerted him, awakened his senses, and probably saved his life.

But this time there was something more. Louisa was in his dream. She was in danger. She was in danger of being arrested for a murder she did not commit. In the absence of any other suspects, Malone was fixed on her.

That damn capsule.... He didn't know where Deirdre had gotten it, but he was certain about Louisa. Just before the attack, he'd let some of James Malone's frustration and cynicism get to him. He'd gotten out of touch with his instincts. You couldn't always trust the faces of things, but instincts were a sure test. Lying in this hospital, he could not help her. He couldn't even tell her how much he wanted to help. He couldn't even talk to her with that tap on his phone. She was in peril, and he couldn't do a fucking thing to help her.

That wasn't all. That damn woman who shot at him. Malone's theory about a wife or girl friend so jealous she'd killed Deirdre, and so afraid of what Deirdre had told him that she'd tried to kill him too, was an improvement over his theory about Louisa's plot against SUM. But who? And worse—how? Was it someone from Deirdre's past? He reviewed all the faces he'd met in Scranton on Tuesday. Had one of those woman been at the marathon? Watched Deirdre die? Killed her, in fact?

The idea was preposterous. But nothing was as preposterous as the shadow that now lay across Louisa. She was no longer at war with him. The strain she was under had broken her down. He wanted her to know that he was on her side. She was strong, and she was fighting for herself, but she was losing heart. She needed help, but since he was confined to his bed, he could help her only by using his brains.

Think. Remember. The faces at Deirdre's funeral. The faces in front of him in the ballroom. Marathoners began to line up in his mind, passing in review. By the end of a marathon, he could usually see every face. But he hadn't been with these people long enough. He didn't know them.

It was a bitter truth to swallow. He might not be able to help Louisa at all.

TWENTY-ONE

HELPED ALONG BY the crowd of commuters at the Times Square station, Louisa took the passage from the Broadway line to the shuttle platform. Her search for Deirdre's pictures, above and below ground, had taken her into the rush hour. She'd had no luck.

At the end of the white tile tunnel, down a short flight of stairs, the hundreds heading for the shuttle met the hundreds coming off it. They converged, pushing and dodging in the subway rider's ritual dance. Louisa ducked out of the stream to wait a few minutes until the crowd had abated. She was not in such a hurry to get downtown that she had to suffer being pushed and shoved. She hated subways. She'd spent far too much tense and anxious time in them already this week.

She found herself in front of the Corner Camera Stop. A hand-lettered sign said "We open at 8:50 A.M." Four minutes later, when she re-entered the stream of commuters pushing toward the shuttle, Deirdre's pictures were in her bag.

Triumph bubbled up in her. This had to be the turning point. Luck and proximity had saved her the hours of trial and error which would, eventually, have led her right to this spot. It was a logical place for Deirdre to have dropped off her film on her way uptown to the marathon. She would have planned to pick up the pictures on her way home that night, or the next day.

Louisa was swept aboard the shuttle. She had to stand, clutching one of the overhead straps for support. She scarcely noticed the crowd now. She could go home. She didn't have to trudge around the East Village and Alphabet City looking for photo shops. She didn't want to risk even a peek at Deirdre's pictures while she was standing pressed against other bodies in this jammed train. When she got back to her apartment, she'd be able to look at them carefully.

The conductor bellowed, a few more bodies shoved themselves into the mass. The doors shut, and the shuttle jerked to a start on its short trek. Someone squeezed in behind Louisa. A hand reached up to clutch the same strap as she was hanging onto. Louisa felt claustrophobic. The car was unbearably hot. She was sweating in her down jacket. She felt as if she could hardly breathe. She raised her head to get some air.

The shuttle gained speed. Louisa's hand on the strap tightened. The other hand crowded hers. She looked up.

A man's hand. Slender. White. It had dirty fingernails. It had a flattened, deformed thumb.

Jack. He was right behind her. His body was pressed obscenely against hers. His breath was in her ear. He whispered—she couldn't hear what he said—but the force of it was unmistakable. She twisted, felt a hard pressure. A knife? A gun? She was going to be sick.

The shuttle jerked to a stop. The doors opened. Slowly the pressure eased as the pack began to break up, move out. There was space around her now. She could breathe. She could look.

He was still behind her, still holding on. She got one look at his face. It was inches from her own. He was no taller than she. His skin was dull and pasty. He had a face like a ferret—narrow and pointed—all the features drawn toward the nose. He was wearing a khaki jacket and a close-fitting stocking cap that hid his head.

His mouth was moving, still soundlessly, but she could see thin, colorless lips framing words: "Hand them over."

His eyes—it was his eyes that terrified her. They were light and they stared without blinking. They were filled with a hatred she could never have imagined human eyes could express.

He was insane. Or he was mad with rage.

The man in the seat she was standing in front of was getting to his feet. "Move it, will you!" he yelled. His bulk pushed her back. She was shoved towards the door of the rapidly emptying car. When she looked around, Jack was no longer behind her. He'd gone out the door in the middle. He was out there on the platform somewhere, waiting for her.

The surging commuters bore her along to the IRT and nudged her down the stairs to the uptown platform. She saw so many heads with dark caps that she began to imagine multiple Jacks, closing in on her. She was paralyzed by indecision. She should leave the subway. She would be safer on the street.

She looked back. There he was, on the stairs, near the bottom. She could see his pale face searching the crowd. He was between her and the way out. It was too late. Her only hope now was to get on a train before he did.

The homebound commuters continued to pour down the stairs, adding to the crowd already there. Somewhere in that pressing crowd behind her was Jack. She hoisted the strap of her canvas bag firmly up on her shoulder and held the bag tightly against her side. What he wanted was in this bag.

A train came, but it was too full. Louisa fought, but she could not manage to squeeze in. Then there was a delay. Something had slowed the arrival of the next train. The crowd on the platform continued to build. She waited with increasing unease. A cab would have been impossible to get at rush hour, but she could have walked. If she hadn't been terrified earlier, she would have split away from the IRT crowd and gone up the stairs to Grand Central when she got off the shuttle.

She was aware of being uncomfortably squeezed. She couldn't move enough to even look back. The press behind her was so great that she was being pushed involuntarily closer to the edge of the platform. She fought to control her panic—she had enough to fear from the madman behind her. This was no time for her terror of subways to flare up. If she started to scream, the whole mob would go berserk.

"Stop that!" she panted, trying to see who was pushing her from behind.

Voices cried out in Spanish. A woman muttered unintelligibly behind her. Then a man bellowed in her ear, "It ain't me, lady!" He yelled over his shoulder, "Cut that out!" More voices took up the cry. "Stop pushing!" "Move the fuck back!"

Louisa felt the strap of her bag start to slip off her shoulder. She tried to shrug it higher, but the bag itself seemed suddenly to have gotten heavier. In the instant she realized what was happening, she heard the rumble of the oncoming train. She took firm hold of the strap with her other hand and tugged against the force that was trying to relieve her of her bag. She struggled to peel off her gloves to get a better hold. She had to let the gloves drop; there was no way she could get them into her pockets. She twisted around, but could not see to which perspiring face the unseen hands belonged. She did not see Jack.

The train was closer, now, the rumble growing louder. The crowd surged forward. At the top of her lungs, Louisa screamed, "Get your hands off my purse!" She felt the bag slipping from beneath her arm. She clutched the strap with both and pulled hard.

The strap broke. It slid through her fingers. With her fingernails she caught the corner of the bag. A leather bag would have slipped from her grasp and been gone, irretrievably, into the hands of the purse snatcher, but this bag was cloth, and she got a grip on it.

Her backward lunge cost her her balance. She was teetering on the edge of the platform. Then someone grabbed her just as the train, with a roar and a blinding flash, shot out of the tunnel.

TWENTY-TWO

MS. EBERLE'S EYE MAKEUP reminded Rhonda of Morticia—the mother in a TV show she used to watch as a kid—about a family of freaks who lived in a big spooky house. "The Addams Family."

Ms. Eberle's name was Janet, a name that did not go at all with the face made up in exotic eye paint. She taught graphics at SVA. "Harvey?" she shrilled. "Oh, yes, I suppose you'd say he was a good photographer. Not brilliant, you understand, but competent. And adequate as a teacher. Quite adequate."

"Can you tell me anything about his private life, his friends, whether he's involved with anyone?"

Janet Eberle's eagerness to tell all she knew about Harvey made Rhonda wonder if Eberle had been slighted. "Harvey's discreet, I will say that for him. Everyone knows he's, you know, open-minded. Not the slightest scandal until this student of his was murdered. She was really off the wall."

One of Harvey's students, Mike Rivers, added his bit to Ms. Eberle's analysis. "Sure, everyone knows Harvey swings both ways—that's no big deal. He doesn't put it up in neon. But the thing with Deirdre had us wondering if he'd flipped. Someone did him a favor, getting rid of her."

"No one here thinks Harvey did it?"

"Harvey? Are you kidding? I know about twenty people who were pissed-off enough at Deirdre to at least fantasize about killing her."

"Their names, please."

"Oh shit! Shoulda kept my mouth shut. Do I have to?"

"Yes."

The twenty turned out to be three, all of whom were angry at Deirdre for offenses ranging from cadging cigarettes to failing to repay borrowed money. To them Deirdre had been nothing more serious than a freeloader, a whiner, and a pain in the ass.

Rhonda was fed up. All of this was taking an enormous amount of time, and it was getting her no place. She showed Louisa Evans's picture to everyone she questioned. No one had seen her with Harvey.

In a private room in Lenox Hill, Vivian Wardley was propped up in bed. She looked at Rhonda's badge and summoned up a condescending nod, in the manner of Queen Victoria granting an audience to a commoner. "I suppose this is about that student of Harvey's," she said coldly. "He told me the police would come to ask me questions. What you can possibly expect to find out here is beyond me. I've been here since Thursday night, and I know nothing about this sordid business. What kind of girl was she, to get herself killed like that? So ugly, so public! Harvey did not tell me."

Underneath the waspish resentment, Rhonda detected a gleam of curiosity. Vivian Wardley wanted to know what was going on, and Harvey had wanted to spare her. Rhonda said, "You're absolutely right about that, Mrs. Wardley, it is sordid. I'm here just on routine business. We have to talk to everyone who knew Deirdre, or who might have known her, even in the most unlikely connection. Your son seems like a very fine person. Talented. Devoted to you, I'm sure."

"Harvey's a good boy," Vivian Wardley conceded. Her resentment was fading, as was her Queen Victoria act. She was a sick, lonely old woman who felt left out.

"I bet it's been a real comfort to you to know he's been here for you—all through the operation and when you woke up."

Vivian Wardley said, "Every time I opened my eyes, Harvey was here, I will say that for him. I was so groggy that both Friday and Saturday are hard for me to remember."

So much for Harvey's alibi for Saturday. Rhonda took Louisa Evans's picture from her purse. "Have you ever seen this woman, Mrs. Wardley? Or heard about her? Her name is Louisa Evans. We think maybe she had something to do with the girl's death. She might be someone Harvey knows."

Vivian took the photograph in thin, trembling fingers. "Attractive woman. No, I've never seen her. Why don't you ask

Harvey? He never tells me about his girl friends. Never brings any of them to meet me. I'm not going to have grandchildren.'' She pressed her lips tightly together and handed back the photograph. In her eyes was sadness and resignation. And something else.

"Maybe Ms. Right just hasn't come along yet," Rhonda said cheerfully. "People are marrying late nowadays. Take me, for example. I'm thirty-four, and I'm in no hurry."

"Harvey's forty-three."

"And has a good job, doesn't he?"

"A job, that's right. He's known ever since he was young that I expected him to be independent. I can well afford to support him, but I've not given him a penny."

"Well, I'm sure Harvey's a good catch. Some lucky woman . . .''

Mrs. Wardley's pale cheeks flushed slightly. "I worry sometimes that he'll never marry. I hear things . . . read things."

"What kind of things, Mrs. Wardley?"

"You know, about men who don't seem . . . to like being with women. Harvey didn't go out with girls when he was in his teens. I worried about him having no social life. Then I began to wonder, to be afraid. . . .'' Her hands twisted the sheets. Her face was a dull red now.

"I'm sure Harvey has no problem like that."

"His father would be so angry. Harvey's father died when he was only four, you see. I brought him up alone. I was very strict with him. There's never been any scandal in my family, nothing—irregular. I wouldn't put up with it if there had been."

No wonder Harvey had been so angry about the police questioning his mother. He had been terrified that some hint of his sexual adventures would get through to Mrs. Wardley. The secret life of Harvey Wardleigh. Wardley the mama's boy and Wardleigh the bisexual swinger.

"I won't bother you any more, Mrs. Wardley. It was this woman's picture I needed to know about. Thank you for giving me the time. I hope I haven't tired you."

"What did you say your name was?"

"Rhonda Lord."

"And you're a detective, you said?"

"That's right, ma'am. Detective Rhonda Lord. I've been on the force eight years."

"You don't look like a detective." To Rhonda's surprise, Vivian Wardley reached out one pale, shaky hand. Now Rhonda could see the loneliness. And beneath it, barely held back, the terror of dying. "Thank you, Detective Lord."

"For what, ma'am?"

"For listening."

TWENTY-THREE

SHOCK. That's what it was. Louisa clutched her bag with its broken strap. Deirdre's pictures were still there. She was alive. This was her building, this man in uniform was her doorman. She must be real to him—he was holding the door open for her. His face showed that he saw her. "Ms. Evans! What happened? You look . . ."

She knew how she must look. Disheveled and scared out of her wits. "I'm okay, Dan," she said shakily. "It's been a bad day." She did not add that it had almost been her last.

Inside her apartment, she slammed her locks with enough noise to make the fact that she was locked in penetrate her brain. For good measure she brought over a chair and propped it at an angle under the police bar. She checked her windows to make sure they were locked before she drew the curtains across them.

She turned on all the lights in her living room. Locked doors, lights, covered windows—they would never be enough to make her feel safe.

She dropped her jacket on the chair by the door. As she passed the foyer mirror she saw why Dan had exclaimed at the sight of her. Worse than she'd thought. Her face was without color, her lips bitten and dry. Her hair hung limp and tangled.

But she still had her bag. She still had Deirdre's pictures. She had come close to dying for them.

The shock was wearing off. She was trembling. Her teeth chattered. Soon she was shaking uncontrollably. A drink was out of the question, alcohol would loosen the floodgates. She went into her kitchen and put water in the kettle. Her hands shook as she got a mug off the shelf, a tea bag out of the cannister.

With the comforting mug of hot, sweetened tea in her hands, she sat in her rocker and sipped until she was warm, and the shakes had passed. She felt limp and drained. Her body, that in shock had seemed weightless, was heavy again.

She tried to remember what had happened. She was on the crowded platform. Then she'd felt the snap as the strap broke. She'd clutched desperately at her bag. Then she'd felt herself falling. Had Jack actually pushed her? Or had her lunge after her bag thrown her off balance? She'd been pulled back from the edge just before the train came in. Its doors had opened, and she'd been shoved aboard.

She remembered the anxious faces. "You okay, lady? You okay?"

"Looked for a minute there like you was gonna fall."

"I'm okay," she said shakily, holding her bag with both arms.

"You one lucky lady!"

These two, one on each side, were her saviors. Two muscular young men in tight jeans and leather jackets. They were scarcely as tall as she was. Their brown faces were beaming. Even packed shoulder-to-shoulder with their fellow New Yorkers, they seemed to swagger. They nodded, smiled, said a few words in Spanish. She tried to thank them, knowing how disjointed, how inadequate she sounded. They didn't seem to mind. They disclaimed any heroism. She'd lost her balance, they'd reached out and caught her. Simple.

Their names. Even in her distracted state, she knew she had to get their names. "Pablo. I'm Pablo. He José." Last name? "Diaz." Where did they live? "Bronx."

The onlookers began a litany. "Nice going, Pablo! Right on, José!" Faces beamed. Hands reached over to touch Pablo and José. They grinned. Louisa forced out more words of gratitude. She struggled to reach into her bag, to get out her notebook to write down their addresses. No, please lady, they didn't want no reward. They were just in the right place at the right time.

"Did anyone see...?" She tried to ask if anyone had seen the man who had tried to snatch her bag. But then the train was at Seventy-seventh Street, and she was propelled out of it and onto the platform with words of advice ringing behind her.

"Go right home now, lady!"

"Have a stiff one and forget this ever happened!"

She thanked the little group that got off with her and refused an escort home. She was alive. That was all that mattered. She had the goodness of New Yorkers, and the reflexes of Pablo and José to thank.

She was alive, but she had almost died the way Deirdre had almost died. It could not be a coincidence. Deirdre had almost fallen in front of a train when the strap of her camera was seized.

She had not been imagining that she was being followed. Jack had discovered her trick; the claim slip she had left in the phone booth had netted him only pictures of her Thanksgiving weekend in Boston.

He'd followed her to the shuttle platform, and he'd seen her come away from Corner Camera. He followed her onto the shuttle, but he would not risk stabbing her in that crowded car. He'd been behind her at the uptown IRT platform, and somehow he'd managed to slither his way through the crowd to a place close enough to grab the strap of her bag. In that press of arms and hands and bodies, she'd not been able to see whose hands were where.

The pictures. She got up from the chair and went to the foyer for her bag. The mirror showed her face again, still pale, but calm. She brought the yellow packet into the living room. Her fingers did not shake when she opened it and pulled out the inner envelopes. Deirdre had taken two rolls of thirty-six pictures.

The first set was just as Harvey had predicted. Deirdre's city faces were true to the banal. A pretzel and chestnut vendor by his wagon on Central Park South. A skater at Rockefeller Center launching out onto the ice. Children in line for the Christmas show at Radio City Music Hall.

Deirdre was also true to her reputation as a photographer. Faces were blurred. Some shots were too dark, some too light. Several shots had Deirdre's thumb over the lens. Deirdre would have been hard put to meet the requirements for this assignment no matter what leverage she had over Harvey.

Louisa opened the second envelope. If Deirdre was a bad photographer when she was relatively sober, she was a disaster when drunk. At first the pictures didn't even make sense. Then they began to reveal themselves.

Here was a blurred figure in white that must be Jack in drag for his performance. His blonde wig was askew, and he was pounding a guitar. Here was a huddle of black-robed figures—the Abelards in monks' habits—with guitars and basses, and white objects dangling from their necks that must be the dildos Clare said were part of their get-up.

Here was Jack again, little more than a white blob.

Here was a waiter. One hand balanced a tray with drinks on it, the other held up one finger.

Here were a couple of men at what seemed to be the bar. Their faces turned away from the camera.

The waiter again, so close to the lens this time that his face was one big open O-shaped mouth.

The men at the bar. They were looking at the camera this time, but their faces were so far away, they were unrecognizable.

Here were tables in front of the performers' platform, tables with drinks on them. The clientele all seemed to be women. None of them had distinct facial features, only outlines of hair and clothes. All were visibly dressed up for their evening at the club. They looked strangely innocent, like a group of suburban matrons in town for an evening of carefully selected risqué entertainment.

She was baffled. She took the pictures over to her desk and spread them out under the bright light. Then she took a magnifying glass, and she scrutinized each picture carefully, the backgrounds as well as the subjects.

She was still baffled. Twice Jack had attempted murder on subway platforms to get his hands on these pictures. He'd succeeded in killing Deirdre in such a visible and dramatic way that a full-scale, well-publicized police investigation had resulted. He must be insane.

She was counting on these pictures to save her from arrest for a crime she didn't commit. No threat to anyone seemed posed by these pictures. The only recognizable face was the waiter. Had he later regretted his cheerful obscene pose? She looked at him again. He looked not unlike her rescuers, Pablo and José, and just as insouciant. Whatever he'd done hardly seemed worth killing for.

The only possible answer was that Jack didn't know how innocuous the pictures were. He'd gotten Deirdre thrown out of the club for taking them. That was clearly what she'd meant about his being so pissed-off he had her "thrown outta the place." Then he'd gone to desperate lengths to get hold of the camera, and failing that, the film. Somehow he'd figured out that Louisa had it. He'd failed to get the pictures from her. He would try again.

Now what? If she gave these pictures to Detective Malone, what would they prove? They had seemed her only chance to prove her innocence. Malone would wonder why she'd waited so long to turn them over to him. He wouldn't believe the subway story any more than he'd believe that Jack—or one of his friends—had dressed like Deirdre to terrify her. He doubted Jack's very existence. The fact that she'd held back on the pictures might be the last bit of proof he needed to make a reasonable case against her.

What was she going to do now? She had to save herself and Clare, if it was not already too late for that. She had to think of something. She needed someone to talk to.

Tony! His eyes had told her he was on her side. She could call him.

By the time she had looked up the number of Roosevelt Hospital and gotten the switchboard to ring his room, she was having doubts. She was shaking again. Surely she had not misread what he'd tried to say without words. He knew she wanted to talk. He knew she couldn't talk in front of the police.

The phone rang several times. She could picture him straining, with the pain in his ribs, to reach for the phone on the table beside the bed. Maybe this was a mistake.

The receiver was lifted. There was a long silence. Then his voice. "Hello?"

She was strangely out of breath. "This is Louisa. I hope I understood this afternoon. It's all right for me to talk to you on the phone?" To her surprise her voice was shaking as well.

"Ah . . ." He paused. Then, curtly, "Negative on that!"

She waited. That was all. His silence was like a blow. She managed to get out, "Sorry—goodbye." She hung up.

She was numb. She had misunderstood him. She'd bothered him, wakened him from sleep perhaps, and caused him pain reaching for the phone for a call he did not want to get. Whatever she thought had dawned between them this afternoon was dead now. In her loneliness and desperation she'd imagined that he was moved by her situation, and he wanted to help her.

Unshed tears were making her throat ache. She closed her eyes. A couple of hard tears squeezed from beneath her lids. Another failure. Fortunate, she thought bitterly, that this time hope had been brief. She had to let go of it. She had no time to grieve over Tony Cazzine.

What was she going to do about these pictures?

She could burn them, pretend they never existed. She could send them anonymously to Detective Malone. She could . . .

She flipped through them again. She was missing something. If she looked at them again, if she looked at each one long enough, maybe she'd see it.

The waiter. The women. The men at the bar. Jack in his dress and long blonde wig.

A man in a dress and a wig?

Impossible!

Impossible? No!

It was exactly what Jack would do! Heloise—Deirdre—how could she have missed it?

It was so simple, so clear, so perfectly in Jack's character. He was a person who took big risks. Cocaine made its users bold, even foolhardy while the high lasted.

How could she prove it? Detective Malone would laugh out loud this time.

She didn't have to talk to Detective Malone.

She had misunderstood Tony, and maybe she was wrong about this too, but if she didn't do something she was doomed. What had Tony said about being responsible for your own life?

One risk was very much like another at this point. Neither she nor Clare would ever be safe until Jack was under arrest.

Her mind was working again. Her idea was crazy, but it was all she had. She opened her notebook, took a piece of paper from it, and reached for the phone.

TWENTY-FOUR

HARVEY WORE A PALE BLUE terrycloth bathrobe. A towel hung around his neck. His wet hair was plastered against his pink scalp. "Really, Detective Malone!" he exclaimed irritably. "I just got out of the shower! I got home only a short time ago, and as soon as I'm dressed I'm going to see Mother. Can't you wait until tomorrow?"

"Sorry, no. Just a few minutes."

Harvey's shrug was eloquent. "Sit down. I'll put on some clothes and be back in a minute."

Malone sat down in a leather sling chair. He already knew it would bear his weight. He'd sat in it the first time he questioned Harvey. He looked around the small living room. It was more to his taste than Louisa's apartment. But he liked it less this time. It was too stark, too sterile, like its owner was trying to prove something about himself by choosing browns and beiges and furniture made of metal frames. It looked like a display room in a department store. Not even the large photographs that decorated the walls had any animation. He supposed those male nudes with their serene faces and contorted bodies were considered art photography. For a moment, he even wondered what kind of place Tony Cazzine lived in, what he had on his walls.

Harvey was back. He'd toweled his hair. It stood up in thin wisps. He was wearing a purple sweatshirt and jeans that had a name on the back pocket. His feet were still bare.

"How is your mother?" Malone asked.

Harvey sat down. "She's not getting any better. Monday they're going to begin some radiation therapy. If that's too hard on her, I'm going to let her decide if she wants to continue it. It will prolong her life, but if it makes her violently sick, what's the point? She's capable of making that kind of decision for herself. You're *not* going to try to question her, are you?"

"No, no," said Malone hastily. "I'm sure Detective Lord found out everything we need to know from your mother."

"And what more can you possibly want from me? On Tuesday I told you everything relevant about my acquaintance with Deirdre Doyle. My friends at SVA have been phoning all day. Your partner must have gotten my entire life history. There can't be anything about me—social, sexual, or professional— that you don't know!"

"How long have you known Louisa Evans?"

"Before Wednesday I knew her by name. You might even say I'm a fan of hers—I read everything she writes. But I never met her until the cemetery in Scranton. When I saw she was being hounded by the media, I offered her a ride back to New York."

"What did you and she talk about while you were in the car?"

Harvey chuckled. "Trying to prove a conspiracy? It won't make it through the wash!"

"I have Ms. Evans's version of your conversation, I just want to hear yours." Malone tried to keep his face blank. Harvey was a pain in the ass.

Not a stupid one, however. His voice was edged with malice when he said, "I told her about my relationship with Deirdre. Louisa told me what had passed between herself and Deirdre just before Deirdre died. Nothing any different from what I'd read in the papers. We commiserated with each other on being your chief suspects. We speculated about what Deirdre had taken pictures of."

"Did she tell you she'd found out that Deirdre had another lover, a rock musician?"

"Yes. Deirdre told her. What of it?"

"She told you Deirdre told her that?"

"While they were talking before the marathon started up again. Deirdre told her quite a lot in those few minutes."

"Did Louisa Evans mention to you another source of her information about Deirdre?"

"No."

"Do you know this other man, this musician?"

"I'm not surprised that Deirdre was seeing someone else, but I didn't know him, no. She was a bitch, capable of almost any kind of scheme that she thought would get her something. I told you the other day, I made a mistake getting involved with her, and I got out of it as best I could. I won't be hypocritical and say I'm not relieved she's dead. I could curse the day I met that green-haired . . . ! But I didn't kill her. And I'm sick and tired of having you turn up on my doorstep, and I'm furious that you question my sick mother, my colleagues, and my students behind my back!''

"The girl was murdered. You were intimate with her. And I have a job to do."

One of Harvey's bare feet beat impatiently on the floor. "I have a job to do too. I have to visit my mother. With your permission?"

Malone stood up. Harvey did the same. Malone glanced at the photographs on the wall and said, "You told me you had given your class an assignment to take pictures of people's faces—was that it?"

"City faces. Yes, I assigned that last week. The students turned them in on Monday."

"You never saw the pictures Deirdre took for that assignment?"

"No, I didn't. I read in the papers about the camera she brought to the marathon, and the speculation about what happened to the film that should have been in it. Do I infer correctly from your question that you people have not found Deirdre's pictures?"

"No, we haven't."

"They may not even exist. She was perfectly capable of taking a whole roll of pictures with no film in the camera!"

When Malone left Harvey's building, he stationed himself across the street and watched the entrance. Fifteen minutes later he saw Harvey emerge and walk briskly east toward the subway. Malone recrossed the street and entered the building. He pressed the doorbell of 5B, the apartment next to Harvey's. When he got no answer, he pressed the bell for 5C. At 5D, occupied by an M. Santore, he got in.

The young woman who buzzed the door open when he identified himself as a police officer kept her door on the chain even after she had scrutinized the shield he held out for her inspection. He saw only a portion of her face. It looked young and a little frightened. "What do you want to know?" she asked.

"Do you know the tenant of apartment 5A, Harvey Wardleigh?"

"I've seen him in the elevator, I know who he is, but I don't know him, you know what I mean? He's not in trouble, is he?"

"No, this is just routine. Have you ever seen visitors go in or out of his apartment? Or have you seen him get into the elevator with anyone who was obviously with him?"

Ms. Santore considered. "Once I saw him with an old lady I thought must be his mother. That was a couple months ago. She looked kinda sick."

"That would be his mother, yes."

"And a week or so ago I did see a woman go into his apartment. I was just coming out to the elevator and she was standing by his door."

"Was she ringing the doorbell?"

"I didn't notice. The elevator was there, she must've just gotten off it. I hopped on."

He reached into his pocket and pulled out the photograph of Louisa Evans. "Look at this picture and tell me if this is the woman you saw." Her hand came out to take the picture. She drew back from the doorway to study it.

Her hand came back holding the picture. Her face reappeared. "No, that's not her, nothing like her. But this picture looks familiar. Has she been in the papers lately or something? I'm sure I've seen her."

Malone returned the picture to his pocket. He sighed. "You probably have."

It was eight o'clock when he got to the station. Rhonda was still there. For the first time in their association, she was visibly tired. Welcome to the club, he said silently as he saw the shadows under her almond-shaped eyes. Not even the fifteen year age advantage she had on him helped against this kind of duty—the grinding routine of knocking on doors and asking questions.

He'd already heard her report on what she'd gotten this morning from Harvey's acquaintances at SVA. She gave him the details of her conversation with Vivian Wardley with none of her usual spark. "Harvey's an asshole, in my opinion," she concluded. "Playing mommy's darling only son to her face, and behind her back doing tricks with the boys and the girls. And if Louisa Evans was one of them, mommy didn't know about her."

Malone wondered if Harvey took down his photographs when his mother was coming to visit. "'Asshole' isn't allowed in official reports," he said.

"How about 'tough shit'?"

For the first time he felt a fleeing empathy.

"Any luck with the boys in the band?" she asked.

"No Heloise, no Abelards. Since Deirdre claimed she was attacked on a subway platform Friday night, I figured she'd gone uptown to see Jack's band. I must have hit twenty-five clubs and all the booking agencies, gay and straight, between Fourteenth Street and Forty-second."

"What's next?"

"I sent a team to that address in Deirdre's pocket. It's a long shot, but it might turn up something. We go back to the marathon tomorrow. We'll start with 'Did you ever see Louisa Evans before the marathon?' Then we'll ask the same thing about Harvey, and this invisible musician, Jack. You get a picture of Harvey?"

"Yeah, from the yearbook at SVA. What are you trying to prove?"

"Conspiracy between Louisa and Harvey. As for this Jack, if he exists, it's conceivable that a marathoner knows him or has heard his band. Some of them might be into the, uh, kinky kinds of entertainment." His phone rang. "Yes?" He listened and his eyebrows went up. "She's here." He put his hand over the mouthpiece and turned to Rhonda. "Pick it up at your desk. It's Louisa Evans. She wants to talk to you."

He kept the receiver to his ear. He heard Rhonda say "Detective Lord here." Then Louisa's voice, low and urgent. "I want to talk to you alone, Detective Lord. It's late, you probably want to go home, but—would you meet me first for coffee?"

TWENTY-FIVE

THIS TIME THEY MET in the Caffe Lucca on Bleecker Street at Sixth Avenue. They had picked it with the gravity of two superpowers agreeing on a site for treaty negotiations. The Caffe Lucca was neutral ground. It was not far from West Fourth Street, where Rhonda could pick up the F train to Brooklyn. Its interior was highly visible from the street and from Father Demo Square, where James Malone was shivering on a bench trying to look like a Greenwich Village deadbeat.

Rhonda, who was hungry, ordered cappuccino and cheesecake. Louisa asked only for an espresso. Rhonda was shocked at the way Louisa looked. She'd changed a lot in the two days since Scranton. Whatever Louisa had on her mind, it was keeping her awake nights and giving her a lot of grief. If she acted like she was about to confess, Rhonda knew what to do. She didn't need any of the instructions Malone thought he had to lay on her.

When their order came, Louisa took a nervous sip of the dark brew. Then she took a deep breath and said, "I think I know how you can find out who killed Deirdre Doyle." Her voice stumbled a little. She sounded like she'd rehearsed what she was going to say.

Rhonda took up a forkful of cheesecake. "Okay. Let's hear it," she said, as noncommittally as possible.

"Replay the scene in the Ladies' room last Saturday. Get someone to play Deirdre."

Rhonda dropped her fork. "That is the most absolutely off the wall thing I ever heard!" she exclaimed. Then she cursed herself for lack of professionalism. She was glad Malone hadn't heard that. Cops were supposed to keep their cool. Women cops especially had to work at it, according to Malone.

Louisa sat back in her chair. She seemed to collapse. She put her hands over her eyes. When she looked up again, her face was frightening in its weary desolation. "I should have known better," she murmured. "I didn't give Deirdre that capsule. I thought replaying what happened in the Ladies' room might show who did." She took another swallow of her espresso. "I'll go now. Thanks anyway, for meeting me."

"Hold it!" Rhonda said. "You aren't going anywhere. You gotta give me time to think. That's a big one. It won't go over with the Man. Look, Ms. Evans, I'll feel a whole lot better scarfing up this cheesecake if you'll have something to eat too. And have a cup of hot chocolate, not another espresso. You look like you need nourishment."

Obediently, Louisa ordered a cup of hot chocolate and a piece of cheesecake. Resistance, as well as energy, seemed to have drained out of her. They ate in a silence that was, strangely, without tension. A little color came back into Louisa's face.

Rhonda ordered an espresso. Now her brain needed all the help it could get. "Okay," she said. "Run that whole thing by me again."

"Detective Malone . . ." Louisa began, a little uncertainly as if she did not know whether she should risk her thoughts about Rhonda's partner.

"Say what you have to say—he and I aren't lovers. Or even friends, for that matter. We're a political arrangement."

"From the beginning he's been fixated on me. He didn't like an article I wrote about gays and police. I probably sound paranoid, maybe by this time I am, but I think he's so sure I killed Deirdre he's not looking for anyone else. I was sitting beside Deirdre, I saw the capsule and described it, therefore I gave it to her. It's as if ever since he stepped into the ballroom and found out that Deirdre died of poison, he's had that old cliché in his head."

"What cliché?"

"It's an old saying—poison is a woman's weapon. And I got to thinking about the women in the restroom, about how close together we all were, and how someone could have put the capsule into Deirdre's pocket. I know you questioned all the women who were in there, and no one saw that happen. But suppose one of them wasn't in the marathon? The restroom is off the lobby, it's available to anyone in the hotel, what if...?''

One part of Rhonda's mind noted that Louisa Evans was running off at the mouth as if she'd needed someone to talk to. The other part of her mind was snarling at James Malone. Him and his fatuous, sexist remarks—that's what he'd started to say on the phone when she was talking to him from Scranton. She hoped he was freezing his butt off in the square over there.

Louisa's flood of words had ceased. She was looking at Rhonda hopefully now. Her face was alive.

Rhonda mentally called herself back to duty. "You have a point, Ms. Evans. But like I say, it's going to be hard to sell this to the Man. And he's the boss of this investigation. Now if you had something to offer in return...."

"My source's name is Clare. I don't know her last name. She lived in the apartment below Deirdre's. She was about to move out of the building. She helped me after I was mugged, and she told me what she knew about Deirdre. She didn't want whoever killed Deirdre to know she'd given information."

Neat, Ms. Evans, thought Rhonda. But just a little too prompt. Louisa Evans was still holding out on something. But her idea about the restroom, bizarre as it sounded, would either smoke out someone or prove there was no one to be smoked out.

The windows of the Caffe Lucca had steamed up with the warmth and the moisture from the espresso machine. Louisa picked up her napkin and wiped a section clear. She looked out. "I don't believe it! There he is!" She was looking across Bleecker to the square. "See—he's sitting over there! Detective Malone! When I went to the hospital today, he wouldn't let me talk to Tony without a policewoman in the room. Now he won't even let me talk to you. Did you know he was there?"

"Yeah, I knew. You can cool it, Ms. Evans. I don't think you're the only one he doesn't trust."

TWENTY-SIX

SWEAT WAS BREAKING OUT on his face. He put a finger into his collar and tugged at it. James Malone had never been so uncomfortable in his life. This was the most goddam unprofessional thing he'd been involved in since he joined the force, and he was fucking mad he'd let himself in for it. He and Rhonda, along with fourteen women, were crammed into the Ladies' room at the Park Summit the following Saturday morning—the second weekend of the Marathon. Rhonda was playing the part of Deirdre. He was representing Louisa Evans, whose fool idea this was. He should never have let Rhonda handle that meeting alone. She'd made a deal that had them doing this stupid play-acting, instead of questioning that ballroom full of people. He was getting a headache from the cries and occasional hysterical peals of laughter that bounced off the tile walls.

"Okay, let's quiet down!" Rhonda was taking charge with zest. His job was to play the part of Louisa, and to observe. And at this point in the script, to add indignity to stupidity, the part required him to be in the john. He put the lid down and sat on it, listening to the bedlam outside the partition. In his hand he held notecards he'd made after last weekend's questioning, should prompting be needed.

After the women quieted down, Rhonda said, "You're all lined up like you were when you first heard Deirdre, right?"

"No, Amy, you were behind me, remember?" That was Marge Lindskey.

"I was just coming out of the booth and I started over to wash my hands." That was Helen.

"Okay, start moving. Now, who finished up at that wash basin when Helen came over and stepped up to it?"

"Me, I think. I was just walking out of the restroom when I heard Deirdre."

"I was combing my hair. It was a mess. I was standing there when Louisa came over." That was Cassie of the frizzy hair.

"There's no one at the last basin."

"She must be in the john. She'll come out when the action starts."

"But I was sure..."

"Ready? Take one!" Someone was getting into the spirit of the thing.

"Roll it!" cried Rhonda. Malone heard some shuffling of feet. Water was turned on and off. He sincerely hoped he was not going to hear any of them actually urinating.

By a miracle, the fourteen women, who according to his original interviews had been in the Ladies' room with Deirdre, were here. Louisa did not come. That had been part of the deal she'd made with Rhonda. She did not want her presence to have any effect on the outcome of the experiment. The others had all agreed to take part in the re-enactment with an enthusiasm that astonished him. Alex had handled the hotel management. This restroom was temporarily closed to the hotel patrons.

"Anybody got a trank? I'll buy whatever you got!" Rhonda cried. Her imitation of Deirdre's whine, according to the admiring chorus, was very close to the original.

"Never mind the reviews!" cried Rhonda. "Just go on with what you said."

"The contract, Deirdre!" cried one voice.

"You signed it same as the rest of us!" cried another.

"You want to get someone else in trouble?"

"Gimme a break!" Rhonda whined.

"Will ya?"

"What do you mean, 'will ya'?" Rhonda asked in her own voice.

"Deirdre said, 'Gimme a break, will ya?' Isn't that right?"

Voices chorused agreement. Rhonda thanked her prompter and said in Deirdre's voice, "Gimme a break, will ya? I got problems!"

"Flush!" A loud whisper came from somewhere.

"What the hell?" Malone cried.

"You're Louisa, aren't you? She flushed the toilet right then." The voice came from the booth beside him.

He glanced hastily at his notecards. Louisa had not heard the rest of the conversation. Obediently he stood up and flushed the toilet. Now what? How long did it take women to do what they had to do? He hoped he'd waited the appropriate number of seconds before he opened the door.

He walked over to the wash basins. "Is this right?"

"That's right," said Cassie, whose hands were fluttering around her mane in pretense of combing. Next to her was Veronica, who was actually washing her hands, then Helen. "Louisa reached between me and—hey, who's supposed to be standing at this basin?" said Cassie.

"Someone's missing a cue?" Rhonda's voice came from a booth. At this point Deirdre had not been in Louisa's sight. Everyone agreed she'd gone into a toilet.

"Someone's missing, period! There was a woman standing next to me all the time I was here combing my hair. She was putting on makeup."

"I saw her," Marge said. "She was still there when I came out."

"I saw her too," echoed Amy. Both voices came from the booths.

"Come out here, all of you," Malone said.

Doors clicked open. Rhonda, Marge, Amy, and a fourth woman emerged. "Everyone look around," he said. "Is the woman who was at that basin in this room?"

Only Malone and Rhonda knew that a policewoman was outside the door in case anyone tried to leave. No one did. They all looked around, at him, at Rhonda, and at each other.

"She's not here." Marge was positive.

"No, she's not," Cassie agreed. "I remember her now. Her name was Sue. I was standing next to her, and I remember it looked funny backwards in the mirror, like 'euS', you know?" Cassie was talking directly to Malone now, and she said, "You reached between us to wash your hands, and you said 'excuse me'—oh, I don't mean you, I mean Louisa Evans!"

"Sue was the one I told you about," Marge said, "doing a whole makeup job—foundation, blusher, eyes—when her face looked completely made up to me."

"What did she look like?"

"Brown hair. Brown eyes. Not really good-looking. Her face needed makeup to be attractive."

Malone consulted his notes from his questioning of Louisa. Louisa hadn't seen the name tag of the woman at the last basin. She thought that woman was the one who had come out of the toilet she'd gone into. Louisa remembered Cassie, who was doing her hair.

His eyes met Rhonda's in the mirror. "We missed one?"

"We can find out easily enough." She turned to the women. "Okay, all of you—you can leave the Ladies' room, but don't go back into the ballroom. Sit down in the lobby and wait. We'll be with you shortly."

When the room was empty, he said, "You're in charge of this caper."

"We get Alex and the marathon roster. We see how many women there are named Sue."

There were two Susans and a Suzanne. Alex had them located in the ballroom and escorted to the lobby by assistant coaches. One Sue had gray hair. The other had long blond hair worn in a braid down her back. Suzanne had black hair in a less violent version of Deirdre's styling. All three faces were innocent of makeup except for lipstick. The three Sues were mystified. No, none of them had been in the Ladies' room when Deirdre was. Each of the fourteen women waiting in the lobby looked at the three Sues and said the same thing—the woman at the last basin was not one of them.

"Are there any other Sues on the marathon roster? Women who are absent today?"

Alex went into the ballroom and came out with Kevin Mulroy. They consulted the name tags on the table and Kevin's envelope of the name tags of marathoners who had called to say they weren't attending. There were no absentees named Sue.

Malone thanked the three Sues and sent them back to the ballroom. For the next twenty minutes he and Rhonda questioned Cassie, Helen, Veronica, Amy, Marge, Muffy, and the others. Did they see Sue after they left the Ladies' room? While they were there, did they see her give anything to Deirdre? Did she at any time stand close enough to Deirdre to put something into her pocket?

Two women said they thought they'd seen Sue in the ballroom after the shutdown. No one had seen her in proximity to Deirdre in the restroom or anywhere else. She'd left the Ladies' room before Deirdre did, said Muffy, who had walked behind Deirdre back to the lobby.

As each woman finished answering questions, she went back to the marathon. When they were all gone, Malone sat down heavily on a leather couch. He didn't want Rhonda to know how chagrined he was. If he'd had time to be more thorough when he first questioned the women, if he'd gotten descriptions when they couldn't recall names, if he'd drawn a diagram, he would have discovered sooner that he had not questioned all the women who were in the Ladies' room.

"If she was wearing a name tag, she made it herself," said Alex. "Not hard to do. The plastic shields you can get at any stationer's. The names are written with a green felt-tip pen."

"She must have been out here watching for the marathon to shut down. She went into the Ladies' room and waited," Malone said.

"Or she was in the marathon all along!" Rhonda cried. "After she gave Deirdre the capsule, she went back into the ballroom so she'd know Deirdre swallowed it."

"If she did that, we would have found her name tag at the dinner shutdown. She couldn't get out of the room without turning it in." Alex turned to Kevin. "You didn't report anything amiss with the tags."

Kevin turned scarlet. "Oh, God!"

"What's the matter? *Was* there something wrong with the name tags?"

"I swear to God, Alex, I didn't see how it could be important! I mean, one blank name tag—it just looked like an extra one got thrown into the basket, you know?"

"You found a *blank* tag in the basket? When?"

"After they went out on the dinner shutdown. I was counting them to line them up for when they came back. There were a hundred and ninety-nine tags. Louisa Evans had hers pinned on when she left. So did Deirdre, in a manner of speaking, you know? There was one extra. It was blank."

"Blank or empty?" Rhonda asked.

"Blank. The tag in the shield had no name written on it."

"She knew we'd pick up on a name tag with a false name. So she dropped a blank tag in the basket," said Alex. "She probably took care that it fell in upside down, so the assistant coach at the door didn't notice. She took the fake tag away with her. She got away with it, didn't she, Kevin? Why?" Alex's voice was very quiet.

Kevin shrank. His eyes actually filled. "Because I fucked up! I should've told you as soon as I found the blank. You would have known on Saturday we had an imposter!"

"As long as you know who's responsible, that's all that matters. Now if these detectives are finished with you, you can go back to the ballroom and do your job."

"We're finished," said Rhonda. They watched Kevin slouch across the lobby with his head hanging.

The three of them continued to sit on the leather couches. Malone absently shuffled the notecards in his hands. He had to say something to Rhonda—she'd done a hell of a job no matter how crazy and unorthodox it had been. She knew it, too. She was sitting there looking smug. Did she have any idea how much work this meant they had to do?

Where would they start? Obviously the same place they had before—hours and hours of questioning the marathoners. Now they had to ask if anyone besides the women in the Ladies' room had seen the woman who called herself Sue. How had she passed Deirdre the capsule?

He looked across the lobby to the bell captain who seemed to be frantically enjoying his job. He was handing brochures to tourists setting out from the hotel, he was answering his phone, he was waving for bellhops. He didn't miss much. Malone looked at the card that held the testimony he had taken from the bell captain last Saturday.

Rhonda was looking at him. She followed his gaze from the cards to the bell captain. "You see something—what is it?"

He heaved himself up from the couch. "I know how she did it!"

TWENTY-SEVEN

CERTAINLY, the bell captain said, he remembered Detective Malone. Certainly, he'd be glad to go over his answers to the questions he'd been asked last weekend, but he was pretty sure he didn't have anything new to say.

"You said that all the time Deirdre Doyle was in your sight in the lobby, no one came near her?"

"That's right. She was all alone until one of those assistant coaches, whatever they call them, came around the trees there to tell her it was time to go back in."

"She smoked a cigarette while you were watching her?"

"She was smoking one when I first saw her. She finished it, then she put it out in the roots of the tree there. Guess she didn't see the ashtray."

"Maybe she didn't want to see it."

"How's that, detective? I don't follow you."

Malone consulted his notecard. "You told me that another woman also put out a cigarette in the planter. Was that before or after Deirdre Doyle put out hers?"

"Before. She put it out and moved on just before Deirdre got to where she was standing while I was watching her."

"What did she look like—the woman who put out the cigarette?"

The bell captain considered. "Brown hair. Not a big woman, but not little, either, you know? Ordinary looking. Not like Deirdre with her green hair and all."

Role-playing had worked in the Ladies' room, they might as well try it here, too. "You watch while Detective Lord and I try to act it out. I'm the woman, she's Deirdre. You tell us if we've got it right, okay?"

The re-enactment required three takes before it was as the bell captain remembered. The woman had come from the direction of the Ladies' room. She had paused by the planter to fin-

ish a cigarette and put it out. She was not close enough for
to see the name on her tag. She had walked away just as Deir
dre came around the tree and took up her position. Yes, come
to think of it, Deirdre had put out her cigarette in just about the
same spot.

"And picked up the capsule," said Rhonda. "A wink, a nod
in the Ladies' room, maybe while they were both looking into
the mirror. Deirdre got the signal and followed her."

"Did you see where the woman went? Back toward the ballroom? Out the main door?" Malone asked.

"No, I'm sorry, I wasn't watching her then. I was so taken
by that Deirdre I couldn't look anywhere else!"

The ballroom door burst open. All the heads in the lobby
turned as Kevin Mulroy ran toward the little group by the bell
captain's desk. "Detective Malone!" he cried. He caught
Alex's warning eye. He stopped, panting in front of them, and
dropped his voice to an intense whisper. "You better come in
here, both of you," he said to the detectives. "There's a man
inputting right this minute who says he lied when you questioned him last Sunday. He says he did see Deirdre Doyle before the marathon."

Ten minutes later Malone was sitting at the desk in SUM's
weekend office, with Ernie Grimes across from him. Ernie was
rigid with fear. He was almost painfully preppy—Shetland
sweater, corduroy jeans, gray Nikes with socks the same pale
blue as the sweater. He could be a lawyer, a banker, a computer programmer.

They had questioned so many people that Malone could not
immediately recall the young man's face. That face was, at the
moment, gray under the eyes and white around the mouth.

Rhonda said, "Thanks for being willing to let us ask you
questions. We knew when Kevin told us what was going on that
you could be a big help to us." Ernie relaxed a trifle.

"Before we get started, may we have your full name and address?" Malone asked.

"I'm Ernie Grimes, and I . . ."

Ernie Grimes? Ernie's was one of the marathon data sheets
he'd pulled out because what Ernie wrote about himself
sounded like the guy could be hiding something. Tony had ex-

plained Ernie's problem with his sexual identity. He wrote down Ernie's name. "What do you want to tell us that you didn't say on Sunday?"

Ernie's hands clutched the sides of the chair. "Last Sunday you asked me if I'd ever seen Deirdre prior to the marathon. I said no. That was a lie. I did see her—the night before."

"Where?"

"It's a club, like, I go to it sometimes. It's called the Queen of Hearts. It's on Sixty-sixth Street, between First Avenue and York."

"And you saw Deirdre there Friday night?"

"Yes. When I saw her at the marathon on Saturday, I could hardly believe my eyes. But there was no mistake. She was, you know, distinctive?"

"Even dead she was that," Malone agreed. "Was she at the club as a customer?"

"Not exactly. I couldn't quite tell. She was taking pictures."

"Of the customers?"

"No. Of the musicians and the waiters mostly."

"Why didn't you tell me this on Sunday?"

Ernie twisted. His face reddened. "I was afraid you'd think..."

"Think what?" He had to force himself to be patient. Maybe he should have let Rhonda handle this.

"The Queen of Hearts has both kinds of customers, but it's mostly a gay bar, you know? And—I'm gay. Up until last Saturday at the marathon I hadn't, you know, come out, as they say. And Sunday, when you asked me about Deirdre, I didn't want to tell you I'd been at a gay bar. Some cops despise gays, you know? I wasn't ready to take the risk of you looking at me that way—disgusted, you know?"

Malone quickly made his face blank. "Look at me, Mr. Grimes."

"I am." Ernie's eyes met his quickly, then dropped.

"Do I look disgusted? Look at Detective Lord. Does she look disgusted?"

Ernie shot a glance at Rhonda. She flashed him a sympathetic smile. She said, "We're detectives, Mr. Grimes. We're investigating a murder. We need to know anything that will lead to the killer, and we don't care a lot where our information comes from. Detective Malone and I know that it takes guts to go to the police, especially if you didn't level the first time. So tell us now what you held back."

Ernie sighed. "The Queen of Hearts is a special kind of gay bar. It caters to men who like to dress up. They—I, I mean—wear women's clothes, wigs, makeup, perfume, the works. I know it sounds sick, but it's really—I mean we don't hurt anyone. We're not into the bizarre—we're into more like, glamour, you know? And we're not into pain or bondage or anything like that. So what's the harm in it?"

"You tell me," Malone said. Ernie paled. "What do you mean?"

"Why did you lie to me the first time? Why are you having such a hard time telling us now?"

"I was afraid you might think I killed Deirdre because she saw me there and might tell."

"Saw you there and took a picture of you, don't you mean?"

Ernie nodded miserably. "But even if she did, she wouldn't have known it was me when she saw me, you know, like this. I—we—all look entirely different. Plus the fact she was so high, sort of bopping around, bumping into tables, stuff like that. Her pictures couldn't be any good. You could tell by the way she handled the camera she wasn't a pro. She was giggling a lot, having a ball. I got the idea that she knew the lead guitar in the band. He kept yelling at her, and she yelled back, but the music was so loud you couldn't hear what they were saying."

"Tell me about the band."

Ernie rolled his eyes and shrugged expressively. "The worst! The pits! They couldn't play, and they were obscene beyond belief. The manager of the Queen was getting complaints from everyone. I mean, our dressing up is, you know, by your standards maybe, a little peculiar, but this guy in his wig, and those monks with dildos, calling themselves Heloise and the Abelards, I mean!"

Malone exchanged a quick glance with Rhonda. He had to fight a peculiar impulse to slap Ernie on the back and invite him out for a drink. "This is really important, and I want you to think carefully. Did you see anyone at this Queen of Hearts that you recognized—or that you would recognize if that person were wearing ordinary clothing?"

"No. We're very careful about our anonymity. We have special names, never give our real ones."

"Deirdre was taking pictures pretty indiscriminately, you said. Did you see her asking permission of the people she photographed?"

Ernie suddenly got it. "You think someone in the marathon . . . !"

Rhonda spoke up. "Think back, Mr. Grimes. Did you see anyone who was at the club, other than Deirdre, who was also in the marathon? Dressed in different clothes, wearing a different wig, made up to look older or younger, maybe?"

Ernie shook his head. "I really didn't. Besides, it would be hard to spot a person like that. We look so unlike our real selves, and we can be one person one time and have a totally different look the next."

"You said some of the patrons are straight."

"Yeah, they come mainly to watch—they hang out at the bar mostly. We go to the back room where the show is. They, like, watch us come in."

"Does the Queen cater only to male cross-dressers?"

"Sometimes we get a few women dressed like men. I don't remember any on Friday night."

"Did you see Deirdre leave the club?" Malone asked.

"I didn't actually see her leave, but I became aware that she wasn't there any longer."

"Any idea what time that was?"

"One-thirty, two."

"What time does the place close?"

"Three A.M. is the regular closing time."

"Did the band play the whole night?"

"They started about eleven-thirty. The manager threw them out right after they finished the first set. By popular demand. They were so bad we wouldn't put up with them any more."

"Describe this Heloise and the group."

"Heloise is very fair, skinny, light eyes. He was wearing a white dress and a long blond wig. Lots of eye makeup. The monks all looked like Rasputin—big and hairy. Two of them were white, one black."

"Did Deirdre and the lead guitarist leave together?"

"I couldn't say. I didn't see them go."

"You didn't see him without his costume?"

"Yeah, when he took it off, he was wearing a garter belt and black lace stockings. He didn't have a good body. No muscles except in his arms."

"I mean, you didn't see him in male clothing?"

"No, I didn't."

He thanked Ernie Grimes and told him he could return to the marathon. He listened, with a tolerance that surprised him, to Ernie's effusive expressions of relief and gratitude. Kevin came to escort Ernie back to the ballroom. Kevin walked beside Ernie as if they were linked by handcuffs.

When the door closed behind them, Malone looked inquiringly at Rhonda. She'd started this, he'd let her see where it had gotten them.

"Deirdre took a picture of someone in that club who didn't want to be photographed," she said. "He tried to snatch her camera on the subway platform. Slipped into the marathon in women's clothing and passed her poison to make sure she didn't tell anyone."

"Where's the film?"

"She left it at home. The killer searched her apartment after he was sure she was dead. He found it and destroyed it."

"Then you don't believe Louisa Evans's story that the apartment had been tossed before she got there?"

"Okay, I see what that means. Try it this way—the killer tossed the apartment *before* he killed Deirdre. He didn't find the film, so—disguised as Sue—he went to the hotel, gave Deirdre the capsule, went into the ballroom, and when they all went out for the dinner shutdown, he took Deirdre's bag from the table. Why didn't he take the camera while he was at it?"

"Too risky. Kevin says it was the only camera brought to the marathon. The killer was afraid someone would know it belonged to Deirdre."

"I bet he sighed all the way down to his socks when he read in the paper that there was no film in the camera."

"He already knew that. He had the film. It was in Deirdre's bag."

"Or it wasn't there, or in her apartment because she'd already left it to be developed."

"Or she gave it to Louisa Evans."

"You won't let her off the hook, will you?"

"I'll concede that she did not kill Deirdre. You and she proved me wrong. That was—uh—good work. But you tell me—do you think she's leveled with you all the way?"

Rhonda considered. "No," she said finally.

"She told Harvey she got all that about the men in Deirdre's life from Deirdre herself. Nothing about her source. What else did she get from Deirdre? What's she holding out?"

"I don't know."

"Maybe Deirdre wasn't so bombed Friday night that she didn't know what she was doing. Maybe she knew exactly. She said to the woman sitting beside her in the marathon, 'I've got a roll of film that's worth a lot of money to somebody. If anything happens to me, I want you to make sure it doesn't fall into the wrong hands,' something like that. Louisa saw a chance to make a buck."

Rhonda shook her head. "She doesn't seem the type for blackmail."

"She's writing a book. Think of the promotion—'sensational revelations—facts the police don't know—shocking pictures.' She left the marathon and went to Deirdre's apartment. I don't buy her story about her rendezvous on Rivington with the man who mugged her. She's too smart to agree to meet a man she knows is violent. She's lying about something. This new evidence clears her of murder, but it does not clear her of complicity."

"Can I tell her our play-acting worked?"

"Not yet. You don't have to lie, just don't call her. Let her sweat. She may call you again, ready to give us more."

"Who tried to kill Tony?"

"Whoever killed Deirdre thinks she told Tony something during their interface. You start the questioning in the marathon, I'll go to this Queen of Hearts and try to get a lead on Jack, a.k.a. Heloise, maybe a.k.a. Sue."

"If the guy gets off on wearing women's clothes, I wonder why he didn't want her to take his picture in black lace stockings and a garter belt."

The phone on Alex's desk rang. Malone picked it up.

"Yeah? Speaking." He listened to the brief message, and a sick sensation began in the pit of his stomach. "Be right there. Thanks. We better put out an alert—also notify the media." He hung up and looked at Rhonda. "Sixth Precinct has a death from cyanide poisoning. Guy swallowed a capsule he thought was an upper. They're holding his friend who called the ambulance."

TWENTY-EIGHT

SATURDAY AFTERNOON. Still no call from Jack.

Every time the phone rang, Louisa froze. She kept the machine on with the volume up so she could pick up if a call came through.

No call from Rhonda either. That meant one of two things. Either she had not been able to persuade Malone to stage the re-enactment, or they'd done it and found no one who remembered a woman who might have been Jack in drag.

Nothing was working for her. She'd pinned her hope on Rhonda Lord. Her last chance was a slim one—its outcome depended on Harvey. She would show him Deirdre's pictures. He had assigned them, he might see something in them that she'd missed. Or they might bring up in something for him, some anger or disgust that would break down his resistance to admitting he knew Jack.

He'd joked about the number one suspects' club, but surely he could see the advantage of clearing both of them of the suspicion of conspiracy. She didn't like Harvey, but now he was all she had.

Harvey was unreachable. He was either at Lenox Hill with his mother, or like her, he was at home with his phone machine on. She did not want to leave a message.

She would have to go to him.

Somewhere out there Jack was waiting for her. Behind those pale, mad eyes, his brain was busy devising another way to get the pictures. This time he would have to make sure he killed her—she knew what the pictures showed.

She had slipped an envelope to Dan and told him to say that she was out if anyone asked for her. Jack, with his flair for disguise, might appear in a form that got him past the doorman. Her locks would keep him out of her apartment, but he could lie in wait in the hall as he had done with Tony.

Her phone kept ringing. She listened to the messages. SUM was still begging her to come back. Hal reported that he was firming the contract for her book. No more calls from reporters, Deirdre's murder had ceased to be a sensation.

At five o'clock she hung up on Harvey's recording. She would wait no longer. Whatever happened was in her hands. She had no one to go out with her and protect her.

Her hands were icy as she dressed to go out, and she had to make herself breathe deeply. But the panic that last night had made her a helpless, frightened child was under control.

Just barely. She jumped when her phone rang again. Tony's voice. He spoke rapidly, urgently, as if he had to cram as much as he could into the allotted seconds, "The cops put a tap on my phone. That's why I cut you off last night. I'm in a phone booth. If you're there, for God's sake, pick up!"

She picked up.

TWENTY-NINE

BOTH THE DEAD MAN and the friend who had called the ambulance looked like throw-backs to the sixties. The corpse had a mane of thick, blond, dirty hair and a full beard. The smell of cyanide still hung around his mouth. He had died as Deirdre had died, swiftly, and in agony. An expired California driver's license in his wallet identified him as Robert Coates, of Long Beach.

His death-throes had been witnessed by his friend in a one room walkup on East Eighth Street. The furnishings consisted of two mattresses, three guitars, and a bass. The search of the premises had yielded a plastic bag of uppers and downers, a supply of grass, and the paraphernalia of serious drug users.

The friend twitched and sniffled. He clawed at his hair—a bushy Afro. He was wearing patched, worn jeans, a T-shirt printed with a picture of Ché Guevara, and a cast-off military fatigue jacket. He smelled.

He was clearly sorry now that he'd panicked and called for an ambulance. "Hey, man," he said to Malone, "this the kinda shit I get for bein' a Good Samaritan? You got nothin' on me— you gotta let me out of here. I'm in pain, man."

"Your name?"

"Darryl Johnson."

"Address?"

"I got no permanent address. I been hanging out with Bobby and the other dudes. We work together."

"What happened to Bobby?"

"He, you know, was feelin' down this morning—needed somethin' to rev him up—so he pops a black. Next thing I know he's chokin' and thrashin'! Shit, man, I never seen no one OD like that. I was scared outta my skull. I runs an' dials 911. Just my luck the medics come in four minutes an' they got cops tailin' them. I shoulda took off an' let the mother die."

"You may have done yourself a favor."

"Sittin' here with you ain't no favor. Man, I'm sick. Can't you see how bad off I is?"

"Where did Bobby get the black? You tell me straight, and I'll get you into detox today. You'll get medication to get you through the worst of it."

"A friend gave it to him. Don't know where he got it. The mother give us a bunch of stuff—blacks, yellows, bennies."

"Where can we find this friend?"

"I dunno. He split. We ain't seen him in a couple days. Man, you gotta let me outta here!" Saliva hung in strings from his mouth.

"The friend who gave you the pills—his name?"

"You gonna get me a fix, man? I'm gonna die!"

"His name?"

"His name's Jack. We a group—Jack, Bobby, Lester, an' me. We do rock. We got an act, you know? But Jack's split, I ain't seen Lester since Saturday, an' now Bobby's dead. An' I'm gonna be, man, if you don't...."

"Any idea where Jack is?"

"No, but I hope you find that motherfucker. I knowed he was up to somethin' Friday night—hanging out at the bar, talkin' to some dudes. He be actin' funny lately, talkin' about scoring big. That sucker was gettin' ready to shaft us. Only thing I don't dig—how come he hadda give us poison blacks?"

Malone's next stop was the Queen of Hearts, where the manager blanched when he saw Malone's shield. "This is about last Friday night, isn't it?"

The manager's name was George Schwebel. He looked like he should have been managing a hardware store in Queens, not a transvestite club on the Upper East Side.

"You've been expecting me?"

"That girl with green hair who died Saturday at the hotel. It's about her, right?" A dew of sweat had broken out on George's forehead.

"Tell me. Don't leave anything out."

George was more than ready. He'd been sitting on this so long he seemed relieved to pour it out. "Okay it's like this. She comes about eleven-thirty, says she's the lead guitar player's girl friend. Hell, maybe she was, maybe she wasn't. Maybe she was his boy friend. Dressed like that, who could tell? I don't discriminate, see? She pays the cover, she comes in. Next thing I know she's taking pictures of the band. That's no problem, except some of my customers are getting uptight, you know? Like they were afraid they might accidentally get into the picture. Some of them are what you might call sensitive. So I was about to tell her to put the camera the fuck away or get out, when the lead guitar starts yellin' at her to cut out the picture taking. She yells back at him and laughs and holds the camera up like she's snapping him. He's playing, see, he can't leave the stage in the middle of his number, so I see I gotta put a stop to this. I goes over an' tells her to leave. She's pretty pissed, says a lot of rough things, gives me the finger, but she goes.''

"What time was that?"

"One-thirty, about."

"Anyone follow her out?"

"Not that I saw. Some customers did leave about that time, though. They were pissed-off about the band. That band was a mistake I do not intend to repeat, believe me.''

"Why did you book them?"

"I was in a bind, see? The act I lined up got sick. Guys who come here, they like a certain type entertainment—impersonators, drag dancers. I mean, don't get me wrong, I got no prejudices. The guy who got sick on me says he knows a Jack Janyck who's got a group that dresses up, you know? And they play some pretty good rock. So I get hold of the guy, and he's free that night. I shoulda known—no good act is available on short notice on a Friday night. So they came, and they played—tried to play, I shoulda said. And their act, I mean, this ain't no *Cage Aux Folles*, but I got standards. There's kinky that's like, artistic, you know? And there's kinky that's disgusting. They didn't get into that until the second set. That's when I cut them off, told them to pack it. Had to give out free champagne to calm down the clientele. The evening cost, believe me!''

"How long after the girl left did the musicians leave?"

"Half an hour, maybe."

Malone showed him the picture of Deirdre taken in the morgue. "This her?"

The manager's sallow face turned an ashy yellow. "Christ. Yeah, that's her. I knew it as soon as I read the Sunday papers."

"So why didn't you come forward?"

"I figure I'm in up to here." The manager made a gesture across his throat. "First there's her with her camera, I mean hell, she coulda been an FBI agent. Then he strips down to his skivvies and does this gross act with his monks. And between sets, he—Heloise he called himself—is tryin' to talk between sets to some guys at the bar I don't like the looks of. Like I say, I got no prejudices, but I draw the line at dealers. They wanna do business, they do it in someone else's bar."

From habit more than anything else, he showed the manager Louisa's picture. George looked at it admiringly. "Transvestite? Or cross-over?"

"Neither, far as I know."

"Then you've got to be kidding. No one like that comes into the Queen."

THIRTY

RHONDA HAD ASKED the question so many times, the words came automatically to her lips. "Did you see or talk to a brown-haired, brown-eyed woman named Sue at any time in the marathon on Saturday?"

The negative answers seemed to come automatically, too. So much that she was surprised when Stan remembered the brown-haired woman whose name tag said Sue. He'd been sitting beside her when the marathon logged-on after the bathroom shutdown.

In SUM's weekend office on the mezzanine of the Park Summit, Rhonda was questioning Stan. Sue had not said anything to him, Stan said. She'd stood up to look during the commotion when it was evident that Deirdre had collapsed, but she had shown no emotion different from anyone else's. She had seemed fidgety during the long wait before the police let the marathon start up again, but who didn't? Two hours later they'd been let out to go to dinner. Marathoners never took the same seats twice, he did not see Sue again.

It wasn't much, but it did establish that Sue had gone back into the ballroom to see that her capsule did its work.

Stan was aghast. "You think this Sue person gave Deirdre the poisoned capsule? And shot Tony too?"

"That's the approach we're working on now. You see why we want to identify her."

"Yeah, wow, sorry I can't help you."

She thanked Stan, sent him back with the ever-hovering Kevin. Her watch said four-fifteen. She'd had nothing but coffee since breakfast. She needed a shutdown. She'd go out and walk around and get something to eat. This kind of questioning was a drag. Today she envied Malone his right, as senior partner, to choose to do the legwork. He'd called to tell her that he'd gotten what they needed from the manager of the

Queen of Hearts, and he was on his way to see Tony Cazzine at Roosevelt Hospital.

This morning she'd felt good. The plan she and Louisa had devised had worked beyond their wildest dreams. How it must have griped Malone to have to admit she'd done good work. He'd almost choked saying it. She wondered how long she would put up with this man. Expediency had made them a team, but they would never have a partnership.

Malone didn't want her to tell Louisa that the performance in the Ladies' room had succeeded. That was unfair, even cruel. Louisa was desperate. Wouldn't she be more likely to give up what she was holding back if she knew her innocence had been proved?

She was tired of lies. SUM's philosophy must be rubbing off on her. She would tell James Malone she wanted out of the partnership. She would tell the captain what to do when he brought up the bullshit about how important their team was to public relations. She'd...

The phone rang. A message from Detective Santos, one of the men Malone had sent to investigate the people who lived at the address on the paper in Deirdre's pocket. Apartment 7A, one of the largest and most expensive in the building, was owned by Vivian Wardley, Harvey's mother. She was not in residence at present because, the doorman informed him, she was in the hospital.

Before she dialed Roosevelt, Rhonda dialed another number. She wasn't going to hold out any longer on Louisa. But Louisa did not answer her phone.

THIRTY-ONE

LOUISA DRESSED CAREFULLY in tailored slacks, a white silk shirt, and a cardigan. She did not want to intimidate Harvey, who was a little shorter than she, so she wore flats.

She said good-bye to Dan at the door and stepped cautiously out onto the sidewalk. She looked up and down Eighty-first Street. No loiterers of either sex. She walked over to Fifth Avenue. As she had the night before when she went out to meet Rhonda, she let three cabs pass before she waved one down. It would be a long time before she went down into the subway again. Not until Deirdre's murderer had been arrested and could no longer be waiting for her on the platform.

If Deirdre's murderer was caught. Rhonda still had not called, nor had Jack. Deirdre's pictures were in her bag again. She'd left the negatives in her desk. If Harvey didn't agree to tell the police he knew Jack and help them locate him, she would have to give Rhonda the pictures and take her chances.

Harvey didn't have as much to lose as she did. He was completely free of suspicion of giving Deirdre the poison, much as he'd wanted her out of his life. Still, she thought, if he'd been angry enough, he could have acted in collusion with Jack. What if they'd planned this together?

She felt as if she was grasping at wisps of possibilities, nothing solid. There had to be an answer to the puzzle of the capsule! There had to be a way to prove Jack had gotten into the restroom and given it to Deirdre.

She drew a deep breath. Nothing had changed for her since the phone call from Tony. She was still under suspicion of murder, and she still had to save herself. Inside, everything had changed. Tony believed she was innocent. He was on her side.

In a few days he could leave the hospital. They could be somewhere by themselves. Not the hotel—she never wanted to go there again. Her apartment. She wanted to know him better. What was he like when he wasn't in his role of coach? Maybe she was ready to take a risk. She was attracted to him. She knew so little about him—his experiences had been so different from hers. Vietnam. Recovery from addiction. SUM was his life and his career. Even the fact that his home was in California made him seem alien.

A week ago she'd despised him. She'd wanted to discredit him and SUM publicly. What she'd been through the past few days had shocked her out of all the fixed ideas she'd ever had, as if everything in her head had been shaken up and thrown out. She was still wandering about among the pieces. The new pattern had not fallen into place yet. Maybe it never would. Maybe that was what SUM was all about—being open to the new and the unexpected popping up in life.

But no matter how open to the unexpected she became she wanted no more Deirdres, no more Jacks, and no more Malones, suspecting her of murder.

She paid the driver and got out of the cab in front of Harvey's building. Its plain brick facade made it look like an Amish cousin among the curving fronts of the brownstones in this part of Chelsea.

Tony had been furious when she told him she was going to talk with Harvey. She had treated the expedition very lightly. In his anger, Tony couldn't help her; having him worry about her wouldn't do either of them any good.

She took a deep breath. "Oh, God, please let this work!" She blinked back a sudden attack of tears. This weepiness was so unlike her! She was coming unraveled.

She opened the door of Harvey's building. While she was studying the names beside the bells, the door opened behind her. "Can I help you—are you looking for someone?"

"Harvey Wardleigh," Louisa said. "Do you know which apartment he's in?"

The woman stared at her. Her face had a slightly stunned look. Louisa was used to seeing that expression. Her work brought her into contact with so many people that she frequently got an "I know I know you but I don't remember where or when" look from strangers.

Odd though, that she felt the same way. She'd seen this woman before, and very recently.

Then Louisa laughed. In her raw emotional state, she had gone from tears to euphoria in a matter of minutes. "I know you!" she cried. "You're in the marathon. You were in the Ladies' room. We shared a space at a wash basin, remember?"

THIRTY-TWO

Tony was in his bathrobe taking shuffling steps around his room.

"You supposed to be doing that?" Malone growled.

"Doctor's orders. I get out of here on Monday."

"Out of the hospital, maybe, but not out on the street until we get whoever aimed at you. Don't get any ideas about going back to California."

Tony gave a small groan and eased himself back onto the bed. Some of the stitches had been taken out of his face, leaving angry red scars. "What's happening?" he asked.

"Looks like you had an imposter in the marathon."

"The hell we did!"

"Probably a man dressed in women's clothes. She—he—apparently left the capsule in a planter in the lobby where Deirdre picked it up. A plain-looking woman with brown hair and eyes. Her name tag said Sue. You remember her?"

Tony shook his head. "I interfaced with a blond Sue with her hair in a braid on Sunday, but no brown-haired Sue, no."

"Saturday, this would have been. When she left, she put a blank name tag in the basket."

"Louisa is cleared?"

"Of giving Deirdre the capsule, maybe. We still have to find this guy and prove he did it."

"But Louisa still stands suspected of complicity, conspiracy, lying, evasion—what else?" Tony sat up. "You've put her through hell!"

"I'm not going to argue this with you again! One step at a time. Do you or don't you want to know what we've got?"

The phone on the bedside table rang. Tony answered it, handed it to Malone. "Rhonda Lord."

"What's up?" Malone asked, taking the phone.

Rhonda's voice was puzzled. "That address in Deirdre's pocket? It's where Harvey Wardleigh's mother lives."

"Like maybe she and Harvey had a date to meet there while his mother was in the hospital?"

"Puts a different light on Harvey's insistence his affair with Deirdre was over, doesn't it?"

"Meet me in front of his apartment in twenty minutes."

When Malone hung up, Tony was scowling. "What was that all about?"

"Don't know yet. That slip of paper in Deirdre's pocket—it was Harvey's mother's address."

"I'm going down there with you." Tony swung his legs over the side of the bed.

"What for? You get back in there!"

"Louisa is on her way to Wardleigh's apartment right now."

"How the hell do you know that?"

"I wanted to talk with her without eavesdroppers. I called her from the pay phone in the lounge."

"What time?"

"Five o'clock. She was just leaving. She doesn't know there was an imposter. She still thinks you believe she's guilty. She thinks Harvey knows this Jack, and she's going to try to get him to tell her where Jack hangs out."

"Oh, Jesus, he's the one! Deirdre's ex-lover, just like she said in the marathon. 'Pissed-off' about her taking pictures Friday night in a club for queers. Deirdre may have snapped his picture while he was talking with some dealers. His name is Jack Janyck—he does a drag act. One of his buddies just bought it with a cyanide-laced amphetamine capsule, which I hope to God aren't being handed out all over the city."

Tony shuffled from the bed to the locker. He opened it and began to pull out his rumpled, bloodstained clothes. "I'm going with you."

Malone kept his face tight. He hoped Tony would never find out that he'd kept back from Louisa the success of the Ladies' room drama. If he'd let Rhonda call her, she wouldn't be out looking for Jack on her own. "The hell you are! Get back in that bed. I don't want to have to worry about you, too."

"Then don't." Tony had tossed off his robe and was already pulling on his pants.

THIRTY-THREE

"LOUISA EVANS? Of course!" The woman smiled delightedly. "Now I know who you are. You're the one who was sitting next to Deirdre! Tell me, have you been back to the marathon?"

"No, have you?"

"I stayed the rest of that day, but that was enough for me! What are you doing here? Did you come to see Harvey about something connected with the murder?"

"More or less," said Louisa. She had found Harvey's bell, 5A, and she was pressing it. "But he doesn't seem to be at home."

"He's not. He's a—at the hospital with his mother. You know how ill she is?"

"Yes, he told me. Forgive me if I'm out of line, but are you a good friend of Harvey?"

"You might say that. I live with him. My name's Sue."

"Oh." Louisa tried not to let her surprise show on her face while she did a hasty reappraisal of her known facts about Harvey. She wondered how much this woman knew about Harvey's involvement with Deirdre.

Sue laughed. "In case you're wondering, Harvey and I have no secrets! He'll be home soon. Why don't you come up and have a drink with me while you wait for him? You can tell me what's going on with the investigation." She unlocked the door.

"I don't know the latest. I've been ducking detectives for days."

"So has Harvey!"

In the elevator Louisa covertly studied Sue. A woman less like Deirdre could hardly be imagined. She was in her late thirties, Louisa guessed, and she was decidedly plain. She obviously took pains with her appearance, however. Her brown hair was so carefully coifed that she must have just come from a beauty salon, and her face expertly made up. Her eyes were brown too, as were her brows and lashes. In high heels, she was about Louisa's height.

Sue unlocked the door of 5A. It opened directly into the living room. She turned on lights and said, "Sit down and be comfortable. I'll change quickly, and then I'll fix us a drink." She disappeared into a bedroom beyond.

Louisa looked around. Either Sue had not been living with Harvey long enough to make her mark on his surroundings, or she had as little individuality as he did. The room was decorated in Bloomingdale trendy, masculine version. She wondered if the terribly arty photographs of nude males were Harvey's work, and if they reflected his taste or Sue's.

She heard the sound of running water, then the toilet flushed. The bathroom was off the bedroom. In a few minutes Sue came back wearing Calvin Klein jeans and a purple sweatshirt. She had changed from high heels to a pair of running shoes. Her figure was angular and slim, and she had an enviable bustline. "What'll you have, Louisa—wine, Scotch, gin?"

"Nothing alcoholic, thanks. Anything else will do." She didn't want to cloud her mind. She was going to have to be very persuasive. If she could enlist Sue, she might have a better chance at cooperation from Harvey.

Sue pulled open a louvered door that ran across the end of the living room. A minimal kitchen was behind it. She busied herself with taking ice trays from a playhouse size refrigerator, getting out glasses, reaching under the sink for a bottle of ginger ale.

"Do you know anything new from the police?" Sue asked. She handed Louisa her ginger ale and passed over a cocktail napkin from a pile on the chrome and glass coffee table.

"Not from them. But on Wednesday when Harvey and I were driving back from Scranton, we talked about the possibility that Deirdre had taken pictures so incriminating that someone killed her to keep them from being shown."

"Yes, Harvey told me about that. The police haven't found the pictures, have they?"

"They haven't, but I have."

"Really!" Sue cried. "And are they—incriminating, I mean?"

"Not at all. At least I can't see anything. I've got them with me, but I'd like to wait until Harvey comes to show them to you."

"Of course." Sue smiled. "He'll be really interested. Here, let me get you some more ice. Those little cubes melt so fast." She reached for Louisa's glass and lifted it from the coffee table. The glass slid through her fingers and landed with a crash on the edge of the table. Ice and ginger ale splashed into Louisa's lap. Louisa jumped to her feet.

"Oh my God!" Sue cried. "My hand was wet. Louisa, I'm so sorry! Go right into the bathroom and sponge off your pants. Ginger ale makes stains. Help yourself to a towel." She swabbed at the glass table top with the wad of napkins.

Louisa's ginger ale had needed no more ice. Sue had deliberately let the glass slide.

Sue wanted the pictures. She did not want to wait for Harvey. Louisa stood in a moment's frozen indecision. As soon as her back was turned, Sue would be into her bag. If she picked up the bag and took it into the bathroom with her, as if she wanted to fix her face, would Sue realize why she was doing it?

Too late. The bag was lying on the couch. Between it and Louisa was Sue, who was on her knees picking up ice cubes.

"I can use a kitchen towel," Louisa said. She was beginning to have deep misgivings. This woman was trying to manipulate her. She walked over to the kitchen, took up a towel from the counter, and dabbed at her pants. From the kitchen she could see into the bedroom. It was as austere as the living room. Sue's dress and pantyhose, flung on the queen-size bed that almost filled the little room, and a tidy line-up of cosmetics on top of the chest of drawers, were the only signs the room had occupants. The mirror above the chest reflected what could be seen of the bathroom through the open door.

What could be seen was the toilet. The seat was up.

Sue was still on her knees. She had stopped picking up ice, she was looking at Louisa's bag. Louisa's hand paused in the act of blotting ginger ale from her pants. They were figures in a freeze-frame. In a second, action would resume. In that still moment Louisa saw what she had not seen before.

The careful coiffure was a wig. Eyebrows and lashes were darkened. Harvey's pale irises were concealed by brown contact lenses. The shapely bust was padding.

In the Ladies' room, Sue had come out of the toilet Louisa went into. Louisa had been too urgently in need to wonder why she'd found the seat up. Sue had stood at the basin until Deirdre came out. Somehow, Harvey, in the guise of Sue, had contrived to pass Deirdre the poisoned Darvon.

Louisa's eyes were still locked with Harvey's. The silence seemed to scream. Louisa felt the blood draining from her face. They'd all been conned—she, Rhonda, Malone. Now she was in terrible danger. She must not lose her wits the way she'd lost her powers of observation. Her only hope lay in not letting Harvey know that she had finally seen through his disguise. Tony knew where she was going, but he had no inkling that she was walking into danger. No one was going to come to her rescue. She had to get herself out of this.

Louisa was the first one to move. She put the towel back onto the counter and said, "Thanks a lot, Sue, I don't think I'll wait any longer for Harvey. Have him call me, will you? We'll all get together and look at these pictures." She had to keep thinking of this person as Sue. That was the only way she'd keep her voice neutral.

She took the first casual steps back toward the couch and her bag.

Sue seemed not to have heard. Her back was still to Louisa. Then she reached, not for Louisa's bag, but under the brown tweed cushion of the couch. In one motion, she stood up and turned around. In her hand she had a gun.

She kept her eyes on Louisa and leaned down. With the other hand, she picked up Louisa's bag. She shook it, weighing it, and then as if satisfied it wasn't heavy enough to hold a weapon, she tossed it underhand toward Louisa. It landed at her feet.

"Pick it up, Louisa. Open it. Take out the pictures and throw them over here." The face was still Sue's, but the voice was Harvey's.

Louisa did as she was told. The thick packet of pictures landed with a thud on the coffee table.

"Negatives there too?"

"No," said Louisa. "I've been stupid, but not that stupid. I put them in the mail last night, addressed to Detective Malone. He probably has them right now."

"You're lying," Harvey said.

Louisa could feel sweat breaking out on her body. When Harvey opened the pictures and looked at them now, he'd realize how little he had to lose. If he'd been in that club and was afraid Deirdre had gotten a picture of him, he would fear no longer. Louisa's one chance to control her fate would be lost.

"The bitch threatened to tell my mother what she and I and Jack were into. Mother has very firm ideas about sexual propriety. She also has a lot of money. I'm her only heir. She would call her lawyer and cut me out of her will in two minutes if she had any hint of the way I choose to live my life."

Sue's face and Harvey's voice. The unreality was making Louisa dizzy. So was the absolute reality of the gun. She wondered if she was going to pass out. And what Harvey would do if she did.

"I was prepared to pay Deirdre off until Mother died, or until she went into a coma and couldn't change her will. But when Deirdre came into that club Friday night with her camera, I knew it was more than coincidence—it was fate. Deirdre was meant to die, and I was meant to kill her. She probably didn't recognize me then, but she would have when she looked at her pictures sober. We used to dress up a lot—she'd seen me in drag, though never in this particular persona."

"You went to the marathon as Sue."

"Yes. I slipped Deirdre the capsule after we came out of the Ladies' room. Left it in a planter in the lobby. She came along and picked it up. I went back to the marathon, saw what happened. Deirdre thought she and I had a date to meet at my mother's apartment after the marathon shut down on Saturday. In case she didn't take the capsule at the marathon, I planned to walk her down to the terrace there at the end of East Fifty-ninth Street and persuade her to take something to calm herself. I'd left doctored capsules—different kinds—in her bathroom stash. It was only a matter of time. But Mother was in full possession of her marbles after she came out of the operation, and if Deirdre managed to get to her, my inheritance was out the window."

"You tried to get her camera from her on Friday night," Louisa said. If she kept him talking, he might get it all out. Then she might be able to get him to be reasonable.

"She was bombed as usual, but not too bombed to fight to keep herself from being pushed onto the tracks. I couldn't be sure the camera would be destroyed by the train when she was, so I gave that up. In the morning, after I knew she'd left for the marathon, I went into her apartment to look for the film. I left the insurance capsules in the bathroom. Then I visited my mother for a couple of hours. After that I went home, put on my Sue face and clothes, and went to the Park Summit to wait for the marathon to shut down for pee time."

"Did you take Deirdre's bag from the table?"

"That was easy—I took it when they broke for dinner. Picked her little kid's bag with the doggie on it off the pile and slipped it into mine. There was such a crowd at the table no one noticed. But I was afraid to go for the camera. It was at the bottom of the pile. I didn't want to rummage for it for fear one of those beady-eyed assistant coaches remembered the camera was hers."

"Did you try to get my bag from me last night on the subway platform? You almost killed me, too!"

Harvey grinned. "I've been following you around for days, Louisa. In fact, I've just come from your apartment! I followed you and watched you get into a cab. Then I got a cab myself and came home. Imagine my surprise when I found you here!"

Louisa brought her hands up to her face. She was going to faint.

The gun pointed purposefully. "Sit down! I don't want you keeling over on me. You're going to show me those pictures."

Louisa's knees gave out. She sat down heavily on the couch. Harvey remained standing with the gun aimed. Her limbs were like jelly, and her mind seemed to have deserted her.

"Like I said, Louisa, I started following you as soon as I let you out of the car at the SUM office on Wednesday. I parked my car in a garage, and I waited for you to come out. And I soon found out something very interesting—I wasn't the only person following you!"

She raised her head. "Jack!"

"It all made sense then. You see, when I searched Deirdre's apartment Saturday morning, I didn't find the film. The police reported that the camera was empty. That meant she'd left it to be developed. Or she hid it someplace. Or she gave it to someone. Your theory about Deirdre's death was so close to the mark that I was sure she had given the film to you. And when I saw Jack Janyck following you too, I knew it. He was pretty desperate to get hold of it too, but I think for different reasons. He was meeting with some unsavory looking types at the bar that night—I suspect they weren't too pleased at Deirdre's indiscriminate photography."

She roused herself. "Jack was the one who mugged me in Deirdre's apartment. He got my name and my address from my wallet. He thought Deirdre had given me the film, too. She hadn't. What she'd given me was the claim slip for it. She wrote her address on it in the marathon. I didn't realize what it was until Wednesday."

"So Jack was following you, and I was following Jack following you." Harvey gave a chuckle. "Yesterday you picked up the pictures at the shuttle platform. He followed you onto the train. So did I. He got lost in the crowd on the uptown IRT, but I got close enough to cut the strap of your bag. How you kept hold of it, I'll never know!"

"You tried to kill me."

"That wasn't my intention. Not then. All I wanted was the pictures. And now I've got them."

"Did you kill Jack? He hasn't called me today."

"I left enough cyanide-filled capsules in Deirdre's bathroom to kill quite a few users. The police report said that no drugs were found, they thought the search was drug-related. If Jack took them, and I'm sure he did, he's bound to swallow one sooner or later."

Up until now, in Louisa's benumbed state, she'd listened to Harvey as if he were discussing the plot of a suspense novel he had written. Now horror got through to her. She was sure he could see it in her face.

Suddenly she saw something in his face, too. Harvey was beginning to show through the face of Sue, the way an old painting reveals its secrets when restoration cleans away the top layer of paint. She could see the peevish creases around his mouth under the heavy makeup. She could see now the faint shadow of his beard.

"You were involved—made love—with Deirdre. And with him too? And you could kill them both with no feeling, no pity...?"

"I didn't kill them, Louisa. Their own addictions killed them. As for making love—I never 'made love' with either of them. What a naive little romantic you are! It's called sex, and it was my addiction as strongly as cocaine was Jack's. And I got off it cold turkey the instant Deirdre wondered out loud what my mother would think of our little games. You don't understand, Louisa. I'd have done anything to keep that slut away from my mother. My mother is worth a cool two million, plus a co-op on Sutton Place! It's all mine if I can keep undefiled my image as her straight and dutiful son!"

Louisa's brain began to work again. She was alone with this killer, who was more than a little mad, and she had only one more card to play. It wasn't a strong one.

"Look at the pictures, Harvey," she begged. "You know what a terrible photographer she was. No way could anyone recognize you or anyone else from those pictures. You have nothing to fear from them. Or from me. Deirdre's dead. If you're right about Jack, he's dead, too. We'll make an agreement we'll never reveal what went on in this room, and we'll destroy the pictures and the negatives."

Harvey smiled. "Nice try, Louisa. But, to use the cliché appropriate to this situation, you know too much. We're going to wherever you have those negatives and retrieve them. Then we're going to Staten Island."

"Staten Island!"

"Have you ever been to Tottenville, Louisa? Very scenic. Parts of it look like the forest primeval. You'll never believe you're in New York City. Sandy roads lead off into the woods and then to the dark, deserted shores of the outer bay. That's where we're going. So pick up your bag and put on your coat."

"I wasn't lying about the negatives. They're in the mail."

He considered. The dark contacts gave his eyes an opaque, glassy look. "Get up, Louisa. Come over here." He backed away to keep her in range. "Kneel down there beside the coffee table and lay those pictures out where I can see them."

She did as she was told. As she knelt down and began to pull the pictures from the envelope, she heard him skin off the wig. She sensed the movement he made to drop the contact lenses from his eyes. He was rubbing his face to get off the makeup, first with one hand, then the other. She could hear the rasp of his palms against his whiskers. When the pictures were on the table, he stood behind her with the gun only inches from her head. She wondered what was going through his mind when he saw how worthless the pictures were and realized what a price he had paid for them.

"I'd do it again," he said in answer to her unspoken thought, "and now I know the negatives are no threat either. Thanks." She looked up. Harvey's sandy hair and pale eyes were strange with dark penciled eyebrows, but he'd gotten off most of the foundation and blusher and lipstick. He gestured with the gun. "Put your jacket on. Pick up your bag. We're leaving."

When they emerged from his building, he took her arm. She could feel the gun poking into her ribs underneath the bulky sleeve of her down jacket. They walked close together like lovers on their way to cocktails and dinner. Harvey managed, while keeping the gun on her, to shrug into a windbreaker.

Louisa took a quick look around.

"Keep your face to the front!" Harvey hissed. "And if we pass any cops, you look at me and smile."

There were no cops. If Tony had told Malone, the detective had left her to her fate, thinking she was in no danger from Harvey.

She was not going to be rescued. Only Louisa Evans could save herself. It was a forty minute drive to where they were going, Harvey said. She had that much time to think of something.

His car was parked on Nineteenth Street. "You're going to drive while I hold the gun on you, so you do exactly as I tell you." He gave her the keys. "Unlock the passenger side. Get in and slide over."

She drove down West Street along the river. The lights from New Jersey shimmered on the cold, dark water of the Hudson. Ahead, the twin towers of the World Trade Center knifed the sky. Soon she could see the Statue of Liberty imprisoned in scaffolding. How could she have thought Deirdre's city scenes banal and trite? She had never seen anything so beautiful in her life.

"Head for the tunnel," said Harvey. "We won't take the ferry." He sounded almost regretful. Except for terse orders— "Turn left, pass that Honda, get over"—he had said nothing since they started out. The gun, in his right hand, was resting on his left arm.

She wondered what he was thinking. He'd killed two people indirectly, through poison they had taken themselves. He'd tried to kill Tony. Was he thinking now how he would make sure, this time, that his victim didn't survive?

She would start talking, try to engage his attention. "Do you have a permit for that gun?"

"Yes, I do. I got it last year when I was robbed at gunpoint in my building. So they won't get me on weapons possession!"

"Why did you shoot Tony?"

He laughed, the same forced way he had during their ride back from Scranton. "I've been wondering when you would ask me that! Can't you guess? I wanted to divert suspicion from

me to you. When you welcomed me to the number one suspects club, I began to figure how I could make sure that you
were the 'number one' number one, if you get what I mean. So
I dressed up and perfumed up and went to the Park Summit
and waited for him. I swished around, and I did not aim to kill.
Tony Cazzine had to be alive to tell the police his assailant was
female. I'm not a poor shot, Louisa—especially at close range.
Does that explain everything for you? I know how important
it is for you writers to tidy up everything in the last chapter.
And this is the last chapter, Louisa.''

He would make her turn off the highway onto a road that ran
out into a sandy lane through trees and scrub. They would drive
without lights so they didn't attract attention. He would tell her
when to stop. Then he would tell her to get out of the car. He
would get out, too. He would make her walk ahead of him. She
would feel the cold, salt air on her face. She would hear the lap
of waves on the beach. Her feet would sink into sand. She
would smell the sea.

And she would die.

The Toyota entered the bright tile tube of the Brooklyn-
Battery Tunnel. Traffic was moderate, flowing along with no
bunching. She looked in the rearview mirror. A car was close
behind them. It was not a police car.

She glanced at the gun. There was no way she could grab it
while she was driving. They would have an accident, and the
gun would go off. They would have to slow for the toll booth.
That might be her only chance. Whatever happened, she would
not make it easy for him. If the end came, and she was on the
beach with the gun at her back, at least she would scream and
run.

Deirdre was dead. Jack was dead. She would be dead soon.
And Harvey's mother would soon be dead too, and her will
would leave everything to Harvey.

They were out of the tunnel now and moving into the broad,
glaring plaza where the lines of traffic fanned out to the toll
booths. The gun poked her sharply. ''On the other side of the
toll, get onto the expressway. We're going to the Verrazzano
Bridge.''

A horn honked sharply. Louisa veered. "Watch it, will you!" Harvey shouted.

Suddenly Louisa began to cry. Tears spilled out of her eyes and rolled down her cheeks. The bright lights blurred. She blinked. Blindly she headed for a lane that lead to a toll booth.

THIRTY-FOUR

AN UNMARKED POLICE CAR driven by Detective James Malone had just double-parked across the street from Harvey Wardleigh's building when the door of that building opened. Harvey Wardleigh and Louisa Evans came out. Harvey looked up and down the street. Then, arm in arm, they turned and walked toward Ninth Avenue.

"What the hell?" cried Tony from the back seat.

Malone gave a grunt of satisfaction. "Looks like they're a lot friendlier than they let on. We've got a whole new ballgame!"

Rhonda tapped on the car window. Malone reached and opened it. "We picked up the wrong ex-lover, man!" she said. "He's got a gun on her. I saw it when he took her arm. I was in the entrance to the basement apartment in the building next door. They didn't see me."

"We'll stay out of sight until we see where they're going." Malone got on the radio, calling for another unmarked car to rendezvous and follow them.

At the corner, Harvey and Louisa turned onto Ninth Avenue and went north.

"Hell!" Tony cried. "One way the wrong way!"

"I'll follow them on foot," Rhonda said. "You go around the block. Pick me up at Ninth and Nineteenth, northeast corner. If I'm not there. . . ."

It took an agonizing four minutes for them to go down, over, up Eighth, and back to Ninth. Rhonda slipped out of a doorway at the corner. "They're halfway up the block. Just got into a gray Toyota. He gave her the keys and stood behind her with his hand in his jacket pocket while she opened the door on the passenger side. He waited until she had slid over to the driver's seat, then he got in. There they go!"

The Toyota slid through the intersection of the yellow light and turned onto Ninth Avenue. When the light changed, Malone eased away from the curb and followed. Another car slid in behind them. He radioed them to keep pace.

The Toyota, with Louisa at the wheel, turned right at Fourteenth Street and continued across town to West Street, the road along the river that carried traffic all the way from midtown to the Battery. It turned south.

"What are you going to do?" Tony demanded. He was hunched over as the motion of the car aggravated the pain in his ribs, and he was furious at his helplessness. This was no dream. Louisa was in terrible danger, and he could only watch.

"We follow until they stop, or until they do something that warrants a chase. Then we'll make an assessment. We don't want him to panic. Or her either. In an accident, a gun usually goes off."

The three cars were no longer in line. Two cars had come between the police cars and the Toyota. "Not taking the Holland," said Rhonda when the Toyota passed Canal Street. The lighted towers of the World Trade Center loomed ahead of them.

"Don't lose them!" Tony begged.

Malone stepped up the speed and passed the two cars that were between them and the Toyota. When the road dipped into the Brooklyn-Battery Tunnel, they were right behind them. He could not see the back of Louisa's head because of the Toyota's headrest, but he tried to will her to look into the rearview mirror, to see that he was with her. But, of course, even if she did look back, she would not be able to distinguish the faces in the car behind.

Louisa had been driving smoothly, competently, at a safe speed. So far no sign of panic showed in her handling of Harvey's car. But at the Brooklyn end of the tunnel, where the traffic spread out to go through the toll booths, she seemed to falter. She veered into the lane of an oncoming truck and swerved hastily back into line when the driver honked his horn.

"They don't seem to know whether to go into the exact change lane or the manned lane," Malone said. He had to drop back until she made her choice. He radioed for all available units to come to the scene. By the time Louisa settled for an exact change lane, another car had slipped in front of them. They were now two cars behind her. Three cars were ahead of her. They inched forward. They stopped. Arms reached out to throw coins or tokens into the metal basket. The gate rose, the car passed through, the gate came down again.

The Toyota reached the gate. It stopped. Nothing happened. The window did not roll down. Louisa's arm did not come out to throw the toll into the basket.

"What's she doing? What's going on?" Tony cried.

The car ahead of them slipped forward. Its driver was leaning on his horn. Behind them a car tried to get out of the line and couldn't. Its frustrated driver leaned on his horn also. A cacophony of blasts began. The man in the car ahead stuck his head out the window and yelled something they could not hear.

Louisa's hand came out the window. She flung coins at the basket. In a second the gate would go up.

It didn't.

"Let's go!" said Malone. "We won't get another chance as good as this one." He called to the car behind them to back them up. Then he stopped the engine. He reached for the gun in his shoulder holster and put one hand on the door handle. On her side of the car, Rhonda pulled her gun from her bag.

Malone looked back at Tony. "You stay put! We handle this." He was in the act of opening the door when their attention was riveted by what was happening in front of them.

THIRTY-FIVE

"LOOK WHAT YOU'VE DONE, you stupid bitch!" Harvey screamed. "You're in the exact change lane. I hope to hell I've got it!"

Awkwardly, because he was holding the gun, he dug in his pants pockets, one after the other, and came up with a handful of coins. "How much do we need?"

"A dollar and a half."

"Here, take this—count it."

Louisa's fingers were shaking. Tears were still running down her face. She could hardly hold the coins. "Fifty, seventy-five, ninety—we need sixty cents more."

Cars were honking behind them. Above the honking was the sound of sirens. "Shut the fuck up!" Harvey yelled.

He was beginning to panic. She had to do something. Her tears ceased. She handed him her bag. "Look in my change purse."

"You look, damn it!"

She fumbled in her bag for her change purse, finally got it open, and found two quarters and a dime.

"Now open that window, throw it in and get out of here!" Harvey's voice had risen to a high pitch, and the gun was jabbing at her side.

She opened the window and flung. The coins rattled into the basket. The gate remained closed. Behind them, horns were honking furiously. Voices were yelling now.

"It's stuck! Of all the fucking luck!"

"It's not stuck, Harvey," she said, trying to sound calm. "The dime slipped out of my fingers. It fell outside the basket. It's down there beside the car."

"You did that on purpose! You're trying to screw up, you fucking bitch!"

"I'll open the door and get out and pick it up and put it in the basket. Then the gate will open." She was shaking so hard her words were coming in gasps, but she tried to keep her voice patient and reasonable. The dropped dime was her only chance.

"No you don't! Go through the gate! Floor it!"

"There's a patrol car on the other side. See it? Look, there comes another one. They'll be on us in a second if we do that. Just let me pick up the dime—it's the only way."

Louisa unsnapped her seat belt. She looked at Harvey. He was staring wildly straight ahead, looking at the patrol cars. She opened the door. He still didn't move.

She did. As soon as her feet hit the ground, she ran. "Help me!" she screamed. "He's got a gun!"

The doors of the second car behind her burst open. Voices shouted. "Back here! You're covered!" Detective James Malone. He had a gun in his hand. Detective Rhonda Lord ran past her on the other side. She, too, had a gun.

Cars honked. People screamed and ducked down in their cars. She heard Rhonda yelling, "Police officer! You in the car—throw out the gun!"

Louisa did not see whether Harvey complied. She ran back to the car. Someone else was getting out of it, moving slowly and painfully. He straightened up. He held out his arms.

THIRTY-SIX

SHE WAS BACK in the marathon. She was bored, restless, hungry, and aware of an urgent need to go to the bathroom. Tony would have a hard time persuading her that this was worthwhile.

SUM had her back. She was a heroine now, and forgiven for deserting the marathon. Alex Meigs personally greeted her when she arrived this morning. Mark Mayer shook her hand and told her what a wonderful person Tony was, and what a privilege it was to be standing in for him.

The capture of the alleged "Marathon Murderer" was in the Sunday morning papers. A horde of reporters and people aiming TV cameras were in the lobby trying to get interviews with marathoners, Alex, assistant coaches, and Louisa. Wishing she could disguise herself like Harvey, she escaped them only by going up the mezzanine with Alex and entering the ballroom by the secret stairway the coach used.

Louisa wished that she was with Tony, anywhere but the Park Summit. She was sick of this hotel and the memories this ballroom evoked. Tony was upstairs. He had absolutely refused to go back to the hospital last night. He'd given in ungraciously to the doctor's insistence that he stay out of the ballroom and in his room in bed.

"I'll bring you chicken soup," Louisa told him.

"I have a better idea," he said.

Laughter had bubbled up in her as easily as tears had only a short time ago.

She and Tony had sat in the back seat of the police car last night, his hand holding hers, and they watched the drama at the toll plaza. Sirens wailing, police cars came from Brooklyn and through the tunnel from Manhattan. The whole area was suddenly filled with flashing lights, cars, and uniformed officers shouting and holding weapons.

But no shots were fired. Harvey threw the gun out the window and surrendered meekly to Rhonda. They saw Rhonda handcuff and take him to the car behind them. Traffic was somehow unsnarled and routed around the lane where the Toyota still blocked the gate. Then Malone was behind the wheel again, and they were making a U-turn, crossing the plaza to the other side to go back through the tunnel.

"Ms. Evans," the detective said, "I have to ask you to come to the station and make a statement about what went on tonight from the time you arrived at Wardleigh's until you got out of his car."

"I better start with some things that went on quite a bit earlier than that," she said. "Starting with Deirdre giving me a claim slip for a roll of film."

In the rearview mirror she caught his startled look. "Yeah, I'll say you better start with that."

"Unless Harvey confesses, my story will be uncorroborated. He gave Deirdre the capsule. He went to the marathon disguised as a woman."

"We have evidence now that we did not have before," Malone said austerely. "It supports that statement."

"He dressed as a woman and shot Tony, he said, to put more suspicion on me."

"Oh?" She caught his glance in the mirror again.

He'd taken her statement with only one comment. "You would have saved yourself, and us, a lot of trouble if you'd turned over that slip as soon as you knew what it was." That was when she told him about Jack's threat to Clare.

The next day the entire marathon was gripped by euphoria. One by one they got up to share their relief that the murderer had been caught, and their excitement that they'd been part of a tense human drama. They were elated and self-congratulatory.

Ernie was applauded and cheered for admitting he'd been at the Queen of Hearts. The women in the Ladies' room drama took bows for their role in unmasking the killer in drag.

Louisa knew everyone wanted her to get up and say something, but she kept quiet. Her hysterical joy of the previous night had worn off, leaving her strangely numb. She had out-smarted Harvey and gotten away from him and his gun. This week-long nightmare was nearly over. She was alive and Tony was alive, and just perhaps she was on the edge of something new and wonderful.

Harvey had made a confession at the police station Saturday night, and Rhonda had called in the morning to tell her. Harvey's confession had not made the morning papers. His story confirmed hers in every detail. He would be out on bail. How long this sensation could be kept from his mother was anyone's guess.

Harvey confessed he'd made a dozen cyanide capsules. The deaths of Deirdre, Robert Coates, and the as yet unconfirmed death of Jack Janyck accounted for three of them. When the capsules found in the plastic bag in the Abelards' room were analyzed, five of them were found to contain cyanide. These were the supply Jack had taken from Deirdre's bathroom and brought back to his friends. Lester, the third Abelard, had not been seen since Saturday. Like Jack, he might be holed up somewhere alone, already dead of a poisoned upper or downer. The East Village was swarming with police putting up posters, driving up and down the streets blaring warnings over the speakers about the deadly capsules still unaccounted for.

The marathoners settled down to more serious inputting. Louisa lost interest in it and returned to her own thoughts. The claim slip Deirdre had given her—that piece of paper that had started it all—was the wrong slip. Both Louisa and Malone believed that Deirdre had fished in her pocket, and in her confused state, brought out the wrong piece of paper. It was the other slip, with Harvey's mother's address on it, that she didn't need any more because she'd memorized it.

Jack's face, with its mad, malevolent eyes, would haunt Louisa for a long time. Somewhere, still plotting to get his hands on the pictures, he had reached into his pocket for one of Deirdre's tranks and died horribly and alone.

The marathon went on and on. Louisa felt too self-conscious to let herself fall asleep. She was still being eyed covertly from time to time. Mark was working so hard to live up to Tony that she felt it would be rude for her to go to sleep on him. The self-congratulation had subsided. People were talking about guilt. Mark was saying earnestly, "You should clean up your unfinished business with people you've hurt or have hurt you. And log-off guilt if those people are unwilling to accept your amends. That's their problem if they won't." She would complete her unfinished business with Glen before she let herself get more involved with Tony. It would be like starting clean.

At last it was over. Marathoners were leaving the hotel after a noisy celebration with floods of tears and much hugging and kissing. Most claimed they were on-line, and all were riding a high cloud of exaltation.

Louisa came out of the ballroom. Tony was sitting on one of the leather couches under the ficus trees. He looked tired, but he too, looked rather exalted. Beside him to Louisa's surprise, was Detective James Malone.

"You on-line yet?" Tony asked.

"I don't know what being on-line is supposed to feel like," Louisa said, "so I don't know whether I am."

Tony's laugh turned into a gasp. He shook his head. "You won't give in, will you? I see I still have work to do."

"Ms. Evans." The detective had gotten to his feet. He looked tired and solemn. "Ms. Evans, I owe you an apology. I did think you killed Deirdre. I understand, now, why you didn't turn over that claim slip. I want to thank you for your—ah—courage—and for your quick thinking at the toll booth." He averted his eyes from hers and held out his hand.

Louisa shook it. Some of the benign spirit of the marathon's grand finale seemed to have enveloped her also. She could almost forgive him. "Thank you for staying here to tell me that."

"Rhonda Lord signed up for the next marathon," Tony said.

"Really!"

James Malone grunted. "Christ, she'll be impossible! To me, it's still bullshit." He turned and walked away quickly.

"Poor man!" Louisa said. "What was he doing here, anyway?"

"He was telling me some of your story, your subway experience, meeting Deirdre's ghost..."

"Tony, what did you mean in the cemetery when you said if I came back to the marathon I'd find the reason in all this?"

"Don't you know yet?"

"You mean I took risks and I survived them—that's all there is to it?"

"Getting on-line is really very simple. You learn that you can live your life fully, all the time."

"I didn't need the marathon to teach me that. I learned all I want to know about living life fully at the Brooklyn-Battery Tunnel toll plaza!"

"Wonderful lesson, isn't it? And you know what? It works in life's more ordinary situations. Like the one we're in right now."

"What situation are you talking about? The marathon is over."

"I mean how are we going to get to know each other when you live in New York and I live in California and I have to go back there tomorrow?"

"When's the next marathon you're doing in New York?"

"February. Think if I came a few days early, we could get together—go out to dinner, take walks, see the city—get to know each other?"

"You mean—no quarrels, no confrontations?"

He nodded.

"No getting shot at, no being pushed off subway platforms, no seeing ghosts in the East Village?"

"Think you can handle ordinary life?"

She smiled at him. "It sounds boring, but—I think I'll be ready to risk it!"

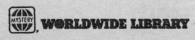

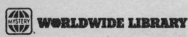